A KIKI LOWENSTEIN SCRAP-N-CRAFT
MYSTERY

PHOTO, SNAP, SHOT

JOANNA CAMPBELL SLAN

WHEELER
CHIVERS

This Large Print edition is published by Wheeler Publishing, Waterville, Maine, USA and by BBC Audiobooks Ltd, Bath, England.
Wheeler Publishing, a part of Gale, Cengage Learning.

The text of this Large Print edition is unabridged.
Other aspects of the book may vary from the original edition.
Set in 16 pt. Plantin.

LIBRARY OF CONGRESS CATALOGING-IN-PUBLICATION DATA

Campbell-Slan, Joanna.
  Photo, snap, shot : a Kiki Lowenstein scrap-n-craft mystery /
by Joanna Campbell Slan.
    p. cm. — (Wheeler Publishing large print cozy mystery) (A
Kiki Lowenstein scrap-n-craft mystery ; 3)
    ISBN-13: 978-1-4104-2798-4 (pbk.)
    ISBN-10: 1-4104-2798-6 (pbk.)
    1. Lowenstein, Kiki (Fictitious character)—Fiction. 2.
Scrapbooks—Fiction. 3. Large type books. I. Title.
PS3603.A4845P47 2010b
813'.6—dc22   2010017707

BRITISH LIBRARY CATALOGUING-IN-PUBLICATION DATA AVAILABLE

Published in 2010 in the U.S. by arrangement with Midnight Ink, an imprint of Llewellyn Publications, Woodbury, MN 55125-2989 USA.
Published in 2010 in the U.K. by arrangement with Llewellyn Worldwide Ltd.

U.K. Hardcover: 978 1 408 49235 2 (Chivers Large Print)
U.K. Softcover: 978 1 408 49236 9 (Camden or Paragon Large Print)

Printed and bound in Great Britain by the MPG Books Group
1 2 3 4 5 6 7 14 13 12 11 10

To my husband, David Slan.
Detweiler's got nothing on you, babe.

ONE

"Anya is all right now," said my daughter's advisor, "but you need to come pick her up please. Immediately."

Three phrases guaranteed to panic any mother: (1) The babysitter called and there's a problem. (2) There's something on the back of your skirt. (3) Your child is all right **now.**

If Anya was all right *now,* what on earth had happened earlier?

"Whoa. What's up? Is Anya okay?" I asked as I waved my keys at my boss, Dodie Goldfader, who owns Time in a Bottle, St. Louis's premier scrapbook store.

"Ye—es." The advisor hesitated. "Anya's okay. But she found a body."

My world came to a skidding halt. I froze in the middle of the store and yelled, "She found a WHAT?"

"A body. A corpse. Uh, someone died. Was killed. In the balcony of the Latreau Theatre here at school. Could you come get her?"

I smacked my cell phone closed and ran, sprinted really, through our stockroom, doing high hurdle jumps over boxes of scrapbook supplies. My co-worker Bama followed me with her eyes. I heard Dodie calling behind me, "Do you need me to drive?"

Bama yelled, "Kiki? You all right?"

Gracie, my harlequin Great Dane, jumped to her feet and yodeled as I ran past.

But I didn't pause for a second.

My daughter needed me. Twelve-year-old girls should not be stumbling over dead bodies.

Two

Okay, I said to myself, calm down. Anya is fine *now,* I repeated under my breath. I flipped on the car radio to hear the dulcet tones of the local NPR broadcaster announcing the next program. If they weren't breaking in with a news bulletin, it couldn't be a crisis. Or could it?

I had this sneaking suspicion something was rotten at CALA, Charles and Anne Lindbergh Academy, the hoity-toity private school my mother-in-law, Sheila, shells out big bucks for my daughter to attend. CALA is the educational stomping ground of the veddy, veddy rich here in St. Louis. I bet there was no news about a death at the school because the "powers that be" had decided to keep this quiet. You can do that — at least for a short time — when you occupy the top rung of the food chain.

Taking a corner with my ancient red BMW, I thanked the good Lord for its superior handling ability. The car was too old to have much Blue Book value, which was exactly why I didn't sell it after my husband met his untimely demise, and I'd been plunged into poverty. I did a couple more two-wheel screeching turns, ran a couple of orange lights (that's when yellow turns red on you), slipped between two parked police cars, and slid into a parking spot near the portico that marked the Upper School Office of the school.

On my way in, I stepped on the school seal.

I was supposed to bend down and kiss it.

Uh, no.

My Keds gripped the marble of the hallowed halls as I barreled past the dean's office. A tight knot of crime scene investigators carried cameras and miniature yellow cones with numbers on them. And yeah, I heard them yell at me to stop, but what did I care? I needed to find my daughter. So I ran through the open double doors of the balcony and didn't give one moment's thought to the crowd on my heels. Nor did I stop when I saw the yellow crime tape. Instead, I did a hurdler's jump right over the top of the plastic barrier. Out of the corner of my eyes I noticed the expression on the nearest cop's face. He was impressed.

As well he should be. I'd cleared the tape in one and not broken stride. I'm not naturally athletic, but because I was concerned about my child, I was super-charged. So, I came down on the other side of the barrier and didn't miss a step. I took two long strides into the balcony and nearly stumbled over the medical examiner and an assistant. (I recognized the M.E. from pictures in the paper.) They were carefully flipping a corpse onto its back.

The expression on Sissy Gilchrist's face was one of pure surprise. I probably looked pretty shocked myself. The difference was I'd get over it, and Sissy wouldn't, seeing as how she was dead.

"Who are you?" The M.E. glared at me. "This is a crime scene. Get her out of here." She gestured angrily to a cop who now had me by the forearm. His grip hurt.

"My daughter . . ." I sputtered. "My child found . . . her." And I pointed to the dead woman on the white sheet. "The school called. I'm Kiki Lowenstein. Anya's mother."

The cop pulled me away. "Your daughter's fine. We have her in an office."

But before I turned away, I took a good look at Sissy . . . or her remains. The back of her head was a pulpy, bloody mess. Atop

11

her long blonde hair sat a crown of carmine. Moving her body had created an uneven streak of red that bore a strong resemblance to a Picasso paint stroke.

The cop led me toward the hallway. "Ma'am, you need to come with me."

"Right," I murmured. A wave of dizziness hit me suddenly, and I felt a little sick. Then came a thought: "Someone killed my husband last year. And he's still on the loose. Are you sure my daughter's okay?"

"She's fine." A familiar voice answered. I stepped away from the cop who was towing me along and stared up into the eyes of Detective Chad Detweiler.

He sighed and rubbed his chin. His Heineken-bottle-green eyes with their gold flecks regarded me sadly. "I got here immediately after they called. I've been talking with her. She's shook up, but she's okay."

I nodded. Detweiler and I stood there. Motionless. Silent. Industry continued around us, with investigators marking spots, taking photos, making notes. We were two rocks in a creek, dividing the flowing water.

I hadn't seen him in months. In fact, I'd purposely avoided him. I'd dodged his phone calls and torn up his letters. I'd fallen in love with him after he investigated my husband's murder. He'd been a frequent visitor to my home, a friend to Anya, and very nearly something more to me. But when I discovered he was married, that was it. The end. *C'est fini.* Cut!

But here's the truth: I was glad, really glad, that he'd come to my daughter's rescue. There was no one else on earth who could have handled this situation better than Detweiler. Of that I was sure.

Now I was certain Anya was safe. At least temporarily.

"Where's Anya?"

"She's in the middle school nurse's office."

"What happened?" I asked.

He took my elbow and guided me down the halls. "Two girls — Anya and Matilda Earhart — were in the hall on their way to class. Coming back from a session in the library. They are working on a project together. They heard a scream. They ran into the balcony area and found the nurse, Thelma Selsner, bent over the deceased."

"Sissy Gilchrist."

"You know her?"

I gave a so-so wiggle-waggle of my hand. My fingers shook a little.

"The girls immediately went for help."

"Why was Nurse Selsner in the balcony? Did she hear or see something?" As I spoke, my stomach flipped over. I had a delayed response to seeing a body. "Uh, excuse me," I said and did a fast trot down the hall and around the corner to a ladies room, all the while praying I'd make it in time. Which I did.

When I returned, Detweiler acted like nothing happened. He handed me a Diet Coke. "They were out of Diet Dr Pepper."

He'd remembered!

I sipped the spicy blend gratefully and tugged at my blouse self-consciously. Over the summer, I'd embarked on an ambitious plan to forget Detweiler. I called it my "eat my way to nirvana" scheme. The plan included eating everything and anything that wasn't nailed down. (I did draw the line at dog yummies. Gracie, my Great Dane, had kept a worried eye on me.) I wasn't a "Rats, I ate an entire carton of ice cream" type of girl. I was more of a "Gee, I started at the top shelf of the refrigerator and ate my way through to the chiller drawer" sort of snarfing fool. Twice I'd made myself physically sick by overeating. Once I'd had food poisoning.

But those were minor inconveniences. Mainly, I just kept chewing and swallowing.

And now all my clothes were too tight. I

bet I looked like a sausage ready to split its casing.

Ugh.

"Mrs. Selsner heard voices from the theatre. She's the upper school nurse. Her office is kitty-corner from the balcony. She wondered what was up and decided to check things out." Detweiler sighed. He wiped his face. A crease was forming between his eyes. It would be one of many. "When the nurse screamed, the girls had just left the restroom and were in the hallway right outside the theatre. The kids ran in to see what was happening."

That was all the police had. No one had seen Sissy go into the balcony. It was supposed to stay locked unless there was a program.

No one had seen anyone leave the balcony. There were no bloody footprints to follow, and none on the carpet. At least, not prints obvious to the naked eye. The crime scene folks would be busy charting, gridding, photographing, and examining the area, but unlike forensic teams on television, the fruits of their work would take weeks, even months.

"The girls didn't see much. Just Mrs. Selsner screaming and bent over someone." Detweiler had read my mind. "Maybe some

15

blood spatter on the carpet."

Thank heavens for small favors.

No one suspicious had been reported by the teachers. Or the janitorial staff. Or the administration. The murderer had somehow blended into our tight St. John Knit community.

What would happen next? How would the school respond? What would CALA do?

"How did she die?"

He shrugged. "Too early to tell."

I reached past him for the handle of the middle school nurse's office. "It was murder, wasn't it? And the killer is running loose, right?"

He nodded.

Through some superhuman effort, I managed to keep myself from falling into his arms and sobbing.

Oh, but I wanted to.

I did not need this. Anya and I had been through so much with the murder of her father, the burglarizing of our home, and the ongoing threats from the person who had master-minded my husband's death. We'd recently moved. It had taken us all summer to "normalize." And we'd turned our backs on Detweiler after I'd discovered he was married, a "small" fact he'd neglected to mention although he'd been a

16

frequent visitor to our home and my fantasies.

Okay, it was good that he'd been here for Anya. But it was bad for *me* that he'd shown up. I wasn't about to let down my guard. Not when it had taken me all summer to put him out of my mind.

Right. Who was I fooling?

THREE

Anya perched on the edge of a chair. Her friend huddled miserably on a cot. Both girls bore that coltish, gawky, pre-teen air of supreme boredom coupled with incredible vulnerability. But the minute my daughter saw me, the walls came down. She flew off her seat and grabbed me. "Mom!" She'd been crying.

I hugged her hard. "You okay?" The middle school nurse stuck her head out of the adjoining office to offer a sad "tsk, tsk."

Anya nodded. "I'm fine."

"Tilly, honey, are you okay?"

The middle school nurse said, "We have a certified grief counselor available. I've encouraged the girls to talk to her."

The girls studied their feet. A certified grief counselor? Wow, how incredibly up-scale. I had attended a public school in Indiana. We didn't even have a college counselor. No reason to. My schoolmates

18

either: got married, joined the armed services, or went directly to jail.

As my mother-in-law would happily explain at length, I was not qualified to appreciate CALA's high standards. Good old Sheila never missed an opportunity to remind me of my humble origins. She and I were getting along pretty well lately, but that was only because she wanted what was best for Anya. Me, Sheila could take or leave. Mainly, leave.

"Tilly, would you like to come home with us?"

She ducked her dishwater brown head and shook it. "Mom will be back in a minute. Then I'm going down and stay with her."

Her mom, Maggie, was a teacher at the school — and a friend of mine. So Tilly was on her way to the kindergarten classroom where Maggie was substituting. The nurse explained since Maggie couldn't be relieved of her charges, her daughter would "hang out" there until the end of the day.

I couldn't wait to talk to Maggie. She'd have the inside scoop on the situation — and she'd know how safe our children were.

I hadn't realized Detweiler was standing behind me, blocking our egress. I turned and nearly walked into his chest, getting a good whiff of him. As usual, he smelled slightly soapy and spicy and very male. Certain parts of my anatomy tingled with joy.

"I'll need to talk with Anya again."

Oh, boy.

Down girl, down! I gave myself a good mental smack. I'd gained all this weight trying to forget him, and now temptation beckoned. I thought I heard the strains of "Bolero," but it was just my heart.

I think I whimpered. (So much for subtle.)

"Let's talk while I walk you to your car," he suggested, quietly. "Anya, you doing okay?" He put a hand on her shoulder, and she leaned into him, slipping her arm around his waist. Which totally undid me. I used the back of my sleeve to wipe my eyes. My poor kid. First her father gets killed by a wacko, and now this. Worse yet, the man she most trusted was the guy her mother had been working hard to avoid.

Detweiler waited until we were clear of the nurse's office. "This is going to be complicated, and . . ." he shot quick glances over his shoulder, ". . . and there's already a lot of pressure, this being Ladue and all. There's the school and its rep."

Charles and Anne Lindbergh Academy was the most desirable prep school in the St. Louis area. The school offers the finest education in the area. In fact, CALA was known all over the world for the quality of its graduates. As one mom proudly explained, "You go to CALA, you'll never be without a job. You are part of a family."

A large, very wealthy family with oodles of connections.

Detweiler had reason to be worried. With connections came lawyers. With lawyers came, well, BIG problems, especially for law enforcement officers.

I wouldn't want to be in his penny loafers. Solving a murder would be hard enough without having all of Old St. Louis breathing down your neck, watching your every move.

Speaking of breathing down someone's neck, I shivered with the thought of him re-entering our lives. Well, parts of me shivered. The other parts jumped for joy.

Then I got hold of myself. I gave myself a lecture which began with, "He's married!"

And another voice inside me said, "Nobody's perfect!"

I groaned. He'd been unfair to me. He'd let me fall in love with him — he'd even kissed me — and not told me he was married. And how about Anya? Huh? She'd fallen for him, too. She adored him. So had our dog, Gracie.

For months after my husband was killed, Detweiler had been wonderful with Anya despite her pre-teen mood shifts, found time to go on nature walks with all of us, patiently taught my daughter to throw "like a boy," and thought our sloppy harlequin Great Dane was just terrific. He was also a competent cook who cleaned up after himself in our kitchen.

By contrast, my dead husband had invited his girlfriend along on father-daughter outings and told our child to keep that little detail a secret. Gee, of course George looked bad by comparison!

But then there was that wife thing.

I sighed. No way around it, Detweiler was off-limits.

And I had other problems. Problems like a killer roaming the halls of my daughter's school.

The three of us stepped outside, squinting against the bright autumn sunlight. The detective opened the Beemer's passenger side door and guided Anya inside. "Try not to think about this. I know it's hard. But we're on it. If you need me, you still have me on speed-dial, Anya-Banana."

At the sound of her nickname — a nickname I was no longer allowed to use since my child explained she had grown up —

my daughter gave him a weak grin. "Yeah."

Detweiler waited for her to click her seatbelt before he slammed her door.

Reluctantly, I started toward the driver's side. Suddenly, Detweiler grabbed my shoulders, turned me to face him, and stepped in close. For one torturous moment, I thought we were going to kiss. Then I pulled back. "No, please . . . I can't do this. You need to leave us alone."

He didn't turn loose of me. He wasn't swooping down for a kiss. Instead, he was pulling me closer to warn me. "Kiki, you don't understand. I think she and her friend saw the killer."

FOUR

I raced into work leaving Anya out front in my car with the engine running — after instructing her to lock the car doors. I grabbed Gracie, asked Bama to take my shift, and drove home trying to ignore my tremors. Had my daughter seen a murderer? If so, was she in danger? We already had my husband's killer sending us ugly postcards and making threatening phone calls to my work. Now what? How would I protect my child? The weight of the world settled onto my shoulders. Being a single mom is tough enough. Now I was a single parent, trying to avoid a married man I lusted after, and hoping to protect my daughter who might be targeted by a killer. Or two.

Time to pull up my big girl panties, and go on.

"Anya, honey, do you want to talk about what happened?"

She turned a pair of blurry eyes and a reddened nose on me. "No," she sniffed.

"Okay. When you do, I'm here for you." I reached over and gave her hand a squeeze. She didn't squeeze back.

The first thing I did after we got home was to let Gracie out for a piddle. The second was to eat an entire bag of Oreos. By myself. With milk. Weight Watchers would have to triple my allowable points to cover this little slip-up.

I brushed my teeth to halt my eating spree. Anya had settled in the next room in front of the TV. I needed a distraction. I dialed the one person who could tell me the school's unofficial take on Sissy Gilchrist's murder. Primarily, I wanted to know what the school's security situation was. Surely the teachers would be the first to be informed of it.

"Is Tilly all right? Are our kids safe?" I asked. Maggie was still at CALA, and I could hear the chatter of busy kindergarteners in the background.

Maggie evaded my question. "Mother? I'll see you at the regular time and place, Mother," she said with special emphasis on the "mother."

"Anything I can do for you? Or Tilly?"

"Yes, Mother," my friend said. "We're all fine. But I'm still here at work and very busy . . . so we'll see you later."

I figured someone was listening in and took the hint.

"Okay." I knew she meant we'd meet for a bike ride out in The Valley, that low-lying space south of the Missouri River, not far from where our kids took golf practice. I understood she couldn't talk, but I felt sorely in need of comfort. I was out of Oreos.

I needed to know how safe my daughter was. According to Detweiler, she might be at risk. But fortified by sugar and chocolate, I wondered what this might mean. Maybe his warning was just an attempt on his part to insinuate himself back into our lives. After I'd discovered he was married, I'd cut off all contact. I'd shredded numerous letters (unopened). I'd dumped an entire bouquet of yellow roses. (That hurt. I'd only gotten perfunctory floral bouquets from George on Valentine's and my birthday. Never roses. Even if they were yellow for peace and friendship, they were roses. Tossing them out durn near did me in. I kept sneaking back to the trash dumpster, pulling up the stepstool and staring down at them through tears. Finally Dodie sent me home for the day.)

I'd dodged his calls. I'd labeled his e-mails

as spam. I'd refused to answer my door when he came round. And my friends — Dodie and Mert and Clancy — had told him in no uncertain terms to stay away from me. They'd all been outraged on my behalf.

And yet, seeing him there at CALA gave me courage. I knew that whatever my daughter had endured, he was there to help and protect her. That he'd lay down his life for her. That's who he was, and how much he cared about my child.

But on the other hand, he'd lied to me. Maybe by omission, but still . . .

I shut my eyes and called up his face as he relayed his worries in the CALA parking lot. Nah, he wasn't being melodramatic. He was genuinely concerned that Anya might have seen Sissy's killer.

After he told me of his worries, we had gone on to discuss what I needed to do to protect Anya.

"She'll be fine at golf practice," he'd concluded. "In fact, anywhere there's a lot of people. I'll phone you if I hear anything different. Try to keep her busy. You don't want her to dwell on this."

I figured the fresh air and exercise couldn't hurt. And Maggie was in the same boat. She would have told me if Tilly wasn't going to golf. That meant she thought the girls were safe. In fact, Maggie could provide me with the most reliable inside information on how the school was coping with the murder, and whether it would be okay for our girls to return to CALA on Monday.

I walked to the refrigerator and stared inside. I didn't find any answers to life's persistent questions. My stomach roiled, bloated with all those cookies, and I decided to give it a rest.

Anya stretched out on the sofa in our small living room, clicking the remote and moving from one sad parody of American culture to another. Nothing like an hour or two of mindless blather to help you zone out. I tried to contact my mother-in-law, Sheila Lowenstein, because I knew she'd be concerned about Anya. Sheila was dating Robbie Holmes, the St. Louis County police chief, so she'd probably heard about the murder at CALA already. In fact, she'd have the official low-down. She didn't answer, so I left a message explaining Anya was okay and promising to phone later.

Except my cell phone beeped twice and signaled my battery was dead. Since moving to our new home, I'd chosen to forgo a land line. Both Anya and I had cell phones, and we could "piggyback" on the Wi-Fi signal from our neighbor, who was a famous author. (I actually owned one of his books and had it by my bedside, but hadn't begun reading it.)

I figured Sheila would be irked when she discovered we were incommunicado. She liked keeping me on a short leash, especially after she forked over a significant portion of the deposit for our new quarters. It was a trade-off I'd been willing to make, but some days I resented her interference.

I filled a water bottle and changed into my bike shorts so I could ride with Maggie while the kids played golf. My friend was at CALA until the end of the year while the regular kindergarten teacher was out on maternity leave. With two kids of her own, Matilda "Tilly" and Matthew, Maggie had her hands full without substitute teaching, but Maggie's one of those incredibly organized women who is so competent she makes you want to puke. And nice? Shoot. Maggie wrote the book on being sweet. As my nana would have put it, "Butter wouldn't melt in her mouth." Maggie never riles anybody. She has no enemies. Zip. None. Consequently, her presence is always in demand.

This serves in vast contrast to *moi*. I've heard that some folks actually shudder when they see me coming. I have this habit of stepping in it. I don't mean to honk folks off, but inevitably I do.

In years past, Maggie has substituted off and on as CALA has needed her. It's a tribute to her broad intellect that she can handle almost any subject at almost any grade level. In truth, the school probably values her for her steady disposition and her willingness to come in at the last minute as much as for her teaching abilities.

I had to nag Anya a bit to get her ready for golf practice. She clearly did not want to leave the sofa.

We pulled into the parking lot of the golf practice range and sat there. I wasn't totally sure if I should let Anya out of my sight. Coach Bosch must have been on the lookout for us. He strolled over to the car and motioned me outside to speak quietly.

"I was in the military, and I'm licensed to carry a firearm. In light of what happened this afternoon, CALA has hired a security guard to attend our team meetings, and the course marshals have been alerted. Your child's safe with me, Mrs. Lowenstein," he said. The steely temperament reflected in his eyes underscored his dependability.

Coach Bosch was the school's former football coach, and although an unlikely match for a team of hormonal and overly sensitive girl golfers, he was a legend to the school's alums. The word was, he didn't want to be put out to pasture (or more accurately an unused football field) after his years of service. And the alums loved playing golf with him and rehashing the ghosts of football games past. So a deal had been struck to keep him on as girls' golf coach. With this compromise, he had access to all the best courses in town, and in return, could jolly up the alums to keep donations rolling in.

I thanked the man, but I didn't quite relax until Maggie pulled up. Anya was still sitting in the car as I walked over to talk with my friend. "Are they safe?" I asked.

Maggie gave me a grim smile. "The day CALA lets anything happen to a golf team will be the day the Chicago Cubs win the World Series. I couldn't talk earlier. Two policemen and Headmaster McMahan were standing outside my room when you called. How is she?" She gestured toward my daughter's silhouette.

"She's upset. How's Tilly?"

"The same."

I went back to the Beemer and opened the passenger side door. My daughter trudged out of the car toward the golf course with her shoulders sagging. Tilly also seemed discouraged. The two dragged their heels toward their chattering teammates. Fortunately, Coach Bosch hustled them along with a brusque wave of his hand. Our daughters teed off right away.

"I figured the fresh air would do Anya good. You must have thought Tilly could use a distraction, too."

Maggie nodded. "Yes. Best to get their minds off this."

"But I'm worried."

"As are we all. Meet you over at the access road."

A few minutes later, she and I strapped on our helmets and straddled our Trek 1500s. Hers was a 50 c.m. regular; mine was a 51 c.m. WSD or Women's Specific Design. I love my bike. With silver spokes and narrow wheels under me, I feel like I can fly. Last summer, Anya and Sheila had decided I needed more exercise. (My weight is a constant concern for Sheila, and with my recent "see food/eat food" diet, she was very worried.) Working together, they bought me this Trek for my birthday. It was one of the best gifts I'd ever gotten. Even if I did fall off a lot in the beginning.

We adjusted our helmets and pulled on our biking gloves. "What happened?" I asked my friend. I didn't want to taint her recollection by sharing what I'd already seen and heard.

Maggie shrugged. "Mrs. Selsner found the body and started screaming." The noise of Highway 40 caught the words and ran over them like they were a cluster of cigarette butts tossed from a car.

"Doesn't give me much faith in her ability to cope with a crisis," I said.

"Be fair. There's a world of difference between chickenpox and corpses. Poor woman. I feel sorry for her. Who wouldn't have been upset about stumbling over a dead body in the balcony?"

"Such a ritzy place, too." I flashed back on the velvet seats and the gorgeous, thick carpet. This was one of the perks of having a child at CALA. Your darling offspring took drama class in a theatre that would have put Broadway to shame. Back when I was a kid, we rigged bedsheets on clothesline tied to bamboo poles and sat on hard bleacher seats to watch the school plays in the gymnasium. But then I grew up poor as dirt. Which begs the question: Why would dirt need money anyway?

"It's odd. Odd that anyone could get in. Policy dictates that the door to the balcony is supposed to stay locked during school hours unless a member of the staff is present." Maggie emphasized "policy" as though it were a person's name. She was a great one for following rules. "Mrs. Selsner saw it ajar, and she decided to investigate."

"Bromo was the first person on the scene?"

Maggie nodded.

Bromo was our nickname for Mrs. Selsner, a battle axe famed for treating every tummy ailment, every headache and non-specific trauma with Alka-Seltzer. Rumor had it that Mrs. Selsner once told a girl with a sexually transmitted disease to rinse with Alka-Seltzer, um, down there. Definitely an off-label use. I shouldn't laugh.

"Why do you say supposed? The door to the balcony is *supposed* to be locked? What's that all about?"

We'd been spinning along at 13 mph, our normal warm-up speed. Maggie shifted her body weight, moved her hands onto the drops, and skidded to a halt. I slid in beside her, dragging one foot along the ground. The toes don't last long in my bike socks because I haven't quite mastered the art of an elegant stop.

"Don't repeat this . . ."

I nodded. The biggest benefit of having a friend who teaches part-time at my daughter's school is The Inside Scoop.

34

"Students have been making out in the balcony of the Latreau for years." She saw the look of shock on my face, and her moon-shaped visage darkened. "Come on, Kiki, you know kids and their raging hormones. Don't act naïve. We can preach morality all we want, but good values begin at home."

She had the good grace to turn red as she remembered my husband's peccadillo.

"But making out in the balcony? Geez Louise, Maggie, we're talking high school kids here. Practically babies!"

She rolled her eyes.

I hate it when people roll their eyes. My nana always said your eyes could get stuck back in your head. She might be right.

"I know we're talking high school kids. Of course, it's inappropriate behavior. Didn't you have a boyfriend in high school?" She pointed a finger at my chest.

No, I didn't. Sign me up as an official Late Bloomer. I had my first real relationship in college, though, and we broke up. That night I went to a frat party and got drunk for my first time. Which was how I wound up pregnant. Which was how I happened to marry George, Anya's father. But I wasn't up for sharing these personal tidbits.

"The school acted responsibly by keeping

the door locked. A couple of faculty members have copies of the key." Maggie tucked both hands under her armpits and looked away. I was staring at the Giro logo on the back of her helmet when she continued, "That's when faculty started having trysts in the balcony."

"You've got to be kidding me."

"It's human nature." My friend gave me a withering look. "Don't act so shocked."

The private school system in St. Louis is its own little universe. And from this unusual solar system comes a greeting peculiar to our city: "What high school did you go to?" The answer can tell the inquisitor your neighborhood, your religion, your IQ, your economic background, and your social standing.

I rubbed my eyes behind my sunglasses. A quick glance at the computer on my bike told me we had less than a half an hour before getting back to the girls. "Let me get this straight. Faculty members were playing doctor with each other in the balcony. Gives a whole new meaning to the phrase 'Show Time,' doesn't it?" I ignored her scowl and went on, "Are you suggesting that Sissy Gilchrist was in the balcony with a playmate when she got bashed in the head?"

Maggie sighed. "It's possible."

"With who?"

"You mean 'with whom' and I shouldn't say." Abruptly, she turned away from me.

"Maggie! I tell you everything." That was an exaggeration. We'd met three years ago at a scrapbook crop and kept loosely in touch since.

"Her son Christopher is one of my kindergarteners. I need to stop talking." Maggie threw a leg over her sissy bar and pedaled back toward our cars, leaving me sprinting to catch up.

I wouldn't give up on finding out more from Maggie. Not yet. One of my best attributes is my ability to encourage people to say more than they should. I have a baby face, blonde curls, and I look a lot stupider than I am. Therefore, with a bit of judicial coaxing and indefatigable efforts on my part, most people open up.

We pedaled to the overpass where Spirit of St. Louis Boulevard meets Chesterfield Airport Road. I put a foot down on each side of the bike and touched the ground for balance. "Thirteen and a half." Or so said the computer mounted on my handlebars. Since we had begun riding together, we'd improved our average speed by a half a mile an hour. "Give me a high five, girlfriend."

"Lance Armstrong averages more than

thirty-two miles an hour," pouted Maggie after slapping my palm.

"Lance Armstrong has no excess body fat and weighs his pasta every evening."

"Obviously he's not responsible for getting a meal on the table for his family."

"Obviously. At least we're moving up in the world. The bike world that is."

Off came Maggie's gloves. Bike gloves, that is. "I will say this about Sissy Gilchrist. If someone else hadn't killed her, I would have cheerfully done the job myself."

KIKI EXPLAINS HOW TO DO THEME ALBUMS — FAST!

If you need to make an album fast, and you don't know the recipient well, these tips will help:

1. Pick a neutral solid paper with a textured surface for all your backgrounds.
2. Choose a simple image, such as a flourish or a flower or a symbol. Repeat this in varying sizes and colors on all the pages to pull your album together.
3. Decide on a single color and use it for all your mats. (This will also save you paper.)
4. Select a single typeface of letter stickers, or rubber stamps, or a computer typeface. Use that in varying sizes throughout your project.
5. Divide your photos into topics. Group like photos together on the pages.
6. Create a thumbnail — a small sketch — of each page. Graph paper works well for this. Figure out where your photos will go before you start assembling your album.

FIVE

Sissy Gilchrist wasn't exactly model parent material. Nor was she a co-worker whom people enjoyed. And she wasn't much of a teacher either, according to Maggie. In fact, she would have been unemployed had her father, Quentin Gilchrist, not been a Class of '60 graduate and a generous donor.

"But kill her? Maggie, that's cold," I said as my friend loaded her bike onto her car rack.

"She beat kids down," said Maggie. "Emotionally. She teased them, made fun of them, and generally eroded their self-esteem. Matt was a straight A math student. He'd attended an accelerated math program for years. The first day of class last year she made fun of him for going to get 'extra help.'"

Maggie went on, "Matt's had problems fitting in. His acne doesn't help. But he's always been proud of his math skills. Then

40

Sissy made fun of him. Stripped him of the one area he was confident."

"Could that be why she was killed? I mean, maybe she did that to other kids as well."

"The Mama Bear Syndrome," we chorused. When mothers become overly protective of their young, they can be dangerous to others.

"All I know is my son loved math. It was Matt's best shot at a college scholarship, and Sissy Gilchrist nearly ruined it for him." She grumbled a moment. "He quit his outside studies. He refused to participate in class discussions. Didn't turn in homework. He started saying math was only for geeks and losers."

Sending Matt and Tilly to CALA put a financial strain on the Earhart budget. Maggie'd once told me, "We spend money on CALA thinking it will help our children get into better colleges. Our fingers are crossed the kids will get scholarships later."

"I'm worried. My friend Detective Detweiler thinks our daughters might have seen the murderer."

"Oh, no," Maggie groaned. "That makes sense, though. The girls were in the hall when Mrs. Selsner screamed. Who knows what they saw? But we don't really have a choice about sending them back, do we? What are our options? Transfer them to a public school? Try home-schooling? Like your mother-in-law would stand for that! Get real, Kiki."

I pinched the bridge of my nose. "I don't know what my choices are. Or yours. The jerk who killed George is still on the loose. Now this. I wish I could get into a witness protection program somewhere. I feel like my fanny is sticking out in the breeze — and my kid is at risk."

"Mine, too. But here's the good news: the school shares our concerns. Before I left, I got an interoffice e-mail. Administration outlined our new security measures. We'll have guards walking the halls, new security cameras installed, and gates blocking all the parking lot entrances. All by Monday. Money may not make the world go round, but it sure can buy you a first-class trip and a set of designer luggage."

Our golfers finished later than usual. The coach gave practice instructions while the girls poured water on their necks. St. Louis is known for beastly extremes of weather. This fall had been gorgeous with cool days and cooler nights. The golf course nestled on the south side of the Missouri River, with only a small levee standing sentinel over the reclaimed bottomland. Players always came away from the fields coated with dust. Spackles of dirt covered Maggie and me. We leaned against our cars and talked.

"Why didn't you ask to have Matt moved to another math teacher?"

"We tried. By the time a transfer was in the works, we didn't have to. After Christmas break, Sissy Gilchrist changed. Or at least she seemed to. Matt said she was being nice. I waited for her to revert to type. But it never happened." Maggie plucked at her sweaty hair with thick fingers. Every part of Maggie was solid. You could take her to the bank and a teller would hand over her weight in gold.

"Wow. What was it? A warning from CALA administration? A religious conversion? Massive medication? Hmm?"

Maggie smirked. "Something more prosaic. She fell in love."

I plugged my phone into the car charger. Anya's rang as we pulled onto Highway 40 to make the journey back home. She handed it over.

"Come by my house," said my mother-in-law. "It's Shabbas." And she hung up.

How very, very Sheila. No "please," no

43

"would you," no nothing but her directive.

I couldn't go directly there; I had to let my Great Dane out for a piddle or I'd come home to Lake Mini-Pee-Pee.

I raced in, let out Gracie, watched her do her business, and mulled over my choices. They were none and none. Sheila's wish was my command. I knew when she loaned me money that she'd extract her pound of flesh. I also knew she'd take it one postage stamp square at a time.

I gritted my teeth. Is it any wonder my dentist Dr. Wallace told me I need to wear an "appliance"? Sounds like a washer-dryer combination, but he assures me it's really a mouth guard like boxers use. I probably need one. The dental tech noticed I'm wearing down my molars. Which probably explains why I've been getting headaches and popping Advil like they are jelly beans. "Stress," said Dr. Wallace.

"Sheila," I muttered to myself.

Anya was half-asleep by the time we pulled up at her grandmother's. I roused her by shaking her shoulder. I followed my child in after Linnea, Sheila's maid, opened the door. Sheila took one glance at sweaty, stinky me and said, "Not on my furniture, you don't. Come back to the kitchen. You can sit on a stool."

Wasn't that special?

She directed Anya to go upstairs and take a shower. My daughter has her own bedroom at Sheila's. I "sort of" have a guest bedroom there, which I guess counts under the heading "making progress."

St. Louis County Police Chief Robbie Holmes didn't care. He greeted me with a hug as I pulled up a seat on the far side of the granite countertop. Linnea slid a huge glass of frosty lemonade toward me and a plate of cheese and crackers. Despite the Oreos, I was famished.

"Don't eat that," said Sheila, moving the plate out of my reach. "You've gotten positively pudgy, Kiki. Robbie and I were discussing what happened today at CALA," said Sheila. "It was irresponsible for you to be unavailable by phone with that happening."

I sighed. I was learning — slowly — not to respond to her jabs. Linnea took the plate from her employer and gave me a small "what can you do" shrug.

"Chief Holmes, will Anya be safe going back to school on Monday?"

His weathered face nodded. He had this expression of tiredness, brought on I was certain, by all the horrible scenes he'd witnessed. Yet, his eyes were incredibly warm and concerned. In many ways, he was proof that opposites attract because Sheila's blue peepers could be so ice-cold. "We should be making an arrest here shortly."

"What's the holdup?" Sheila raised a perfectly shaped and shaded eyebrow.

"We've yet to locate the murder weapon."

Sheila sniffed. "How hard can that be? A gun at CALA? That would seem obvious."

I noticed Linnea struggling not to make a face behind my mother-in-law's back. She slid the plate of cheese and crackers back in front of me. To cover my corresponding grin, I lifted my glass and winked at Linnea.

Good old Sheila. The world was such a simple place to her: She had all the answers and by golly, you were a dope if you didn't.

Chief Holmes smiled at my mother-in-law, who picked up the plate and took it away from me. That man was totally besotted and it showed. He gave her an indulgent little hug. "Sheila, darling, not every murder is committed with a gun. This was a brick."

I added, "Wow. If you're ready to make an arrest, you've been moving right along."

He shrugged. "Everyone connected with CALA wants to get this behind them as fast as possible. But to your question, Kiki, of course, there are safety concerns." He reached past Linnea, grabbed the plate of cheese and crackers and set it back down in front of me.

He continued, "The school is following our suggestions on a variety of procedures. Some public. Some not. And we have our eye on a person of interest. More importantly, I'm concerned about Anya. How's that little sweetheart doing?"

"She sure had a shock."

"Of course she did! It was irresponsible of you to take her out golfing," said Sheila. She reached past Police Chief Holmes, picked up the plate of cheese and crackers and handed it back to Linnea. "She should have been seen by a doctor and given a tranquilizer."

Chief Holmes shook his head at Sheila and ruffled her hair. He had incredibly huge hands, ham hocks really. "Sheila, calm down."

Wow.

I nearly fell off my seat. No one touched Sheila's hair. No one. It was always a perfect coiffure, and now it stuck out every which way.

"Sheila, my darling," he said. He grabbed the cheese and cracker plate and set it back in front of me. "Fresh air and exercise are good for the child. Believe me, when you've seen something like this, you need every distraction you can get. This way she'll sleep well tonight. You don't want to start her on pills. Kids and pills are a bad mix." He tossed a smile my way and then said to her, "I think you're being a little hard on your daughter."

Double wow.

"Daughter-in-law," said Sheila.

Chief Holmes bent her head to his to give her a quick kiss on the cheek, which caused Sheila to flush with pleasure. (Meanwhile I stuffed a cracker and a wodge of cheese into my mouth. I also slipped two crackers down the pocket at the back of my bicyclist's shirt.) "Kiki's your daughter. She stood by your son. She's the mother of your grandbaby. To my mind, you couldn't have done better in the family lottery if you'd had access to the Almighty's own insider knowledge. Kiki's a keeper."

Okay, triple wow. I was now officially in love with Robbie Holmes. What a nice guy.

Sheila did settle down a little. "Daughters are so much more trouble than boys. That Sissy Gilchrist has done nothing but break her parents' hearts. She was a sweet little girl and then something happened. Her poor mother, Paula. If it hasn't been one thing, it's another with that child."

An image of Sissy's body popped into my head. Child? Sissy was a woman and dressed the part. Her corpse had been wearing a low-cut knit top, a dramatic push-up bra, and pants so tight the seams screamed for mercy.

"Something happened to Sissy?" I focused on Sheila's remark. That resonated with me. My daughter had grown increasingly moody. I worried it was the onset of puberty, and I took every opportunity to learn about what to expect. I'd been a very compliant child. But then, I'd grown up scared.

Sheila sniffed. "Something to do with a horse. Or horses. The Gilchrists didn't have the money to buy one for her when she was younger so she rode at . . ." and my mother-in-law snapped her fingers trying to recall the name. "Red Leaf Stables. On the way to St. Albans. The owner was the principal in the accounting firm where Quentin Gilchrist worked. Before Quentin made partner."

"Her personality changed because of a horse?" Chief Holmes sounded as incredulous as I felt.

Sheila brushed away his comment with a wave of her hand. "Not exactly. But something happened. Some drama about a horse. I remember how upset Paula was. Next I heard how Sissy was acting out. She became attracted to inappropriate men." Sheila glanced pointedly at Linnea, who had her back to us.

"Inappropriate? In what way?" I couldn't believe what Sheila was implying. Especially when Linnea was standing two feet away. But, I was fairly certain Linnea knew all Sheila's faults. Probably much better than I did because she was with the woman eight hours a day.

My mother-in-law's jaw tensed. "In every way. Unsuitable in their professions as well. She married outside her station."

Like my husband had. I bit back the angry words forming storm clouds in my mind. Sheila could be so mean-spirited and small-minded. How she'd ever raised a wonderful son like George was simply beyond me. Not for the first time did I wonder if Harry Lowenstein should have been canonized as a saint. But Jews don't have saints, so there you go.

A tight chuckle came from Chief Holmes. "Sheila, Sissy Gilchrist married a policeman, didn't she?"

I could see the hurt in his eyes.

And Sheila did, too.

Six

We lit the candles. Chief Holmes, a staunch Roman Catholic, stood with his head bowed as we prayed, thanking God for the light, the wine, and the bread. The Friday night prayers are a lovely reminder that even in the midst of tragedy, God has blessed us. I took a tiny sip of the wine and sent up my own prayer of gratitude that Anya was safe. I don't ask God for much for me. I figure God's done more than enough on my behalf. I have friends, a roof over my head, and a darling child. My prayers are prayers of thanks, not of need.

Most of the time.

Over the meal, Sheila coaxed Anya to spend the night with her, which was good because I had a Saturday afternoon class to teach at Time in a Bottle. I took Anya aside and asked again, "How are you? Do you want to talk? Or come home?"

She rolled her eyes at me. (There must be

something going around, some eye-rolling virus.) "Moo-oom. I'm in the house with the chief of police and his girlfriend. It's the safest I've been all day. Now, just quit it."

I drove home with my phone plugged into the car charger. I quickly returned calls from Dodie, plus my friends Mert and Clancy, leaving them voice mails that Anya was all right, and the situation was under control. (Whatever that meant.) I said I'd talk with them the next day. As I stood outside waiting for Gracie to finish her business, my cell phone rang. Sheila didn't bother with hello. She started right in on me. "Why didn't you tell me that detective was involved in this? That he talked to my granddaughter?"

"I figured Chief Holmes would tell you."

"He did. Later. But you should have!" She took off on Detweiler, calling him everything but human. She'd been pretty peeved when she discovered (before I did) that the hunky detective was married. He was definitely on her bad side. Sheila slowed down a bit and I managed to put in a word. "Honestly Sheila, I'm glad. Anya was comforted by his presence. I got to the school minutes after they called, but he was there for her."

"Well," Sheila said. "All I have to say is he better not come sniffing around after you anymore." I almost laughed. Sheila was . . . well, Sheila was Sheila. I bet she had her own branch on the evolutionary tree.

I braced myself for more to come, but three beeps saved me as my partially charged phone gave up on my mother-in-law. For once, I was happy that my cell phone battery never lasted as long as Jack Bauer's did on *24*.

"The Major Case Squad has arrested a suspect in the murder of Sissy Gilchrist, a teacher at CALA," said the radio reporter. I listened on the way to a spinning class the next morning. Chief Holmes had been as good as his word. I parked my car and rested my head on the steering wheel. Thank goodness. That was one less thing in life to stress about.

Kelly, our spinning instructor told us to bring our heart rates to 80 percent of max. "Hold them there for ten minutes. Pretend you are at the front of the pelaton. You are pulling away from the pack. Go! Go! Go!"

Forget the pelaton.

I had plenty of other problems to pedal away from. A murder in my daughter's school. My child's blossoming adolescence. Her safety. A married cop I was attracted to. My weight. A guy named Ben Novak I'd been dating but wasn't sure about. My best friend Mert's brother, Johnny, a former felon, who occasionally asked me out for a "good time." My weight. The knowledge my mother-in-law thought I was an idiot. My friend Clancy, who was too busy these days to chat. The fact I owed Sheila money. My weight. And work.

Did I mention work?

My boss, Dodie Goldfader, was having a lump in her breast biopsied on Tuesday. Dodie was scared, and who could blame her? Her mother died of breast cancer. So after finding the lump, Dodie sank into denial. She waited as long as possible. She had a whale of an excuse. Her husband, Horace, had unexpectedly lost his job and their insurance. Had she waited too long? If she died . . . oh, Lord . . . what would I do? She was my friend, and yeah, what about my job? How horrid of me to be so selfish, but it was true.

These thoughts propelled me, plus the worry that my poochy tummy was the first thing anyone noticed when they saw me coming.

I had a real list of concerns. But all my worries faded away when I worked up a sweat on a bike.

Lance Armstrong and I rode together in

my mind.

In my dreams.

In real life, I was one of a dozen in a spinning class practicing drafting. At the end of our ten-minute sprint at maximum heart rate, our instructor Kelly assigned us numbers. We each took turns cranking up the resistance on our bikes and pretending we were "pulling" the other bikers up a hill, just like the team did for Armstrong at Tour de France. For forty-five minutes we took turns riding our hardest, revving up our heartbeats, and conquering an imaginary route over hills and flatlands.

Finally, Kelly ordered us to slow down and cool down.

As we stretched, one biker asked, "Hey, Kelly, how come there are never any valleys on these rides? Just hills and more hills?"

Kelly laughed. "Because valleys don't make you strong, dude. You can do valleys on your own time. And you need to be strong. We're planning that outdoor ride next week. You don't want me passing you up on those hills."

I was dabbing the back of my neck with a towel when I caught a glimpse of a familiar profile outside the spinning room.

"What are you doing here?" I asked Detweiler. "Did you come to talk with someone?"

"You," he said. "Only you, Kiki."

I nearly swooned. My heart monitor beeped as my pulse raced into the red zone. Okay, so he still made my heart pound. I was NOT giving in. No way. I would totally resist his charms.

"Cute outfit," he said as his eyes swept over me.

Um, about resisting those charms. Not so much.

My knees went rubbery. I stood up straighter and pulled in my gut. Thank goodness my bike shorts are made of heavy-duty Spandex. (I'd bought these hoping to lose weight. I had to grease my thighs and lie on the floor to pull the shorts up and on. I'd once lost three fingernails peeling them down to pee. At least I was burning extra calories!)

"Kaldi's on THF?" He grinned at me. "I'm buying."

Gosh, was he ever gorgeous? A few other female exercisers must have thought so, too. I could see them staring at us. Well, at him. Okay, at his backside.

I sucked in my tummy, cut off my air supply, and still managed to stay conscious long enough to nod "yes."

It was only 10:05 a.m. When you rise with the sun, the day is longer than you can stand without a hefty dose of caffeine. I didn't have to be at the store until noon, so I could squander a little time. Okay, I admit: Detweiler still was my favorite time-wasting activity.

And Kaldi's was on my way home, and it featured fabulous baked goods. Why else would I drive all the way out to Chesterfield Valley to take a spinning class? Especially when Maggie had text-messaged to say she couldn't join me?

The line at the counter snaked around the self-serve condiment area and nearly out the front door. I took my place at the end. Detweiler stepped up and paid for my order. He handed me a latte (sugar-free, low-fat, vanilla) and an iced cookie.

He knew me too well.

"I'm part of the Major Case Squad."

I nodded. The sugar cookie was cut into a big lavender flower, the inside soft and the topping buttery.

Detweiler glanced around furtively. We stood on the sidewalk. Without discussion, we headed for the small boulevard of grass between Kaldi's and the street. There we plopped down on a parking bumper to sit.

"Forensics found debris embedded in the skull. Clay."

"Clay?"

"You know the layout of the school. The theatre doorway is not far from the construction site for the new lunchroom. The murderer must have picked up one of the bricks on the skids. No one saw anyone carrying a bloody brick. It'd make sense to wipe the thing off and put it back in the pile. But telling which one it might be is complicated. The architect ordered a mixture of old and new bricks to match the existing building. Esthetics and all that. We can't match the particles on Ms. Gilchrist's body to any particular kiln."

Detweiler pointed and said, "You have icing on your face." He smiled as he lightly traced a spot beside my mouth. His finger tickled. I rubbed the spot furiously. He continued, "Point is we're having no luck finding the murder weapon. Guess how many bricks are sitting on those skids."

I couldn't. I need to make hash marks when we take inventory. My math skills are fine until I run out of digits.

"Four thousand seven hundred sixteen. Luminal detects body fluids, but the bloody surface could be on the inside of the stacks. Or even part of the new wall."

That didn't make sense to me and I guess my face showed my confusion.

"There was a lag between when the murder occurred, and the body was found. Not long, but enough that a bricklayer could have laid the one brick we're hunting for. It might be awhile before we can find the murder weapon, if we find it at all."

I didn't say anything. I was happy. I held a cookie in one hand, coffee in another, and I sat beside one of the two people I loved most — ARGH!

I shook myself hard. This was nuts. Here I'd worked so hard to get over him, and I was close to coming undone.

But we were talking about murder. And my child's safety.

I struggled to concentrate.

"The crime must have happened between 9:30 a.m. and 10. Ms. Gilchrist dropped her son Christopher off in the kindergarten room shortly before then. Several staff members saw her."

I remembered Maggie saying Sissy's son was in her classroom. "The radio said you have a suspect in custody. Seems like all you need to do is tie up loose ends." My unspoken message was, "So we don't have any reason to see each other, do we?"

Detweiler ran his hand through his hair,

pushing away the lick of hair that always threatened to fall over one eye. "Corey Johnson, the basketball coach, has been arrested."

My jaw flapped in the breeze. Maggie had mentioned Sissy was dating. But . . . someone at CALA? Another teacher? Could the coach have murdered her? I reviewed what I knew of the man. Being a very visual person, the first thing that popped into my head was an image. I remembered Coach Johnson as being a nice-looking man with a very pointed chin. He was young, well-liked, and in the mold of our newest president: African American. The school pointed to him at every opportunity to prove their dedication to diversity. More importantly than that, he'd established a reputation as one of the kids' favorites. The man was one of those rare teachers who always managed to make time for his students. He captured their trust and respect. Even Anya, who'd only met him as a visiting "lecturer" for a health class, adored the man. "He remembered all our names the first day, Mom," she said with amazement. "He sees you in the hall, and he stops to ask how you are. And he really listens! He's way cool."

"Corey didn't do it," Detweiler interrupted my thoughts. "Ms. Gilchrist's parents hate him. Can't stand him. They put heat on the department. Mr. Gilchrist is connected. The governor's office called yesterday afternoon. Sent word for us to get on the stick and arrest the coach. Not even twelve hours after the woman's body was discovered!"

Of course the Gilchrists would want the authorities to move fast. So would the school. Despite all the hype about security, everyone at CALA was at risk until the killer was caught. But more importantly, why was Detweiler so certain Corey wasn't involved?

And why did he call the coach by his Christian name? Detweiler and other cops habitually refer to people by their courtesy titles. I think it helps them sound respectful. It probably also helps maintain professionalism and, let's be honest, it would sound better in court, so it was a good habit to develop.

"What makes you so sure he didn't do it?" Then another thought. "Why are you sharing all this with me?"

He blushed and turned away.

My own personal slide show started up in my head. I saw Detweiler kissing me. I saw Detweiler's wife, Brenda. I saw myself looking and acting like a fool when I met her. I felt embarrassed and sad and hurt all over again.

My cheeks flamed red. How stupid I was. I'd barely managed to move on with my life, and here I was, spending time with the man I struggled to avoid.

"I can't do this." I rose, but he grabbed the back of my bike shorts. If I hadn't sat back down, I'd have mooned all of Chesterfield Valley.

"I need your help," Detweiler's voice moved up a notch.

"Hey, how about you ask your wife?" After the words were out, I regretted them.

Detweiler gave me a long look, as a vein pulsed in his temple. "Don't. Just. Don't. Whatever wrong I've done you, that's on my head. I deserve it. But Corey didn't kill that woman. He shouldn't have to pay for my mistakes. I need your help. Even if you won't let me explain about us."

He was right about that. I hadn't let him "explain" his situation. I couldn't. If I had, I would have run the risk of throwing caution — and my morals — to the wind. Instead, I'd stuffed my feelings down with food and tried to move on.

Now here I was. Back at square one.

Would I ever learn? I groaned.

"Please, Kiki," he reached for my shoulder. "You're the only person I trust to tell me about the inner-workings of that school. You've got a good mind and a sharp grasp of details. You're on the inside. I'll never be. And we won't have access to interviews or the people we need. Everyone involved has lawyered up. You know how these people are! The Major Case Squad captain believes we have a good suspect. He's committed to looking for evidence to close the case. I can't count on much cooperation. Not from my peers or from the school."

I brushed his hand away. This time I did stand up. I'll give him this, he sounded desperate. And it broke my heart. The hurt fortified me. I had to be strong. I had to wrench myself away from this man before it was too late. I swallowed hard. "Tell me one good reason I should help you. Why should I take your word for it that you all have the wrong man?"

"I think Anya saw the killer."

"Nice try. You said that before. That's just baloney."

He took a long deep breath and said, "Kiki, it's not baloney. I know Corey. He didn't do it — which means someone else did. And Anya might be in danger! Look at the timeline! Anya and her friend were in the hall right as Mrs. Selsner found the body. They were coming back from the library. They walked down the hall. They stopped in the bathroom next to the balcony door. Then they ran out when they heard the screams. The killer had only one way out — that balcony door. The girls said they saw lots of people that morning."

Anya hadn't told me this. But then, she hadn't had time to. We'd gone from home and television to golf and then Sheila's. Crud. How could I have been so stupid? What was I, contestant Number One in the Bad Mother of the Year show? I shouldn't have left my daughter with her grandmother. Anya hadn't been willing to talk, but maybe if I'd given her more time, she would have confided in me.

Instead, I entrusted her to Sheila and I drove away.

I shook my head as I mentally flagellated myself. What was it about parenting that made the job so treacherous? Every step seemed fraught with the possibility of life-altering mistakes. No wonder God gave kids two parents: Raising a child took the combined mental powers of two adults. And I was one partner light.

The import of Detweiler's words hit me. "Lots . . . lots of people? They saw them? After the murder?"

"There was a sports booster meeting happening about the time Mrs. Selsner yelled." He smashed his cup. "Okay, so Anya and Tilly don't realize they saw the killer, but they might have. Whoever did this probably blended in. He or she could be one of the parents! The girls could have seen something small but significant. They were the only students wandering around that particular hallway."

My mouth fell open. Adults could fend for themselves. But Anya and Tilly? At risk? He was right. This was a very, very bad situation.

But then again, they'd arrested Coach Johnson. Chief Holmes must have felt confident that Coach Johnson was the killer.

Whom did I trust more? Detweiler or his boss?

The detective's face was full of emotion. I could recall only one other time I'd seem him so upset — the night I learned he was married.

"I know I was unfair to you. I know the evidence looks bad. But I also know Corey. Like a brother." Detweiler turned those amazing bottle-green eyes on me, and I thought I saw a world of sadness in them. "I have no right to ask you to help me. Or Corey. But I am concerned about Anya. I couldn't stand it if something happened to her. I couldn't live with myself."

SEVEN

I sank back down on the curb. "What makes you so sure he's innocent?" Last fall I was accused of a crime I didn't do. I knew how helpless a person could feel. But I needed proof that Detweiler wasn't shining me on. I couldn't trust myself, and therefore, I couldn't trust him.

He talked a mile a minute. "Corey and Ms. Gilchrist were involved. Romantically. But they were in love. He'd never hurt her."

"You know this because?"

While Chad Detweiler was training to become a policeman, he'd volunteered for a youth basketball program. "Corey bounced around from foster home to foster home. His adoptive parents both died from complications of diabetes. I guess you could say he and I bonded. He was like a younger brother. I had him over to our family farm in Illinois. My sisters adored him. He helped my dad with chores. My mom even taught him to make pie crust! We played ball together. The kid was a natural. His talent was impressive."

The two remained friends even as Corey was given a college scholarship by an anonymous donor to study history and sports management.

"I visited him on Big Brother weekends at college. We've always stayed close. We've been friends for ten years," he finished.

I had to admit, this was pretty compelling. Still, I couldn't keep silent.

"You said he'd never hurt Sissy. What do you base that on? A man can be one way with his guy friends and another with women. You know that."

"I taught Corey to drive. He had his permit, we were on a city street, and he ran up a curb rather than hit a baby bird that was in the street. He worshiped his adoptive mother. Loved both his parents, actually. But she was a really strong role model. And he treated my sisters and my mother with total respect.

"I'm not saying it couldn't have happened. I've been a cop too long to say a person would never snap. But I can tell you they were going to get married. He knew she was flawed. He knew she had a past. They talked about it. Seems to me, if you can talk, you don't need to resort to violence."

I agreed with his logic. "If they were planning a future together, why is he under suspicion?"

"They'd been seen together having a disagreement early that morning. He doesn't have an alibi for the time she was killed. He says he was in his office working on baseball rosters. You know how it is, he teaches and is in charge of three sports rotations."

My mind raced ahead. "Let's go back to yesterday. You said the girls saw a lot of people. Any idea who?"

"We have the list of those who RSVPed to come to the sports booster meeting. I doubt it's accurate. The girls gave us a few names. But we haven't been able to interview anyone on our list."

"Why not?"

"The school's attorney stopped us. He's throwing all sorts of motions at us . . . breach of privacy . . ." Detweiler sighed. "No one will confirm who was at the event. They say they don't take roll."

That was true. The RSVP was merely a head count for refreshments and a chance for the school to prepare gorgeous name tags. Which half the time people didn't bother with. Other than what folks reported, there'd be no way to tell who attended.

I told Detweiler this and his shoulders sagged. "Every request we've made is followed by, 'Do you have a warrant?' "

"But surely Elliott McMahan, the headmaster, wants to help you build your case. It's to his advantage to get this over with."

"As far as he's concerned, it is over because Corey is in custody. Mr. McMahan hates the idea a staff member was involved, but frankly, he's got his hands full. Parents are raising Cain. Mr. McMahan is spending hours on the phone, calming parents down. The Major Case Squad captain's phone lines are jammed. The more time we waste on stupid phone calls, the less progress we make. The upshot? We've got nothing so far." He stopped to take a breath and grumble, "Except suspicion. And a small amount of circumstantial evidence. So he had brick dust on his clothes and in his office. There's dust everywhere, and his office is close to the construction site."

Detweiler rubbed his face with both hands. "I feel like I'm storming the gates of a medieval castle. Everybody who is anybody is connected to CALA. I'm beginning to think all of Old St. Louis went there."

"They did."

There was that term: "Old St. Louis." A

phrase Sheila delighted in bandying about. "Old" was certainly a relevant comparison.

Detweiler must have read my mind. "We're not talking ancient civilizations here or landed gentry. I'm sick of hearing, 'Talk to my attorney.' "

What he didn't say, and we both knew, was that Corey Johnson didn't have a prayer. Not only was he the wrong color, he wasn't Old St. Louis. If all of them thought he was guilty, he was in deep doodoo. The kind of doo-doo these people scraped off their shoes.

Detweiler ran a hand through his spiky hair. At this rate, he was going to rub it all off. That happened to my Ken doll. That was before Mattel quit gluing flocking on their heads and painted hairstyles on all the Kens. Pretty weak, if you ask me.

"There's a problem with opportunity. You've got 1,562 students. And 257 faculty and staff. Spread that over a hundred wooded acres, plus volunteers, parents, grandparents, nannies, babysitters —"

I raised my hand in surrender. I got the point. CALA was a world unto itself. Of course, it was that way by design.

"I don't suppose you know anything that might be useful?"

I thought a minute. I stared hard into the

flowers planted thickly around the THF Boulevard signage. The effect was darn pretty. Pink, purple, and white petunias blanketed a small area.

There would be a lot of flowers at Sissy Gilchrist's funeral. Wasted flowers. That's why the Jews don't do flowers at funerals. The dead can't enjoy them. Why not give the money to a cause that will ensure the person's memory lives on?

"What do you need from me?"

"Inside dope. Who's connected to whom. Who hated Ms. Gilchrist and why."

I thought about Maggie and what she'd said. Detweiler was asking a lot. If calm, kind Maggie would have cheerfully strangled Sissy Gilchrist, you could bet there were lots of folks who wanted to see her dead and gone. I didn't want to rat out my pal, Maggie. She'd been talking to me in confidence. And what was it Sheila had said? Sissy and her inappropriate men? Ugh.

Nope, I had nothing to say. There was no currency in getting involved. I'd just tick a lot of people off.

I was about to open my mouth and tell him I wouldn't — couldn't — help when a woman and her daughter walked toward us, clearly on their way into Kaldi's. The girl must have been about fourth grade, because her permanent teeth were oversized for her mouth. Her hand rested confidently in her mother's. A pink and white polka-dot bow rode up and down on her ponytail. A stuffed animal in a decidedly grubby hue of pink was tucked under her free arm. She was a bit old to be carrying a lovey, but so what?

Sissy Gilchrist had once been a child. She had a mother. Whatever Sissy had become in the years between fourth grade and now, she began as we all do, as an innocent. Maybe her mother didn't much cotton to the woman her child had become. Join the club. Mine wasn't too thrilled with me either. But that really didn't matter. Sissy was another mother's child, and every one of us deserves justice, no matter how tawdry our lives.

But why me? Why should I stick my neck out?

The little girl stopped two feet from us and threw her arms around her mother's thighs, freezing the woman's progress with the ferocity of her hug. In response, the mother leaned over and held the child close, stroking her hair and planting a kiss on the top of her head. Then they broke apart and walked hand in hand into Kaldi's.

What if someone had — God forbid — murdered my Anya? A chill went through my body, followed immediately by a hot wave of anger.

Detweiler was watching the duo, too. His eyes softened as he saw the little girl swinging her stuffed animal.

I found my voice. "Okay. I'll help you."

EIGHT

Two hours later, my harlequin Great Dane and I climbed out of my beaten-up BMW and entered the back door of Time in a Bottle. I carried a fruit salad I'd thrown together by mixing a can of cherry pie filling and two cans of drained fruit cocktail. Scrapbookers are always hungry, and I was determined to try to feed our croppers at least one healthy dish per get-together.

My boss, Dodie, was in the backroom, next to Gracie's empty doggy playpen. "About time. How's Anya?" Her voice was gruff, but she bent to love up Gracie, and I could see that Dodie wasn't angry.

I put the salad in the refrigerator and told my boss about Anya's scare. Dodie loved Anya. When I'd accepted the job, Dodie agreed my daughter would come first, and she's never gone back on her word. "CALA has too much at stake to take this crime casually. Oy. Just because you can talk doesn't mean you are making sense," she said, dipping into her plentiful store of Jewish sayings.

Reading the confusion on my face, she added, "CALA will do a lot, but that doesn't mean the school will do what's right."

She was right. She flipped open her cell phone and dialed a number. "Horace? She's here," she said.

I wondered why she'd stop and tell her hubby I'd come to work, but I didn't ask. Tuesday was her biopsy. She'd been grouchy as all get-out, but I didn't blame her. I knew she was scared. And unfortunately, Dodie seemed resigned to a bad result. No matter how often I tried to convince her that survival rates are excellent these days, she turned deaf to my preaching. On an elemental level, Dodie had decided she had cancer. Maybe she was simply in tune with her body, and knew it to be true, but I was pretty confident she'd been unable to separate her mother's fate from her own. I recalled visiting Graceland and hearing how Elvis Presley had died the same day and month as his mother had, too. Perhaps this was more common than I realized.

"I'm all ready for the crop. I finished everything yesterday," I said. "See? We're making family trees. All that's left is to bag up the individual project pieces." From a shallow box I retrieved our project and held it in my outstretched hand. A sense of satisfaction swept over me as I saw that Dodie was impressed.

"Where on earth do you come up with this?"

I smiled. "I think it up in my little head, I do. I'd better get to work."

Dodie put up a hand to stay me. "Horace will be here in a minute. We need to talk with you."

My stomach churned. I wondered what was up, and naturally being the worry-wart I am, panic consumed me. I come by this naturally. Once my sister Amanda suggested we all take turns worrying. "I'll take Monday, Kiki can take Tuesday, Catherine can take Wednesday, Mom can take Thursday, and Aunt Gwen can take Friday. That way we'll worry more efficiently. If something happens to any of us on your day, it's that person's fault — and we can blame her."

Sounded reasonable to me.

I puttered around straightening paper before turning to the die cut machine to punch trees from brown cardstock.

Horace came through the front door, turned our sign to CLOSED, and motioned me to the back. My knees shook as we took seats in Dodie's office, and I fought a mouth so dry my lips caught on my teeth. I loved my job. I really did. This was the first time I'd ever been good at something. Now it was all about to come to an end.

I could tell he was going to fire me. Why else had he come? And why close the shop?

I sniffled and tried to act calm.

Horace nodded to Dodie. She pulled a leather briefcase from her side of the desk, opened it, and pulled out a manila folder. "We have a special project for you, Kiki, but first you need to sign a confidentiality agreement. Horace can notarize it."

"Huh?"

"The customer who has contracted with us doesn't want anyone to see this project and expects you not to talk about it," Dodie said. "Let me back up. Our customer is getting a divorce from a prominent local person. Her attorney has suggested that she have a scrapbook of her life made as an exhibit. This scrapbook will be entered into the court proceedings to show the judge her lifestyle. She doesn't want a settlement that will reduce her standard of living."

Horace sighed. "The man has cheated on her several times. A private investigator is gathering proof as we speak of the latest infidelity. But this man is very prominent and well-off. His wife is confident he'll do everything he can to leave her in the poor-house."

Dodie interrupted. "Petty thieves are hanged, but the big ones go free. This creep has all kinds of connections. Legal, business, political, you name it. He told her years ago she'd never see a penny if she filed. And he promised to make her lose face in the community."

"Are there children involved?" I mused out loud.

"Yes," said Dodie, "but that doesn't necessarily matter."

"What kind of a judge wouldn't make sure he provides for his family?"

"A judge who owes a lot to this man. Or in this case, several judges. If one of them gets the case, this woman is matzoh."

"What does a confidentiality agreement entail?"

"You can't work on this when anyone else is in the store. We suggest you keep all the photos and what-not inside this briefcase. You can see it has a combination lock. You can't talk about what you see in the project. You can't mention it to anyone. I will tell Bama you are doing it, so she doesn't walk in on you, but that's all. You can't contact the client," and here Dodie paused. "This woman is someone you might meet in a social context. So you need to be especially discreet. It would be easy for you to let it slip."

She was calling me a blabbermouth. That hurt. My expression must have changed, because I caught the flare of emotion in Dodie's eyes. "Sunshine, you love to talk about your scrapbooking. You're an addict. But this client asked me to put my best employee on the job, and that's you. I know you can handle this."

I signed the papers, noted the due date of the project, realized I'd be coming in before the store opened and staying late to get it done.

How weird was all that?

I put the briefcase in the trunk of my car and went about my work.

The rest of the day went by pretty slowly, but at six p.m. our croppers started to pour in. I grabbed a Slim-Fast® bar and an apple to tide me over until we broke out the treats. Now that Detweiler was back in my life (sort of), I needed to quit eating like a starved pig at a trough of fresh slop.

Our regular gang was all in attendance. We were delighted to welcome back Bonnie Gossage, an attorney who worked part-time since the birth of her son Felix. She'd finally gotten a regular sitter for her little boy. We used to welcome him to our crops, but now he'd started to "cruise," grabbing on to everything within reach, and we all worried he'd pull something heavy over on his head or snatch up a sharp craft knife.

Addison Kobie was working on a memory album of her high school days. Joyce Casaldi and her daughter Ashlyn brought a graduation album as well. Nancy Weaver was trying to organize vacation photos she'd taken of her husband, Mark, and the kids Eliza, Jackson, and Chase.

My pal Clancy Whitehead showed up to work on her first album. She was making good progress. Each week I could see her grow more confident about her skills. As a divorcee with an empty nest, she needed a hobby. Scrapbooking and taking college courses now soaked up most of her free time. (That left me a little lonely for her, but I was happy she was busy.)

Another friend, Ella Latreau Walden, a mother from CALA, was also learning the craft. Yes, that was "Latreau" like the theatre where Sissy met her demise. Ella's family was very involved in our children's school.

Some days poor Ella was all thumbs, but I admired her for keeping at it. She brought another CALA mom with her, Patricia Bigler. At nearly six feet tall, Patricia towered over me, so I used the cue "bigger" to remember her last name.

Ella was unusually quiet tonight. I figured she too was worried about the murder, especially since it had happened in the theatre that bore her family name.

LaShana Freeman joined us, pulling out an old family album, her toffee-colored skin and inky black hair a strong contrast to Ella's blonde-streaked hair and Patricia's almost ghostly pale skin and hair.

Last but not least, my best friend Mert Chambers strolled in. She was carrying a plate of cookies. I guess my face showed how surprised I was — Mert never cooks — because she shook her head and wagged a finger at me. "This here was made by my baby brother Johnny 'cause he's such a sweetheart."

Mert's hands were encrusted with cocktail rings, and she had a butterfly tattoo on her right ankle. She and Tammy Faye Baker belonged to the "pile-it-on-thick" school of beauty. Mert always "dressed up" for our crops. Her scrawny shoulders sported the last of a summer tan under a bright red strappy T-shirt with a neckline of lace and sequins. She paired it with bottoms that gave a whole new meaning to short-shorts.

I liked Mert. I liked her a lot. She was genuine and good-hearted. I felt much more comfortable with her than I did with the mothers at Anya's school. They intimidated me.

"Heard about the murder at the school."

"Yep."

Mert peeled the plastic wrap off the plate of cookies. We were at a folding card table a good distance from the craft table. This separation of food and craft kept the scrapbooking area clean and free of spillage which could ruin a photo or a page layout. Mert spoke in a low voice. "I know her ex, Sissy Gilchrist's ex, that is. Danny Gartner. Know the whole family, in fact."

I shouldn't have been surprised. Mert had lived here her whole life, and she knew everybody, absolutely everybody. She'd worked for enough people, hung around enough bars, and picked up enough gossip to do a lot of damage. I knew from helping her out on occasion, both in her dogsitting business and with her janitorial firm — I was always keen to pick up part-time work — that cleaning houses was an entrée to dirt, all sorts of it. Although Mert wasn't a gossip, she could be persuaded to share. If she thought it appropriate. Just like Maggie, she took the confidentiality of her work very seriously. But she took our friendship as a higher priority, and for that, I was exceedingly thankful.

"What's Sissy's husband like?"

"His momma gets groomed regular at the vet's office. His daddy is an equal-opportunity hater. They're all racist. Whole family belongs to the Aryan nation. Supposed to hate blacks, but figured hating was more fun than killing cats, so they decided not only to hate blacks, but browns, yellows, and Jews. You can just imagine how they feel about our new president. They call him Oba-mination."

"Oh." That was all I managed. My mental wheels were turning. So Sissy's ex hated blacks. Did he know she was romantically involved with an African American? Could he have decided she should be punished? Local racist groups were not above making examples out of people.

Mert raised an eyebrow. "Spill it."

I motioned for her to help me get the rest of the treats from the refrigerator in our backroom. As we worked, I told her about what Anya had seen and Detweiler's request.

She gave me a long, meaningful look. Mert knew we had a Jewish household even though I never converted. We'd discussed various aspects of religion while giving the baseboards in my new house a wash a couple weeks ago. We had decided we both believed in God, and that our Maker obviously loved diversity, so we had no problem with the differences in our religious views. Instead, we celebrated what we held in common.

"Kiki, you best better stay clear of this."

"How can I?" I hissed. "My daughter may be in danger."

"If you get involved, she sure will be."

I nodded. A dull pounding began in my head.

"The Gartners are mean as snakes with sunburnt bellies. Huh. They believe God made them superior — and they got to fight to wrestle this nation back from Jews and such. Where they get that, I just don't know. Jesus never preached no hate-mongering. I defy them to show it to me in the Bible that he did."

Mert set great store by knowing her Bible. We may have disagreed on how to practice our faiths, but we were united in believing that the underlying principles were the same. Here's how I explained it to Anya: A person who hates a Jew, will hate a black, will hate a Moslem, will hate a Mexican, will hate an Asian, will hate a . . . whatever.

People who hate, hate. It's not about the object of the hatred. It's about justifying an unjustifiable attitude.

I mused over this info about Sissy Gilchrist's ex. I needed to tell Detweiler about what I'd learned. The sooner the better. But there was no way I could call him now.

It was time to get started. I suggested we introduce ourselves, since we had a newcomer in the group. Everyone said her piece and then I turned to Patricia.

"I'm Patricia Krupp Bigler. My daughter Elizabeth goes to CALA with Kiki's and Ella's children." Her voice was barely above a whisper. "I'm working on an album to give Coach Bosch. I was hoping to get to it this evening."

I explained she might have time after we completed our project. If not, she was welcome to drop by the store anytime and use our cropping area. I then directed the women to assemble their materials. We started the project by working on tags. These we labeled with the names of family members. Then we colored the tags with chalk.

Bonnie seemed unusually quiet as she worked. Finally, she turned to Patricia and said, "Is your brother Donald Krupp? The attorney?"

Patricia nodded. Her face should have been lovely with its long oval shape, its cool blue eyes, and its unwrinkled forehead. But she missed the mark, and as I studied her, I wondered why. Taken separately, her features were perfect. But together, she was just . . . blah. Maybe it was her nearly nonexistent chin.

Patricia studied Bonnie. "Are you that woman attorney who defended that . . . Mexican?"

Her tone caused all of us to freeze.

"You must mean Dr. Juan Salvador. He's a U.S. citizen, and he was unfairly accused," said Bonnie. "Which is why the jury found him innocent. I was proud to represent him."

I decided to step in. "Wait until you see how cute this family tree project is. It's a terrific way to display the various branches and how we come together. At the foot, the soil represents the countries of our origins, because most of us are of immigrant stock. We'll label the different mounds with the names of countries of origin."

"How'd you come up with this, Kiki?" asked LaShana.

I explained how Anya brought home her American history book, and I'd read to my shock that Virginia Dare was the first person born in this country. "This can't possibly be right," I pointed out. "There were Indians here. The stork didn't bring them. So maybe she was the first European, but even that's wrong because the Vikings explored Newfoundland and Greenland nearly five hundred years before Columbus."

"Hmm," Patricia brought me back to the present. "I'm not convinced that all this mixing of cultures is always a good thing. Adults get to decide who they socialize with. But our children depend on us to make good decisions. Perhaps it's best for all concerned to socialize with their own kind."

"That can be really hard," said Mert. "Cause I ain't seen no special gathering spot just for turkeys."

I have no idea how we managed to work the rest of the evening without incident, but we did. Perhaps it was because everyone had to concentrate on tearing apart their sheets of words and pasting them to their trees.

True, I wound up copying more sheets because our guests kept complaining, "I ruined mine." I counted six pieces of shredded paper a win, compared to the sort of disaster we'd narrowly avoided. I walked around giving pointers and helping. I admit, I wanted to avoid Patricia, but my job was to be the hostess so I sucked it up and acted as if nothing happened. The group loved the project, added their flowers and a few leaves.

"Aren't you missing one?" Patricia pointed to the tags on Ella's tree.

Ella stiffened.

"I have these sad blank tags. They represent all the miscarriages I had. Remember, Ella? It was awful. I wanted another baby so bad."

"Yes, I remember. That was a very bad time for you."

I did feel a surge of sympathy for our newcomer. I knew I wasn't alone in thinking that to lose a child is the worst thing that could ever happen to anyone. I could see the other women's body stances softening a bit toward Patricia.

"Your tree looks fabulous!" I said cheerily to Ella. Her tags read "Ella, Walter, Frederick, Natalie." She palmed one empty tag.

I tried to dredge up a compliment for Patricia, too, or a sincere comment of condolence, but I couldn't find it within myself. Her tree turned out okay, but a bit sloppy.

Her poor outcome amazed me. But that's how it goes. Oddly enough, I could give the same instructions and products to twenty people and get twenty variations on a theme. A few would always be plug-ugly, no matter what.

"Are you all right?" I asked Ella when I saw her shoulders sagging.

"Just worried about what's happening in the school. How about you? Is Anya okay?"

It was the proverbial elephant in the living room. No one had mentioned the crime during the crop, and I had purposely compartmentalized my thoughts. But I couldn't hold back any longer. "Anya's all right, I guess."

"What do you mean?" Ella perked up.

I reached up to rub my temples. "Sorry," I apologized. "Of course, the situation is upsetting."

"Have you spoken to your detective friend?" asked Bonnie. She knew Detweiler from last year when he'd investigated my husband's murder.

"Um, he was at the scene." I didn't want to say more so I averted my eyes and busied myself picking up stray scraps of paper.

"Thank goodness they have the man in custody," broke in Patricia.

Ella rustled in her purse for her keys. "I need to get home. Will I see you Tuesday at the mothers' book club?"

"Oh, yes," said Dodie. "Kiki is making adorable bookmarks for each of you."

I tried to smile and seem enthusiastic. While my visit to the book club was ostensibly to pass out bookmarks, these would be tucked into an envelope with class listings. So, attending the book club meeting was a job requirement, not a social event for me.

Dodie continued, "Remember, everyone, we're doing a special crop with a special homecoming project. Let me show you." With a ta-dah, she whisked out a layout filled with paper flowers in CALA school colors, royal blue and gold. "Of course, for other schools, the colors will be different, but you can imagine how gorgeous they'll all be. Kiki will teach you to use punches and inks to create this floral display. I'll pass around a clipboard and you can sign up now."

"I can't wait. I promise you that you'll enjoy the homecoming project." And I smiled hard, even though my head split with pain.

HOW TO MAKE KIKI'S FAMILY TREE

This is an adorable project that you can put on a shelf or tabletop to display. It's particularly terrific for the spring.

1. Color copy a page from an old book with the word "family" on it several times. (A children's book is good because of the large type.) Also stamp the word "family" and "love" and "together" in warm brown on a creamy piece of paper or a white piece of paper stained with dark tea.
2. Tear the words apart and glue them to a die cut of a tree with bare branches. (This should be made of brown cardstock, the rougher the paper the better.) Do this on one side only and don't worry if the words stick out past the die cut. Once the words dry, trim them so they are the same shape as your die cut.
3. When the tree is completely covered, dip it in melted beeswax. You can melt the beeswax in the microwave oven very carefully.
4. Twist together several strands of brown wire. This will go on the back of your tree and function as a stand.

Adhere the wire to the tree. (The easiest way is to sew it on with a thread that matches.)

5. Add silk flowers to your tree.
6. Add tiny tags with names of family members.

NINE

After our guests left, I let Gracie out of the playpen and snapped on her leash. I turned to the sound of Dodie's heavy footfalls. She had a habit of clomping along, letting her heavy bulk hit the ground hard with each step. Tonight, she was walking more slowly and awkwardly than usual. I let Gracie out the back, and she quickly did her business.

Dodie stood in the doorway to the stockroom, watching us, and stroking her chin.

"I had a root canal last fall," she said. "It was a whole lot more fun than this evening."

"With any luck, Patricia will never come back."

Dodie gave me a stern look. "Everyone is welcome here."

Oops.

Dodie continued, "But some are more welcome than others."

I laughed.

Mert stepped into the backroom. "You

cain't stop people like her. She don't have a subtle bone in that body of hers."

"That's because prejudice and ignorance go hand in hand," said Dodie. "Like chicken fat and matzo meal."

Not the metaphor that sprang to my mind.

Mert leaned against the wall and shook her head. "You know, folks forget that the father of the American Nazi Party was born right across that river over in Illinois."

This was news to me. Gracie whimpered by my side.

Dodie sighed. "Ladies, I need to call this a night."

Mert jingled her keys. "Me, too. Let's all walk out together, okay?"

That was our new safety routine, one recommended by the local Richmond Heights P.D. While I'd never ask anyone to go with me — I didn't care to be thought a chicken — I felt much more comfortable when we left as a group. As Dodie turned the lock, Mert said, "I got a new pooch for you to babysit. I'm picking him up tomorrow. His name is Mr. Gibbes. Is the kid at Sheila's?"

"Yes." I didn't tell Mert I needed to chat with Detweiler. I knew I should just call him and leave a message. But I thought it possible he'd drop by to hear what I'd learned, and I struggled to come up with a reasonable excuse for why he should. "How about you call me first? Make sure I'm home?"

My friend gave me a long thoughtful stare as we stood beside our cars. "You got plans?"

I blushed. "Uh, no."

Dodie climbed into hers and turned on her lights.

"I'll call first," my best friend said. Her eyes were narrow as she swept them over me.

Mert. She could see through me like I was an acetate overlay.

Drat.

I called Detweiler on my way home. He didn't answer so I left a message. I hemmed and hawed around, feeling like a schoolgirl calling a boy for a date. By the time I sputtered out my thoughts, the ending beep sounded.

Gracie leaned over and licked my ear.

She knew what was up.

I felt about two inches high as I dragged my carcass out of the car. Once inside the house, I noticed I had two messages in my cell phone, one from Ben Novak, a really sweet guy I'd been keeping at arm's length, and Johnny, Mert's brother. Any other woman, any sensible woman, would have been glowing with joy.

Instead, I was ashamed of myself.

I stripped to my underwear and crawled into bed without removing my eye makeup or brushing my teeth. How bad was I? I couldn't stop thinking about a married man, the one man I couldn't have; instead of being tickled to a shade of cardstock pink, I was depressed. How did this happen? How did I let myself care?

And what was I going to do about it?

Sunday once had been a family day for Anya and me. I'd make a special breakfast, and we'd take Gracie for a ramble through a park. However, late last spring my darling daughter had informed me I needed to find friends of my own age. She was tired of entertaining me.

No one ever picked me for dodge ball either. But this hurt even more 'cause no one in gym class had ever given me stretch marks. A black eye once, but no stretch marks.

Sheila was up, bright and cheery, when I called. She practically chirped that Anya had spent the Saturday night at her friend Nicci Moore's house. I rather suspected that

Sheila had a "sleep over" guest of her own, but I didn't say anything. I figured Chief Holmes wouldn't have let Sheila "off load" my daughter unless he was sure Anya was safe.

I threw myself into a frenzy of cleaning. I scrubbed the kitchen floor, washed windows, and I was dusting the ceiling fans when a big black snake fell onto my bed.

I ran out of my bedroom screaming. I sprinted past Gracie and into the front yard, hollering for all I was worth. I was standing out there bellowing like a bull calf in one of those National Geographic specials when Mert's truck pulled up and out hopped Johnny.

"Kiki? Calm down. You okay? You hurt?" He grabbed me and pulled me close so he could inspect me.

"Snnn-snnn — snake." I managed.

"I'll go kill it."

"No!"

That was weird, I know, but see I didn't want to hurt it. I just wanted it out of my bedroom. So I grabbed Johnny and stopped his progress. He smelled of sweet grass and fresh air, with a hint of musk, like he always does. "No, kill, no."

He started to snicker. I had him by one of his huge biceps and I was hanging there like

98

fruit off a tree. "Whatcha planning to do with it? You want it for a pet?"

"No," I was catching my breath. "Just don't kill it. Anya would be mad."

"You beat all," he said, pulling me close before he kissed me. Johnny has these kisses that cause your knees to go weak. Mine always do. One of these days, I'm going to wind up on the ground in a puddle afterward.

We were locked in an embrace when Detweiler pulled up, his tires spinning gravel. He stomped out of his big Impala with his eyes on fire. Johnny turned loose of me, saw the lawman glaring at us, and winked at me. "I'll go take care of the bedroom."

"What the . . . ?" Detweiler's next word was not suitable for a PG audience.

"Snake. Big one. This long," I made a gesture separating my hands.

Detweiler's nostrils flared and he pawed the ground.

Oh, boy.

This was bad.

I added, "In my bedroom."

That didn't help. I tried to clear the situation up. "Uh, Johnny's in my bedroom."

Detweiler snorted. I thought I saw steam come out of his ears.

The door slammed behind us and Johnny's feet crunched along my walkway. "I got it. Holding it in my hands. It's big, too. Wait 'til you see this snake of mine."

I could hear him, but I couldn't see him.

Fortunately, Johnny couldn't see through me to Detweiler. The cop had his hand on his gun. His expression was murderous. I could see him calculating and I could sense him pulling the gun from the holster.

"Stop. Don't you dare!" I thought for a minute I was going to faint.

But Johnny stepped between us. He offered the detective and me a scooped-up section of my bedspread stretched between his arms. "That's your snake, missy," he said.

A four-foot-long piece of clotted dust.

"I'm guessing there was dust built up on the fan, and centrifugal force sort of packed all that dust together and made it thick like a piece of felt," said Johnny, with wonder in his voice.

I wobbled toward my kitchen. "I've got to go sit down."

Johnny brought in Mr. Gibbes. He was the cutest thing, a white puff ball with a lively expression and mischievous eyes. Detweiler stalked along behind man and dog.

100

"He's just a pup," said Johnny as he set down Mr. Gibbes' traveling bag and handed over the pooch. "Inside is his food, dishes, leash, and something extra, I need to explain to you."

Johnny reached into the bag and withdrew a colorful piece of fabric about a foot long and four inches wide with Velcro on each end. "This's a wanker wrapper."

"Huh?" Detweiler and I spoke in tandem. Gracie was leaning against the cop, taking all this in, and staring at the excited dog in my lap. Her tail was beating a double-time rhythm as she stared up at the detective with loving eyes.

"See, this guy likes to squirt. He'll hose down your house in pee, if you let him. So you put on this belt contraption," and here Johnny wrapped the wanker wrapper around Mr. Gibbes' belly. "But you have to make sure his manliness is tucked in or it won't do any good."

All I could do was shake my head.

Detweiler muttered, "I can think of a better use for that contraption."

I ignored him.

Johnny guided me in dressing Mr. Gibbes so he was socially acceptable. After all, I'd just mopped the floor, and I didn't need a mess to clean up. Besides, I've always been house proud. Anya and I had moved in three months ago, and I was still busy fixing up and decorating our new home. I didn't need help from an interior designer whose only color chart was yellow, darker yellow, and really, really dark yellow.

Maybe even a shade or two of brown.

At my front door, Johnny paused to kiss me again. Long and hard. Obviously for Detweiler's viewing pleasure. (I thought it kind of funny, too, so I didn't protest or cut it short.) "I have to run, but I'll swing back by. And don't forget we're going to the Kemp Auto Museum over in Chesterfield next weekend." I could tell by the sparkle in Johnny's eyes that he was enjoying watching Detweiler watching us from the kitchen. That Johnny was such a scamp. According to Mert, he'd always flirted with danger. Unfortunately, it had also landed him a short stint in the slammer.

"I can't believe you let that ex-con hang around," fumed Detweiler after Johnny left. "Much less touch you."

I took a deep breath. "Not your business. Not your problem. And please take note: Johnny has never lied to me."

"At least not that you know about," he grumbled. I walked past him over to the refrigerator. I sort of liked hearing him get honked off. I was glad he wasn't comfortable with the situation. He deserved it. After all, he'd made a fool of me. All my friends had known he was married. And Sheila. That was the worst.

"Would you like some ice tea? I've made some spice bread, too. If you like cinnamon, you'll love this."

I served him and sat down to explain what I'd learned about Danny Gartner. Then I asked, "Any news on your end?"

"Someone stepped forward to provide legal assistance to Corey. Still no luck with the murder weapon. The Major Case Squad captain still believes we have the man who killed Sissy."

"Sounds like you're out there on a limb by your lonesome."

He nodded. "Yeah. I am."

My daughter missed Detweiler by fifteen minutes. Jennifer Moore dropped her off. I promised that Nicci could sleep over next Friday after we lit the Shabbas candles at Sheila's. My mother-in-law had planned a Shabbas dinner party. Actually, it wasn't so much a meal as a cattle call so Ben Novak's parents could examine my teeth and decide whether I was possible daughter-in-law material.

Still, it was our turn to have Nicci over, and her presence would give me a great excuse for cutting the evening short. As soon as I mentioned the idea, though, Jennifer got a skittish expression on her face. "It's fine for the girls to stay at our house. Besides, I still have Stevie at home."

But Stevie was a junior in high school. Why would he be staying home on a weekend night?

Clearly, Jennifer didn't want her daughter to spend the night at our place. I willed my face to stay neutral. I knew what she was thinking. Last year our house had been burglarized twice, and I had been wrongly imprisoned. Spending the night in the county jail had not been a career highlight — at least not yet. Worse, word about my escapades (as Sheila called them) had spread through CALA quickly. I had hoped everyone would have moved on, but once a jailbird always a jailbird. Peep, peep, peep, shoot.

So I chose to be gracious, especially as I noticed the tense way my daughter was standing behind me, hanging on every word of my conversation. I wanted Anya to have friends, a social life, and the feeling that she belonged. I could swallow my pride, put aside my ego, and do what was best for her.

"That would be lovely," I said.

"I'll see you Tuesday right after school starts for the mothers' book club meeting at my house," said Jennifer. "You are coming, aren't you?"

"I wouldn't miss it for the world," I lied. As she drove off, I touched my nose to see how much it had grown.

Jennifer hadn't mentioned Sissy's murder even once. But then, everyone thought the killer had been found. Everyone but Detective Chad Detweiler.

Hmmm.

Anya and I watched a little TV before I forced her to go to bed. With puberty on her horizon, I'd noticed she wanted to stay up later and later. I'd read that this was a natural chemical reaction in teens' bodies, a shift in their circadian rhythms. However, normal or not, she still had to get up early for school. So we went two rounds about "silly" bedtimes, treating her like a child, and so on until I rang the bell with, "Bed now or you'll stay home next weekend."

She slammed her door. I puttered around, too revved up by the adrenaline from our scuffle to settle down. I ironed clothes for her and me. Set out what I needed for the next day. Let the dogs out, carefully unwrapping and rewrapping Mr. Gibbes' wanker.

Then I headed down the hallway to my room.

The light was on and seeping out from under Anya's room. I opened her door and reached for her computer, swiftly turning it off.

"Mooo-oom," she wailed.

"Last warning. I catch you using it after bedtime again, and it's gone." I closed the door and headed to bed. I knew I shouldn't have let her keep George's old laptop in her room, but the house was small and she'd argued she needed a quiet place for home-work.

Another day, another worry.

After hustling Anya through her breakfast, pushing her to get into her school clothes, letting the dogs out for a piddle, wrapping Mr. Gibbes' boy parts, and cleaning up after breakfast, I drove my daughter to school in preparation for my real job. My daughter had resisted every portion of our morning ritual. I'd gulped two large mugs of coffee which I badly needed after my late-night computer intervention, and the caffeine caused me to move double-fast while Anya poked along.

But I bit my tongue and didn't fuss at her. I knew she was worried. "You all right?" I asked a couple of times until she said, "You going to let me stay home?"

"No."

"So what difference does it make?"

I swallowed hard. Pick your battles, I told myself. Of course she's worried.

I glanced at her and thought: You and me both, kid.

Mr. Gibbes bounced around the back seat of my car, crawling over a patient but irritated Gracie. My dog's droopy jowls left a thin trail of drool on the window. I thought about my "to do" list. I needed to add "clean car windows."

"Anya, grab Mr. Gibbes, please." She did, and I noticed that stroking the canine puffball seemed to give my daughter some comfort.

CALA's parking lot was filled with squad cars. A new security gate (as promised) blocked our entrance, and we sat in a long line for fifteen minutes. Clearly, the new obstacle was an impediment (but to whom?) and obviously, the new routine was not going smoothly. Mr. Beacon, the security guard who oversaw much of the traffic flow, waved to me. However, it wasn't a friendly invitation to talk, more of a get-your-bumper-out-of-here type of motion.

"I'm going to be late," whined Anya. "I

am not going to detention because of this. You call them, Mom."

"Yes, your majesty."

The closer we moved to the front of the line, the more agitated Anya became.

"Are you scared, sweetie?"

"Wouldn't you be?"

I dodged that. "Look at all the security. I can see them searching backpacks at the doors."

"Goodie. That'll help if someone brings in a brick. Otherwise, we're on our own. It's every kid for herself."

I didn't know how to respond to that. She obviously knew more than I'd given her credit for.

"Chief Holmes assured me —"

"What else could he say? I'm sleeping with your mother-in-law? Of course he'd say it's under control. That's what CALA wants him to say."

Whoa.

She was right. CALA was a great teaching institution. All the kids memorized one equation early on: Money = Power = Privilege.

I've never felt so incompetent and helpless in my life. I searched my arsenal of parenting tips gleaned from all the books I'd read, all the videos I'd watched, and all the seminars I'd attended. Nowhere could I find words to help us. And I wanted to lie. I wanted to say something cheery and bright and Donna Reed-ish.

Instead, I grabbed Anya's hand. "I'd be worried too. In fact, I am worried. But there are a lot more eyes watching the place today, and I truly think this was about Ms. Gilchrist. I mean, I don't think her death was a random occurrence of violence."

"Yeah," Anya sighed. "I think so, too. She used to be really mean, Mom. Sneaky. And a flirt. I heard she came on to a couple of the seniors." Her fingers gave mine a squeeze.

"Senior boys?" My voice rose an octave.

Anya rolled her eyes. "Mom! They aren't boys. They're grown men."

That was debatable. Did facial hair and big feet make them men? Hardly. "Which boys?"

"I'm not telling you!" Anya pulled her sweater across her chest in a defensive gesture. "That's private."

"Private or not, it was wrong. Whatever the age of the student, teachers should not have . . . uh, romantic relationships with them. It's illegal and immoral."

My daughter shrugged. "Why'd they let Ms. Gilchrist stick around then, huh?"

I couldn't answer that. We pulled up to the gate, I showed my driver's license, the newly hired "guard" waved me through, and I stopped at the walkway to the middle-school cluster. "If you're really worried, you could stay home."

Anya wiped her eyes with her sleeve. "Nope. Chief Holmes told me to stick with other kids, not to go anywhere by myself, to sit close to doors, to get on the floor if I heard a loud noise, and to keep my cell phone on." She pulled her backpack out of the foot well and hoisted it over a shoulder. "Onward, Christian Soldiers, huh?"

Before I could respond, she was bouncing along the walkway, pausing only long enough to chatter to a friend as they fell in step.

Where on earth had she heard that hymn? Certainly not in temple. I chuckled to myself. Anya was really a terrific kid. How quickly my child discovered a world beyond me. A world I had no knowledge of, no access to. It started the first day I took her to preschool. From then on, she had her own life, experiences unknown to me unless someone reported them. As the years went on, more and more of her life would happen without me, which was as it should be . . . a thought that suddenly caused my heart to ache.

I prayed God would watch over my baby and help her through the day.

The dogs and I were the first denizens of Time in a Bottle that morning. I hustled Gracie and Mr. Gibbes into their playpen and turned on all the lights. I opened the briefcase and started to examine the photos for my confidential project.

None of the photos included people. I found photos of clothes (with labels on the back of the snaps detailing the name of the designers and the price tags), interior shots of a home, photos of a second home in Aspen (so said the label) and its interior (plus a clipping detailing the sale price and a list of furnishings and their cost — with the buyer's name blacked out), vacation pamphlets, and shots of cars.

At the bottom of the pile was a letter typed on what I assumed was a laser jet printer. "When you finish with these photos, tell your boss. More photos will be sent to you. Remember to keep your mouth shut."

Deee-lightful.

I started by selecting a three-ring binder style of album. This would allow for shuffling the layouts around. I chose Bazzill Basics' Oslo for the background of each page. The navy paper featured a fine crosshatching on the surface that added subtle texture. That was enough to get me started. Right after I locked the loaded briefcase in my car trunk, I flipped our store sign to "OPEN."

I had lots more to do. I'd designed the coolest bookmarks using brightly colored paper and die cut letters spelling out the name of our store on one side. On the other, my co-worker Bama had written vital information: hours, crop days and times, services, address, phone, blog info, and so on. Bama's fantastic script was whimsical and artsy but very readable. Then we duplicated the image onto strips of cardstock.

Now I punched a hole in the top and tied a ribbon through it. At the foot of the bookmark was just enough room to attach a punched flower with a brad. The final result was a piece that combined handmade art with a ready-made base. Dodie suggested we number the bookmarks to create additional value.

Today I would punch flowers and holes until my palm would be sore, but I wanted plenty of these customized promotional pieces to take to the CALA Middle School mothers' book club at Jennifer Moore's house. Bama, Dodie, and I had discovered these pretty pieces were passed from one admirer to another, creating a wonderful "word of mouth" with a paper backup.

A smarter woman would have punched out one flower from a contrasting solid, punched the hole for the brad in the center, affixed the flower to the bookmark and been done with it.

I am not that smart.

I chose two punches: one with long individual petals like a daisy and one with shorter rounded petals like a violet. Punching the flowers from contrasting shades of patterned paper, I layered the petals (long in back and short on top) and curled the edges over a pencil after attaching them with the brad.

I was exceedingly proud of my handiwork. Here's the deal: Being creative can't fix everything that's amiss in your world, but it gives you a modicum of control. Somehow. Someway. By someone.

At noon, I was joined by Bama. "Dodie has her biopsy tomorrow," she reminded me. She brought in a small locally made chocolate bar and a lovely arrangement of curly willow branches and bittersweet. "How about you making a card to go with and say this is from both of us."

It wasn't really a question.

Over the summer, Bama and I had come

to this mutual respect. I was still prickly about her MFA and my NADA, but she'd proved herself willing to teach and share what she knew. Besides, her calendar was full because she was teaching adult ed classes in art, so I didn't feel so threatened, so worried she'd take my job.

But for all our "togetherness," she drew the line at sharing any personal information. "That's none of your business," she said when I asked her if she was married or had anyone special. Ditto with: "Do you like dogs? Cats? Did you grow up here? What do you like to do in your free time?" And on and on.

Shoot, I was lucky to know her first name.

Or was it really her name? My hand hovered over the punch as I wondered. More than likely "Bama" was a nickname. I sank back into my seat.

I knew nothing about my co-worker. Nothing at all.

Despite the fact we'd worked together for more than six months, the woman was a cipher to me.

I finished the get-well card we'd concocted for Dodie shortly before she arrived. Bama and I then presented her with our gifts

"We're thinking positive thoughts," said

Bama. She continued with, "Dodie, don't worry about a thing here at the store. We've got it covered."

After that, I drove to CALA and picked up my daughter.

"Tilly said the killer is out on bond, whatever that is." Anya turned worried eyes on me.

"But the police are still on the case," I said. "Detweiler is involved. He'll get to the bottom of this."

"Good old Detweiler," she said. "I miss him."

I did, too. Inside me were warring factions: 1) I did NOT want to hear about his marriage. 2) I desperately wanted to hear about his marriage.

I couldn't go there.

I had to. Try as I might, I couldn't believe the man was a cad. That he'd lead me on. He was too fair in all his other dealings. It just didn't make sense.

How I wished I could turn my back on his marriage. Pretend it didn't exist. I knew from my own situation that you could be married in the eyes of the law and of society, and not have that connection that we all dream of. But I also knew I couldn't break that sacred trust. Especially not after what happened to me.

My heart knew Detweiler to be a good and honest man. So why hadn't he told me he was married? Did he have strong feelings for me? Did I want to know what those feelings were? If I knew, would it make my resolve stronger? Or would I weaken?

Really, I couldn't take the chance. My best hope for doing the right thing was to stay away from the man. Oh, I might try to fool myself into thinking we could be friends, but my body was having none of it. Every cell kept shouting, "Friends — with benefits!" And I knew better. I couldn't live with myself if I slipped.

Living this way was pretty miserable, too.

I clenched and released my hands as I held the steering wheel. I rubbed one palm on my thigh. All in an effort to ground myself.

My grandmother's voice floated to me, unbidden, from decades ago. "The right action is often the hardest. But living with yourself after the wrong action is much more painful."

Giving myself a small shake, I turned on a local station to hear a police spokesperson explain that the Major Case Squad was working to put a case together to convict Corey Johnson, and he had every confidence the murderer would be brought to justice.

Surprisingly, a reporter managed to snag an interview with "a representative" from CALA, someone I'd never heard of — maybe a public relations wonk brought in just for this — who said, "Security has been reviewed and increased at the school. We have every confidence this was an isolated, personal matter, but we're using this as an opportunity to strengthen our already extensive system for protecting our CALA community."

Translation: We have no idea what we're doing, but it's costing us a lot of dough.

I mused out loud. "What on earth could be their already extensive system for protecting our CALA community? A phalanx of lawyers?"

"Oh, yeah. They're going to batter the bad guys with their briefcases." Anya began laughing hysterically. The image was pretty funny.

I checked our mailbox and found yet another threatening postcard from the person who'd been behind my husband's murder. This one was from Cozumel. Scrawled on the back was, "You'll pay! I'll get you yet!" I shredded it and put it in the trash. This was getting old.

The nights were getting chilly. I cooked my yummy meatloaf for dinner along with the assorted veggies that my kid loved. We'd stretch out the feast by eating slices reheated tomorrow. On the third day, I'd turn the leftovers into soup for two more days. Anya took Mr. Gibbes and Gracie for a short walk up and down our short block as I watched from the upstairs window. I was tired of being poor, tired of looking over my shoulder, and tired of fearing for our safety. But what could I do? Lock us up in a safe room all night and all day?

Anya went to her bedroom to do homework, and I stuffed TinaB (our nickname for Time in a Bottle) flyers in envelopes with the bookmarks to give away the next day. We watched TV, then went to bed.

All in all, a pretty ordinary night, until I woke up to the sound of screams. I hit the floor running flat out and skidded around the corner into Anya's room. The dogs were on top of her, so I fought my way through the furry guardians to my sobbing child.

"Mom, I saw the blood."

I pulled Anya to me and hugged my child tight. The moonlight lit up her platinum blonde hair as though it were a lunar reflection. I shushed her and rocked her.

That was how we fell asleep.

Amazingly, Anya woke up sunny and in

good cheer on Tuesday. I guess her subconscious had dealt with her worries, screamed out its fears, and put her mental house in order. All I can say is my kid was her happy self. I assembled peanut butter, jam, and banana open-face English muffins for us, poured coffee for myself, loaded the dogs and the bookmarks and away we went.

Anya hopped out at school without a backward glance.

I, however, was the proverbial nervous wreck. While getting dressed, I poked myself twice in the eye with mascara, and managed to hit my shin hard on my bedroom chest of drawers. My stomach was clenched with nerves as I forecasted the book club meeting. I'd rather take a beating, have a tooth filled, and visit the gynecologist all in one day than go to a mothers' outing. Between Anya's late-night hollering and my natural discomfort with social events, I was totally on edge. I took a deep centering breath and headed for Jennifer Moore's home, a place where I'd picked up Anya many a time. Located deep inside one of the nicest areas in Ladue, the house was hard to find because the street signs gave you no help. The general feeling was "if you have to ask, you don't belong here."

The black asphalt wound around a clump

of ailanthus trees and scrub bushes before joining the narrow street. Ahead was a picture-perfect Missouri autumn scene. Flame red-orange maples arched over the one-lane bridge making a canopy of branches laden with bright-colored leaves. Small "burning bushes" formed a line of deep burgundy color, which contrasted with the yellow of scrub brushes. The scenic route did my heart good.

You can tell the size of a house by the number of windows and the space between them or their shutters. The Moore house had six large windows across the front facade, each window bracketed by shutters with at least four feet between. The blocky main section of the house was joined by two smaller additions. The addition on the left opened to a long hallway to the four-car garage. By my reckoning the Moores had at least 8,000 square feet of living space above a full basement.

Cars had already arrived and taken up the available space on the road to each side of the driveway. I had to park quite a ways down the drive. A woman I thought I remembered as Judy "Somebody" managed to pull around me into a small spot I thought was too close to the mailbox.

I meandered my way up the cobblestone walk, paused to admire the gardening and to feed my soul with the mix of colors and textures. Hostas, day lilies, shrub roses, geraniums, and mums made a colorful display. The massive front door, flanked on each side with leaded glass windows, was unlocked, so I let myself in. The discussion had already started. Quietly — and glad I'd worn nice brown corduroy pants with my burnt orange sweater — I eased my shaking self down onto plush carpet on the floor since all the seats were taken in what must be the Moore's family room. I grabbed an armrest of the sofa on the way down and lowered my backside to the wool carpet.

Once I was on terra firma, I tried to concentrate on the book club selection. I'd read Tom Perrotta's *Little Children,* months ago. I didn't know who had suggested the book and how "the leaders of the pack" felt about it. I've learned that if a book is chosen for the book club, that meant one of my contemporaries found it edifying or entertaining. Not that it mattered: the book club wasn't about reading or discussing books. It was an opportunity to get together and gossip.

Since I didn't have anything in my meager social life worth sharing, I never attended until Dodie decided it was "good business." Now my presence was mandatory.

Mahreeya Nichols was talking as I slipped in. "What sort of mother is that? The protagonist has sex with a married man? She kisses him in front of her child and her friends?" Mahreeya's voice commanded almost as much attention as her outfit, a gorgeous light blue gabardine pantsuit that reeked of New York designer wear. The Bottega Veneta purse next to her was one I'd seen in a fashion magazine at a newsstand. The bag sold for $2,000, more than three months pay for me. A diamond and emerald pin sparkled from the lapel of Mahreeya's jacket.

"Her husband is a pervert," added Judy.

All eyes turned to Jennifer. It was an unwritten rule that the hostess led and moderated the discussion. Jennifer squirmed in her chair. I realized with a start that she had lost weight recently. She was slender last year, but now she was gaunt, which I hadn't noticed when she'd dropped off Anya. Jennifer mumbled, "Being a mother is really hard."

The group nodded with approval. Connie McMahan, the headmaster's wife, said, "I'll second that!" rather too enthusiastically. There was Ella, Mahreeya Nichols, Patricia

Bigler, Jennifer, Judy Somebody, and two other moms who left right after I came in.

After her comment, Jennifer's face went blank — a studied sort of forced blah look. The skin on Jennifer's fingertips had been chewed off. Whatever was bothering her, Jennifer's reaction was to literally eat herself alive. Jennifer popped up and walked out of the room.

I uttered an excuse about "helping the hostess." I found Jennifer clasping and unclasping her hands over a seven-foot-long mahogany table covered with a white damask cloth. A stack of neatly folded matching napkins waited at one end, along with fine china plates. Tea caddies held petit fours, sandwiches, cookies, tarts, and miniature cupcakes. A silver tea urn, a carafe of coffee, and a cut-glass pitcher of ice tea stood at attention near glasses and tea cups.

"What can I do?"

Jennifer wrung her hands. "Nothing. But thank you."

"Did you make all this?"

"Pardon?" She must have thought I was kidding.

"Silly me." Of course it had been catered. I held out the envelopes I'd brought with the bookmarks and info about homecoming pages. "What should I do with these? I don't want to ruin your beautiful table setting."

"It doesn't matter. None of it matters. It's all gone wrong." A tear leaked from one eye, trailing a wet streak down her cheekbones. She stepped into her kitchen, and I set down my things before following her.

"Jennifer?" I touched her shoulder. "You all right?"

A phone rang again in the other room. Mahreeya's loud tones boomed, "Senator? Thank you for returning my call."

Jennifer raised bloody fingers to her face and sobbed, "They questioned my son Stevie. The police did. This morning. About Sissy Gilchrist. Now they know. They know!"

They know what? I wondered. That Corey didn't do it? That Stevie did?

"Stevie pretended," she choked out in a whisper. "He made up stuff on My Space to look like he was into older women. I saw it. I should have made him take it down. But he couldn't have been involved. It's just a smoke screen. I know he wasn't involved with her. Because — because —"

She pressed her hands over her mouth and rocked back and forth, trying to sooth herself. "I've known it for years. He's like my brother. I didn't want my husband to know. Not yet, at least. He'll never forgive

Stevie. But he doesn't understand. It isn't a choice —"

"What isn't?" I found a basket of paper napkins and handed her one to use as a tissue.

Jennifer dabbed at her eyes. "Nicci knows. She says she knows but doesn't care. And your Anya knows, too. She's such a sweet girl."

All my internal alarm bells sounded. "My daughter knows what?" I tried not to sound frantic. I was worrying Anya had a piece of information. Something about the murder. A clue that might endanger her. "Jennifer, what does Anya know?"

"Stevie's gay."

TEN

The noise of the women chattering as they entered the dining room made Jennifer blow her nose. I found a dish towel, rinsed it in cold water, twisted out the excess moisture, and handed it over. Jennifer blotted her face with the cloth. We exchanged nods of "let's go" and stepped through the swinging doors to join the book club.

Ella came over beside me, a coffee cup balanced in one hand. She cleared her throat. "Did the police talk with Anya? I heard she ran into the balcony after . . ."

I nodded. Considering my child's safety, I added, "But she didn't see anything. There were two of them. Anya and Tilly. All they saw were a bunch of parents milling around. That's it."

"Don't you help the police? I heard your mother-in-law say you're some sort of Nancy Drew." Judy looked at me over her coffee cup.

Ella cleared her throat. "Actually, Kiki's one heck of a scrapbooker. Did you all see these fabulous bookmarks? She's in charge of a special crop at Time in a Bottle. We'll be making homecoming pages."

Mahreeya closed her cell phone. "How fun. Kiki's managed to turn this into a Tupperware party. I suppose we're all expected to buy something."

My face flushed with shame. Then I remembered a conversation long ago with Mert. She'd said, "You gotta understand how scared these women are."

"Scared?"

"Yes'm. Most of them never earned a cent of their own money. They got nothing but what their daddies or their hubbies give them. So when they see you, they figure what happened to you could happen to them. Makes them nervous. Thinking about what if it all goes away. Most of them couldn't take care of themselves like you managed to do. They don't have the gumption. So what you're hearing is a big wad of emotions. None of which's about you." She winked. "Except admiration. You mayn't hear that, but trust me. It's in there."

I grabbed a sugar cookie and stuffed it into my mouth, completely bypassing the niceties of a plate.

"Are these homecoming pages easy to do?" Patricia asked.

I explained that they were page kits, and that I'd be happy to help anyone create a page or two if she needed assistance.

Mahreeya's cell phone rang again. "Congressman! Hello! It's just me," she continued loudly with what sounded like seating plans.

"That's the third time her phone's rung since we started," said Ella.

"Of course we can make room for the ambassador! We can seat him right next to the undersecretary! Tell him I'm happy he could come." Mahreeya stood in the center of the room talking at the top of her lungs.

"Mahreeya always wanted to be popular. She wasn't much to look at in high school — chubby and flat-chested, with a honker of a nose," Ella whispered to me.

"What a transformation," I marveled. "Are you better today?"

"Sort of."

Patricia Bigler moved closer to us. I gritted my teeth and decided to put the other night behind us. "How are you? And how's your daughter?"

"Uh, fine."

"Isn't it awful about Sissy Gilchrist?" Judy

directed her comments to Ella, Patricia, and me.

"It's horrible." Ella's voice was husky.

"My husband's on the school board. He says Mr. Poland was seeing Sissy," Judy added.

"So was Mr. Frankfort, the bio instructor," chimed in Patricia. "I also heard she was having a fling with that sociology teacher, Mr. Akin."

"My older son says Ms. Gilchrist was fooling around with a boy in the school. A senior. Anyone know who?" Judy asked.

Jennifer stiffened at my side. Suddenly, she was very busy folding and refolding napkins.

"We all know it was that coach," said Judy.

Ella choked a little on her tea.

"I assure all of you," said Connie in a soothing voice, "everything possible is being done to safeguard your children. We're cooperating fully with the Major Case Squad."

I stifled a "huh." I'd always thought a lot of Connie. Now I was forced to revise my opinion. Or accept the fact she was being kept in the dark. If she truly thought CALA was cooperating, she had a pretty weird definition of working together. Detweiler had said the school was stonewalling, and

I'd bet my life he was right.

Judy set her cup down hard. "Connie, Elliott needs to make a strong statement. He needs to be sure that coach gets the death penalty."

"What if he's innocent?" asked Ella, whose complexion now matched the white napkin she held in one hand. "Remember? Innocent until proven guilty?"

But everyone ignored her. Instead, Connie said, "Kiki, do I have your cell number? I might want to come to that crop."

I welcomed the interruption and gave it to her. She repeated it back to me.

Judy grumbled about Corey Johnson.

"I want to emphasize the safety of our children is the school's first concern, and my husband's primary concern as well," said Connie. "I'm sorry, but I have to go to a class now."

I noticed she'd boldfaced "Our children." Of course, the two McMahan kids attended CALA as well.

After the headmaster's wife left, Judy said, "How innocent can he be? They had enough to pick him up. The police don't make mistakes."

"Do they, Kiki?" asked Mahreeya. "You would know, wouldn't you? If they put you in jail, it's because you're guilty, right? That happened to you, didn't it? That's what your mother-in-law said."

Heat rose in my face. "I was falsely accused."

How was that for loyalty? Thank you, Sheila. Good thing Yom Kippur, the Day of Atonement, was right around the corner. Sheila would have a chance to clean her slate. If I didn't strangle her first.

"False accusations can cause someone to be held temporarily. Especially if the accuser has clout," I explained.

"Corey Johnson obviously did something," said Judy.

"So he's guilty based on what? His color?" Ella spat out the words. "This is like a throwback to the 1860s. I thought we'd changed."

"Tradition supplies stability, and respect for tradition is one of CALA's core values," said Mahreeya.

This stilted remark sounded suspiciously like a recitation from the school handbook. Available in tooled leather for twenty-five dollars from the CALA bookstore. I downloaded our copy from the school's website, triple-hole punched it, and stuck it in a cheap three-ring binder.

"Besides," said Mahreeya, aiming her remarks toward Ella. "You can't have it both

131

ways, can you? Have your cake and eat it too? Dump the old traditions after you've benefited? It was good to be Queen, wasn't it, Ella? You had a grand time at the V.P. Ball. You loved being the Veiled Prophet Queen of Love and Beauty. Now you want change? After you've watched everyone bow and scrape? After you decided who sat on the sidelines? Who was in your court and who was rejected? You didn't want things to be different then, did you?"

"Right now we need to worry that the real killer is still roaming the halls of CALA," said Ella. "And whatever happens, Corey Johnson will never live this down. He's ruined. That's two lives taken — his and Sissy's."

ELEVEN

After that dramatic exchange, the party sputtered to an end. The moms hurriedly took their leave. I thanked Jennifer, as she stood there alone with a table full of food and a stunned expression on her face. I headed toward my car.

As I climbed into the BMW, Detweiler text-messaged me. "Big Dawg's? 12?"

If I hurried, I could get there. I texted back, "Yes." I wanted to share the many names that had been flying around Jennifer's house. I also wanted to tell him why Stevie Moore should be struck off his list of suspects.

I drove along the shady lane, enjoying the strobing effect of sunlight through the branches. I glanced ahead to a small blind lane on my right. Immediately following that intersection was a one-lane bridge with wooden planking. The structure was old, sound enough to handle a bigger car, but too open and fragile for my taste. Someone had added wooden guardrails, only for show. I'd paid scant attention to the structure on my way to the meeting.

As I passed the crossroad, my peripheral vision caught a dark blur. A car traveled at a right angle toward me. Overgrown bushes obscured most of the vehicle. But I heard the whine of a large engine. The car was moving fast.

I glanced around.

My cell phone rang. I slowed down and grabbed at it.

"Hello?"

Nothing.

The hesitation cost me.

I looked up.

A huge black car was coming right at my side.

My front wheels faced the bridge. If the big black car smacked my back wheels now, I'd be knocked sidewise into the culvert. Beneath me swirled a swollen creek.

If I were hit, I'd go down the embankment. I'd tumble end over end. My ragtop wouldn't protect me. My car was too old to have a roll bar. I'd land upside down in the water. And I'd drown.

My heart skipped a beat. Sweat broke out on my upper lip.

My mind raced through various scenarios. Stop? Go? My impulse was to slam the brakes. But my mind overrode my instincts. If I stopped, I'd be hit, and hit hard.

My pulse quickened. I swallowed. My palms were wet with perspiration. I froze.

If that car hit me, I would go over the side. My car would flip. I would die. A slow, lonely death.

I thought of Anya. I remembered how she'd reacted to George's death.

I didn't want to die.

I stomped the gas.

TWELVE

My wheels spun. Gravel pinged the back bumper. The car stuttered. I mashed my accelerator hard. I gripped the steering wheel. My car slid a foot or so to one side. The wheels couldn't catch traction. A cloud of dust flew up around me. The spinning stopped. I moved forward.

I shot out the other side of the bridge like a spit wad from a kid's mouth. Once I cleared the bridge, my right foot jumped to the middle. I literally stood on the brake pedal. My body fought the seat belt as I rose up.

But my car skidded to a stop.

Behind me, the black vehicle zoomed past the spot where I'd been and into an adjacent blind lane.

The steering wheel bucked my grip as the car reacted. For a heartbeat, my car skidded out of my control. The backside fishtailed, this way and that. But it stopped. Thank

God, it stopped. I closed my eyes and said a prayer of thanksgiving. Then I heard a honk. Another mother had pulled up behind me. Judy was waiting for me to drive on. I had blocked the lane. Raising my trembling hand, I gave her a weak wave and continued on my way.

"St. Louis. Second only to Boston for bad drivers," I muttered to myself.

Burned into my brain was a sensation of panic. I kept imagining that fatal plunge to the water. I blinked and brought up a sensation of vertigo, of being turned topsy-turvy.

I could have been killed.

All the way to Big Dawg's, I trembled like a leaf in a tornado.

Big Dawg's is a hole in the wall. Fluorescent paint highlights menu items and welcomes customers with "We are Glad to See and Serve You."

Detweiler was waiting for me right inside the door. Other cops were scattered around the seating area. I sighed with relief. I was glad the place was crowded. No way did I want to start trouble with his wife, Brenda. She was muscular and athletic, and frankly, she scared me. She'd showed up at the store to "talk with me," and Dodie had shooed her away.

I'm a lover not a fighter. Well, mainly mostly.

Cigarette smoke prickled my nostrils. I wheezed. St. Louis has the distinction of being the #1 Worst City for Asthmatics in the nation. The fact we don't have a cohesive non-smoking in restaurant legislation is one reason. Another is pollen. But you can't arrest a tree.

I glanced down to see a duo of crushed Marlboros in the ashcan. You could puff away at Big Dawg's. Rats. I hoped the offending smoker had already left. Otherwise, my allergies would really kick in, and I'd be mopping my nose for the next hour. Detweiler motioned to a seat at the far end of the counter, beyond the State Street sign, and underneath a black and white of Marilyn Monroe with pursed lips. I think Marilyn was reacting to the cigarette smoke, too.

The smell of frying onions overpowered Detweiler's cologne, but still . . . he smelled like a guy on a date.

Boy, I wished that date was with me.

My brain said, "Are you NUTS?" But other parts of my self were not so logical. Between the adrenaline from my near miss and my hormones, I felt woozy. I needed to sit down or prop myself up, fast. Added to the general mayhem, my stomach rumbled.

After that buzz saw of a book club meeting, I'd left without sampling Jennifer's offerings. Except for one cookie. And one cookie didn't put a dent in my empty tummy. I wanted food. REAL food.

I climbed onto the stool and studied the menu board. Detweiler offered to buy. "Union employees get a discount," he said.

He stepped to the window and gave our orders to a tough-looking girl with a Slovakian accent, a tattoo, and a "don't mess with me" attitude. Definitely not a Wendy Ward's Charm School graduate. (Which I am. I even made a scrapbook page with my diploma. It's really cute, too.) She shoved a pair of Styrofoam cups toward him and gestured to the fountain drinks dispenser. I took my cup and walked to the dispenser.

My hand was shaky. I poured diet cola all over my fist.

"Self-serve not your bag?" He said as we settled onto our seats.

"Um, I was almost hit on my way back from the book club meeting. Close call." I explained about the bridge. What I didn't say was that being near him made me jittery. My heart pounded in my chest. My eyes measured the space between us at the counter, and I leaned away from him. If we touched, I feared we'd both go up in flames.

Boy, I had it bad.

Detweiler sipped his soda and shook his head. "Drivers here run stop signs all the time."

"Ah, the famous 'St. Louis stops,' right? If everyone else stops, why should I?" I watched him wince. "What's up with Coach Johnson?"

Detweiler ran a hand through his hair. "He's out."

"No kidding! That's good news, right?"

"Maybe." Detweiler lifted a shoulder and let it fall. "He's not talking to anyone, not even me, on the advice of his attorney. I have no idea who paid his bail."

His voice carried a touch of hurt. While Corey staying quiet made sense, Detweiler felt excluded. Worst of all, I wondered if Corey knew his old friend was working overtime trying to exonerate him? I started to ask, but realized, how could the coach know? If Detweiler talked to Corey's lawyer, he'd be going behind the back of his captain in the Major Case Squad. He'd be telegraphing how weak the department's case was. And since he couldn't talk to Corey, Detweiler couldn't pick up any new leads from his friend. A real Catch-22.

The wild card was whatever I could dig up from my snooping around.

"How's Anya?" The detective's voice was gruff with emotion. "She okay?"

I filled him in on her nightmare. Repeating it made me more tired. I shook my head as I said, "I hope she's safe."

He nodded. "She's safer at school and school events, with all the attention being paid to security, than she would be at your house. I flashed her photo to the security guards, so they've promised to be extra vigilant. A lot of them are off-duty cops. We watch out for each other's families."

Families. I swallowed hard. So that was what he considered my daughter? A member of his family? A pricking started behind my eyes and I gulped my drink to push down the pain in my throat. I set down my cup carefully and studied him from under my lashes. A patch of beard had been missed when he shaved. His fingers drummed restlessly on the counter and his leg jiggled frantically. Under his eyes were puffy half-circles, and his lips were chapped. He was definitely not himself. The last time he'd been on a case, I'd been attracted to how calm, cool, and collected he'd seemed.

This one was making him a wreck.

Then I realized. He also thought of Corey Johnson as family. I'd bet my Fiskars Personal Paper Trimmer on it. This new insight

141

warmed me to him all over again. What a good man he was. At the core, decent and loyal.

Except, if that were true, why did he kiss me? Come visit me? When he was married?

I rubbed my eyes hard. "Allergies," I mumbled. "What's the department's response to Corey getting out?"

"What you'd expect. The captain admits we don't have a lot. Chief Holmes is keeping up a PR front. Sorry. I can't tell you more."

I shrugged. I'd sort of expected as much. "I'll tell you what I heard at book club, but what else can I do? Anything? I'm flying blind here."

He repeated how Sissy had dropped her son Christopher off at kindergarten at roughly nine-thirty, and her first class didn't start that particular day until eleven a.m. CALA used a rotating class schedule designed to compensate for the many Mondays that are national holidays. The students adjusted to its quirks quickly, but to me and most parents, it was difficult to keep track.

Corey Johnson hadn't verified his whereabouts for the suspicious timeframe. Detweiler said the man seemed too distraught to think clearly. None of the teachers stepped forward to say they'd seen the coach. So he had no alibi.

"Lots of people had keys to the balcony. Anyone walking the hall — as Anya and her friends did — could have slipped in and out. The amount of blood spatter was minimal, our forensics examiner says. We thought about searching nearby lockers, but that would take a court order," he said as he wiped his mouth with his napkin. "There's that sports booster meeting. We're working our way through a makeshift list of attendees, but folks aren't being helpful."

Our meal was ready at the window. Detweiler hopped up to get it. He slid my red basket with the kid's meal — a hot dog and fries — toward me. "They're all out of toys."

Well, shoot. Now my day was totally ruined.

"Start with the book club." He bit into the first of his two smoked bratwursts. The man had a half pound of pork and veal to plow through, plus a generous helping of fries.

I listed the names I'd heard. I explained about Stevie Moore.

Detweiler's eyes clouded with concern. "But maybe Stevie didn't do it and his mother did. To keep his, um, preferences quiet."

I couldn't believe that of Jennifer. I realized, too, that since Anya was spending a lot of time at the Moores' house, I really needed to know the family better.

I wished Anya hung around more with Tilly, but I couldn't force a friendship on my daughter. I'd tried that before and it had backfired. Anya had bitten the other preschooler during a playdate.

"You know the headmaster's wife? Connie McMahan? Heard she was ticked at her hubby because of Sissy. We don't know the details, but a secretary reported a heated discussion between the McMahans the day before Ms. Gilchrist was killed. A Ladue cop interviewed Mrs. McMahan, with the school's attorney. Didn't get much." His voice lowered. "Could she be the one we're looking for?"

"I know Connie a little. I can't see her doing it."

"Yeah, I was afraid you'd say that. No one saw her the morning of the murder. But she could have slipped in and out. The headmaster's house is on the school grounds."

"She'd've had to walk past the construction workers."

"Right. We're talking to the union workers. Breaks are part of their contract."

Connie had left the book club rather quickly. If memory served me correctly,

144

later today Connie would be planting flowers in preparation for homecoming celebrations. Even though CALA employed a fleet of gardeners, it was a tradition for the women of the school to plant mums along the winding driveway to welcome back the alums.

"I could probably talk to her this afternoon," I told him. "Maybe I can find out what she was upset about. I've got to get to work."

He started to say something. I could tell it was personal. I turned away and wadded up my trash. I kept my back to him, and started toward the door without turning. I could hear him speak my name, in a voice almost pleading. But I didn't stop. I let the hustle and bustle of the restaurant cover for my cowardice.

We walked to our cars. After I climbed in, I looked up to see Detweiler staring at me thoughtfully as he started the engine on his big Chevrolet. It might have been a trick of the light, but he seemed wistful. A dull ache started in my chest, right below my throat. I turned over my BMW and pulled away.

His eyes were on me as I drove out of the parking lot.

THIRTEEN

"Any word yet about the biopsy?" I asked Bama after I'd gotten Mr. Gibbes and Gracie settled in the backroom.

"No. Horace said he'd call, but she's probably still in recovery."

I told Bama about the book club meeting. "Understandably, there wasn't much talk about the homecoming pages. Today folks should be receiving a school bulletin through the Internet with info about the layouts. Maybe we'll get a response tomorrow morning. How's your night class coming?"

"Pretty good. Most of my students want to write family histories. I have plenty of information about safeguarding old photos and creating shadow boxes, but I could use help getting them to write more. They tend to forget current history. Any ideas?"

I had lots of them. I pulled out a form I'd created for people to use while interviewing

146

family members. Bama and I went over it, and she was impressed. "This is great. Can I use it?"

"Of course." Then the green-eyed monster struck me. My face telegraphed my concern.

"You'll get credit. Your name and copyright are on the bottom."

I blushed. A thought: "You know, maybe we shouldn't give this away. Maybe you should teach a class on family histories. That'd mean more income for the store and for you, right?"

I saw her calculating. She cocked her head. Today she was wearing a boatneck sweater with a chiffon scarf at the neck. Bama always dressed artistically. "You have the journaling ideas, the basic scrapbooking know-how, and I have the calligraphy and artistic techniques. Why not work together? We could test what we do as a class and later turn it into an e-book." She went on to explain how that would work. "The only problem is . . . if we do it on Dodie's time, it would belong to her, really."

I thought about this. "She's always been very fair about giving me the lion's share of what I bring in. Couldn't we approach her about this?"

Bama high-fived me. I've never seen my co-worker so animated.

We spent the rest of the day waiting on customers, jotting notes about our family history class, and generally tidying up the store. Dodie was training Bama to place orders, which meant my co-worker needed time to do quick inventories and send e-mails to vendors. Bama could be a bit prissy about her newfound responsibility, but I had to admit, Dodie had chosen the right person for the job. Bama was more mathematically inclined than I (which wasn't much of a trick), and had some bookkeeping background. Since she'd taken over the ordering, we rarely ran out of basic supplies and a steady flow of new papers arrived.

"If I can bug out of here at three," I said to her, "I can drop my kid and her friend off at golf and swing by CALA. I'll come back by for the dogs. The moms will be planting mums for homecoming. I could pass out more brochures for our pages."

Bama nodded. "Sounds good. Or I can drop off Gracie and Mr. Gibbes for you, later."

I was, to put it mildly, stunned. I had noticed Bama warming up to Gracie, and she particularly seemed interested in Mr. Gibbes. She'd picked up the dog and stroked his curly fur with relish. This was the first time Bama had ever offered to do anything out of her way for me. I fought the desire to tell her no, but I remembered what Nana once told me, "People like doing favors for each other. Don't deny someone else the pleasure, Kiki, just because you can't handle feeling obligated."

"That would be very kind of you. I appreciate it." I gave Bama an extra key to my house in case we missed each other.

Anya seemed her usual self as she hopped in the car. Tilly was also talkative, but she paused long enough to thank me for the ride — even though she sat in the back with her clubs half on her lap. I'd consulted the schedule for golf and was relieved to see a local course was the practice location. It was only a few blocks from CALA. We swung by Bread Co., got the girls turkey sandwiches and lemonade, and I dropped them off at the course. I hated to spend the money, but the girls were clearly famished. They lit into their food with gusto. Now that post-meatloaf soup would have to last three days. Ugh.

"Don't forget to pick up all your clubs when you get done," I reminded Anya. She'd been very forgetful lately. The last time Maggie had picked up the girls, Anya had left her backpack in my friend's car. We'd spent half the evening tracking Maggie and the books down.

I drove directly back to the school to help with the planting. This would give me a good chance to talk with Connie. I hoped I wouldn't learn she was inside the school or even on the grounds when Sissy was killed, but if she let slip that she was, I'd pass the information along. At least we'd be making progress.

I parked and walked up the winding drive in front of the main admin building. I was running a bit behind, but not all the flats of flowers had already been planted. The majority of helpers were inside the gym helping decorate for the homecoming dance. I stepped inside and passed out brochures from the store. The festive ambience reminded me of the Opera Theatre function where I'd been introduced to Detweiler's wife, Brenda. She'd tried to contact me several times afterward, and I'd managed to avoid her calls.

As far as I was concerned, I had nothing to say to her. I hadn't known Detweiler was married. Like many cops, he didn't wear a wedding ring. Yes, he'd kissed me once, but otherwise, nothing had happened. I, too, was an innocent victim of his misbehavior.

And all that had stopped.

Except for now, when I needed his help to keep my daughter safe.

With those "cheery" thoughts, depression descended on me like a bad cold. I was working hard not to talk to Detweiler about what I really wanted to talk about: why had he led me on? In fact, there was no one I could turn to. Mert had made it clear she was disgusted with the man. Dodie was having health problems — and she and Horace had a perfect marriage. Clancy had been involved in an acrimonious divorce after her husband cheated on her.

No one in my circle of friends could hear my concerns. I couldn't share the pain, the questions, the emotional tug of war inside me. I trudged up the asphalt, while studying my feet. On my back was a load of worries: fear for my daughter, concern for Dodie, guilt about my feelings for Detweiler.

Of all the jobs I could have chosen, digging in the dirt seemed most appropriate.

Connie looked up from stacking empty plastic pots. Her face broke into a wide grin when she saw me. I think the woman enjoyed my company at school events because she was pleased to have a companion with a mutual interest in writing, even if mine was mainly limited to family stories. She'd told me in a roundabout way our friendship was a welcome break from hearing moms talk about problematic teachers, homework battles, and the notoriously rotten school food for which CALA was famous. Money can't buy you love and at this school, it couldn't buy you a decent lunch either.

"Didn't expect to see you here. Sorry we didn't get to talk at book club. You a gardener?"

"Nope. I'm depressed and I need a way to work it off."

"Lordy," she said. As a South Carolina transplant, Connie had a vocabulary all her own. Her genteel manners and gracious ways were perfect accessories for a headmaster's wife.

"Some days I'm not sure whether I want to shoot myself or someone else!"

I stopped, shocked at what I said. "Oops."

"It's absurd. It's sick, but I can't help it. I said something similar in anger to Elliott, and someone overheard and reported me to the police. The police! You know they tried to push me into admitting that I killed Sissy? 'Cause of a durn fool offhand comment. And a spat I'd had with my husband. Pathetic."

"What'd you tell them?"

"I looked them straight in the eyes and

said, 'Heck, no, I didn't want to kill Sissy Gilchrist. The person I wanted to shoot was my husband!' Anyway, I wasn't even around the school on Monday morning. I was on-line researching my new work in progress all morning. If they push it, I'll let them take a gander at my computer."

"You wanted to kill poor Elliott?"

She nodded. "Ever feel that way about your George?"

The whole world now knew my husband had been cheating on me before he died. "Yeh," I admitted. "But someone else got to him first. Saved me the trouble." Immediately after the words popped out, I covered my face with my hands. "I can't believe I said that!"

Connie laughed. "The question I ask myself is how could a grown man be so stupid? What kind of an idiot hires a woman who plants herself on his desktop like a lounge singer? I walked into his office unannounced and nearly fell over in a faint. And I'm not the fainting type."

Connie pulled off her sunglasses and wiped her eyes on a tissue that had been stuffed up her sleeve. "Sissy was leaning over and shaking her ta-ta's at him. And I thought my husband was a leg man. I told him: 'Elliott McMahan, your brain must have turned to mush. You aren't smart enough to be a school headmaster.' Why on earth would an intelligent man offer a teaching position to a woman like Sissy Gilchrist? Grits for brains, that's what he has."

"What'd he say?"

"He said," and Connie drew herself up, tucked her chin down as though looking over reading glasses, and put one hand on her hip, "he said that he was thinking like a good Christian and giving a sinner a chance at redemption."

"Redemption is for Green Stamps."

"Amen, sister. I told him that Jesus may have forgiven the prostitute, but he surely didn't invite her to come help minister to the little children." Connie gestured to the ground, and we dropped to our knees to get back to the matter at hand. That's what I love about being a woman: no matter what happens, in the end we're brought round to sanity by life's demands. We are nothing if not eminently practical. Straying husbands, sleezy bimbos, stupid choices, none of it mattered. The flowers still needed planting. Back home, clothes would need washing. Dinner would need to be cooked.

Life goes on when you're a woman. And the force of knowing your work never ends carries you along, refusing to let you mope for too long.

Connie and I worked side by side. She handed me a trowel, and I dug holes for the mums. She squeezed and rapped the plastic pots to loosen the root balls. She plunked plants into the hole, and I tucked them in tight. We worked steadily for nearly a half an hour, distracting ourselves with talk about books we'd read, author interviews we'd heard, and other bookish topics.

My thoughts circled round to Sissy Gilchrist. "Connie, was she really as bad as all that?"

"Every bit. It's all about essential nature. That's what I'm talking about." Connie asked me if I knew that cats were exempt from the leash laws in many states. I admitted I didn't. Cats are exempt, she explained, because it is not part of the essential nature of a cat to be domesticated. Nor was it Sissy Gilchrist's nature either. Therefore, to Connie's way of thinking, expecting Sissy to act like a role model was going against nature.

"Elliott knows better. The man's an educator! How many times have I heard him lecture parents about trying to turn a child who's a social butterfly into a scholar? Or a shy retiring child into a performer? All of us have to work within a God-given framework. Sure, you can stretch the limits, but they're still there!"

Despite his wife's objections, Elliott hired Sissy because her father, Quentin Gilchrist, had offered to donate enough money to remodel the lunch room. The irony wasn't lost on either of us.

Connie nodded solemnly. "That's right. She may have been beaned with a brick her daddy paid for. Horrid, isn't it?"

I directed the conversation back to why Quentin was so desperate to get his daughter a job at CALA. Especially considering what an obvious mismatch it was. I couldn't imagine a parent setting a child up for failure. On the face of it, Quentin Gilchrist had done exactly that — and paid for the privilege.

"Sissy was going to move out of state. She wanted to get as far as possible from that cop she'd been married to. Take her son along with. Can't say I blamed her there. Quentin and Paula were desperate to keep their little girl in town. Quentin told Elliott that if CALA would hire his daughter, he'd give the school enough for the new lunch-room expansion in brick, plus double his daughter's salary every year."

I dusted the dirt off my knees and stacked the empty plant flats. I was trying not to miss a word and to commit everything she said to memory so I could share it later. Connie misunderstood my reflective silence. "That shock you? About the donations?"

Heck, no. The lion's share of Elliott's job was stewardship. He was charged with protecting the school's assets, both tangible and intangible, and increasing them. " 'Course not, Connie. I may have grown up in the sticks, but after I fell off the watermelon truck I managed to learn a thing or two."

She snorted. "Endowments, gifts, and donations are a fact of private school life. Speaking of which —"

Another mom came strolling up the driveway dragging a couple of garbage bags behind her. "Connie, I dumped the empty pots in these trash bags. Where shall I put them?"

Connie pointed toward a molded plastic wheelbarrow, sitting off to one side of the driveway. "We'll take them back to the plant store where they'll recycle them."

"I like old wheelbarrows better," I said, running my hand over the molded plastic. "These never look quite real. Too much like those Big Wheel Trikes. I prefer heavy metal."

"That reminds me," and Connie smiled at the newcomer. "How's Sissy's little boy,

Christopher?"

The other mom shifted her weight nervously. "I've heard he's having a hard time of it. A few outbursts."

Connie nodded. "That's to be expected. Good thing Patricia Bigler is working in the kindergarten. The other teachers tell me first thing he does in the morning is ask where she is."

The mom nodded. "She really loves kids. You can tell." With a glance at her watch, she announced she was done for the day.

Time to change the channel. "Speaking of sacred trusts," I edged in my comment, "what on earth were Mahreeya and Ella going on about at book club?"

"You aren't from St. Louis are you?" asked Connie.

"No. Is this place fascinating or what?"

"Sure as shooting. You mean that conversation about the Veiled Prophet Ball? I'd give my eyeteeth to see that. All four of those moms were involved: Ella, Mahreeya, Jennifer, and Patricia."

"Because they all went to school together?"

"As I understand it, the families were friends. All four of them were part of the Veiled Prophet's court."

"Pretty tight knit, huh? I guess diversity

wasn't a goal back then." I thought back to the oblique comments and the implication that Corey Johnson had been arrested because of his color.

"It certainly is now. Elliott works very hard on recruiting families with diverse backgrounds. The school board expects that of him." She rocked back on her heels. "Believe it or not, Kiki, even the old guard here in St. Louis is changing. Slowly, perhaps, but still . . ."

I tamped down the dirt around a mum. "I suppose it would be easier to marry into a family with similar world views." I thought about Sheila a minute and added, "Or at least a family that wanted your marriage to succeed." I didn't add "instead of trying to destroy it and you."

Connie nodded. "I researched the Veiled Prophet shortly after we arrived. The Queen of Love and Beauty serves as the Veiled Prophet's emissary. She's chosen from hundreds of young maidens —"

Maidens? The last time I heard that word I was reading Shakespeare. I laughed out loud and Connie did, too. "Goodness, me, I got carried away. See, the Queen wears white at the Veiled Prophet Ball like a bride does."

"Sort of like a city-wide beauty pageant?"

"You haven't seen their photos, have you?" Connie brayed with laughter. "It is certainly not a beauty pageant. The Queen is a symbol of power and purity, from her bloodline to her conduct. Someone explained to me that the purpose of the Queen is to show the 'less fortunate' what they can aspire to. Ha! Ha! Only if they believe in reincarnation."

Now we both got tickled and laughed so hard I nearly sprang a leak. Connie got hold of herself first, wiped at her nose, and sported a smear of dirt across her cheek. She continued, "Years ago, the Queen wasn't supposed to go to college or get married during her reign. That left her free to make special appearances." With this, Connie waved her trowel around like a scepter, spraying me with fine pieces of soil.

"Get this: even today she's remembered as the Queen for the rest of her life. Ever noticed those big pearl and rhinestone pins some of the alumnae wear? Those were originally parts of their tiaras."

"No kidding? Here I thought they all patronized the same jeweler. Hey, who pays for all this?"

Connie glanced over her shoulder and dropped her voice to a whisper. "It's complicated. Look, Kiki, if you really want to understand what Ella and Mahreeya were feuding about at the mothers' book club meeting, go on over to the library and do a little research on the Veiled Prophet. Meanwhile, we should be careful. I don't want anyone to overhear us."

"Why?"

"You're treading on dangerous ground," said Connie, looking around nervously. "When it comes to the Prophet, opinions tend to get heated."

Less than five blocks away from CALA was the St. Louis County Library. With a modern rounded entry of glass blocks and an unimposing beige façade, it doesn't look like much from the outside, but I've never met a library I didn't like. My mood lightened considerably as I walked through the book detectors to the help desk. I told a librarian what I was after, and she was glad to direct my efforts. She even offered to look through the Special Collection for me in case the library had anything back there that I might want to see.

Halfway into the open reading room, a sharp right led me to the stacks under the mezzanine floor. Truth be told, something about the Spartan shelves and lack of cushy seating seemed to underscore the seriousness of the information offered back here, away from the fiction holdings. No lightweight reading sat on these bare shelves. Calculating the Dewey Decimal numbers quickly, I walked my fingers down spines searching for copies of books about the Veiled Prophet. I withdrew these from the shelves and settled myself at a table to read through each of them.

According to the first author, many African Americans participated in a week-long general strike that paralyzed the city back in 1877. To demonstrate their courage and commitment, approximately fifteen hundred workers marched four abreast through the downtown business district while carrying clubs on their shoulders.

In response to this show of strength, business owners of St. Louis countered with their own citizens' militia parade which was essentially a show of armed power. From this public display came the impetus to create an annual extravaganza designed to make perfectly clear that the elite of the city had the upper hand. Thus the Veiled Prophet was born.

A history teacher of mine once said that to grasp the import of any event, you must view it in the context of the times. In an era devoid of television and video imagery, the pageantry of the Veiled Prophet parade must have been spectacular indeed. At twilight on October 8, 1878, a crowd of thousands gathered by torchlight to watch the waters of the mighty Mississippi River. A cry went up. Rockets exploded. A band began to play. Eyes strained in the fading light to watch a barge make its way slowly to the shore. From that vessel arose a lavishly costumed figure. The Veiled Prophet had arrived to favor St. Louis with his blessing. Once seated on a colorful float, the Prophet and his court were pulled by a phalanx of prancing horses past a cheering throng lining the streets of St. Louis.

I rubbed my eyes. I tried to imagine the times. Less than ten years before, the Civil War had brutally divided Missouri with the northern half of the state supporting the Union, and the southern half supporting the Confederacy. The bloody aftermath of brother fighting brother gave way to a period of grim reconstruction. Men returned to farms left largely untended in their absence. The manufacturing age arrived, and with it came a lack of personal freedom, a new kind of slavery as business owners preyed on cheap labor. Day to day life would have been very dull.

It was hard to imagine the glamour and

drama of the myth created by the city fathers. I wanted to see the images with my own eyes. I skipped deep inside the book I held to the photo section and reeled back in horror. The rotogravure picture from the *Missouri Republican* showed a masked man garbed in a peaked white hat and matching robe. This was the Veiled Prophet? The benevolent bestower of love? Surely not. I went back to the text and read that during the parade itself the Prophet was dressed in dark green, and his face was covered in a veil of white. So where did that original ominous figure come from — and what was his purpose? I shook my head in confusion.

"Anything wrong, dear?" The reference librarian laid a faded October 28, 1946, copy of *Life* magazine beside my elbow.

"No," I said hastily, "and thank you for your help."

The second book on the subject proved more enlightening. This author posited that the Veiled Prophet festival began with the good intentions of reviving the St. Louis economy after the damages wrought by the Union army during its occupation of the city. The brothers Slayback had looked to their former home of New Orleans for inspiration and for floats and decorations to bring to Missouri. The veneration of young white maidens from prominent families was a central portion of the celebration, but it was also a way for a secret society to pledge their familial support as the Veiled Prophet, dressed much as one might imagine a Roman god, descended from his lofty throne to choose the Belle of the Ball and present her with a pearl necklace.

I couldn't decide whether to feel confused or disgusted. Which version of the Veiled Prophet was the truth? Was it a jolly Mardi Gras type event for all to enjoy? Or a thinly disguised show of white power to perpetuate the upper hand of the moneyed elite?

I gently slipped the copy of *Life* from its archival wrapper and turned its yellowed, brittle pages. A musty odor filled the air. "*Life* Goes to the Veiled Prophet's Ball: St. Louis society turns out for its biggest event" crowed the headline. According to the writer, three hundred thousand people witnessed the V.P. parade which featured twenty floats. But only a fortunate twelve thousand were invited to the ball in Kiel Auditorium. I sank back in my seat and did a quick calculation. In other words, if you filled old Busch Stadium six times, you'd have an equal number of spectators lining the city streets.

My eyes drifted to the large black and

white photo covering both pages. A legion of guards in tall hats and carrying lances — I counted twenty-eight — edged an enormous multi-leveled platform. Using my thumb as a measure, I reckoned the size of the elevated stage was at least forty feet long. A woman in a white gown carrying a bouquet that extended past her knees and her tuxedoed escort approached a robed figure in a white mask and snowy wig. According to the accompanying article, this was the queen-designate and the young ladies lining the tiers along her way were members of her court.

As far as I could tell, there was only one ceremony in the world that rivaled the Veiled Prophet Ball, and it was the coronation of Elizabeth I. What would it have been like to be the darling of that ball? To have a rich father who wanted to show you off? To walk like a queen through a crowd of well-wishers?

My fingertip traced the beautiful girl's image. I hated to admit it, but I envied the four alumnae. From all I could see, this was as close to being royalty as you could get.

I pulled myself together and slipped back into research mode. The books noted that the V.P. festivities continued year after year. But the world changed. In the 1960s, civil rights protesters blocked the parade route with nonviolent sit-ins. In the early 70s, activists decried the V.P. festivities as a symbol of exclusion.

The elite didn't give up easily, and the celebrations continued. To enhance security, the parade was moved to the daytime. The ball was moved from the publicly funded Kiel Auditorium to the Chase Park-Plaza Hotel. The timing of the ball was changed from autumn to the Friday before Christmas to uncouple it from the parade. Even so, over the next decade consciousness-raising activities continued and the angry voice of the outsiders grew louder. What was designed as a festival to boost the city's image was seen by some as an embarrassing symbol of economic, social, and racial disparity. Instead of bringing the city together, the Veiled Prophet "celebration" tore St. Louis apart. Again, I turned to the photos to get a better idea of exactly what the words meant. I pulled my magnifying glasses from my purse. Something about an image seemed familiar.

A young Ella Latreau stood shouting at the cameraman with her right fist raised in the well-known salute to black power. Holding her left hand was a tall and equally strident young man, an African American.

FOURTEEN

The golf team was finishing up practice at the course. No other cars with CALA stickers were in the lot when I arrived, so I stayed in my BMW, reading my new library book about the Veiled Prophet Ball and its participants.

The air in the car grew stuffy. I stepped out and leaned against my car hood, nose deep in the library book. Since childhood, I've always had the ability to lose myself in what I was reading. I often read a couple of books a week, weighing open the pages with whatever's handy. And if I'm not reading a real book, I indulge in borrowing books on tape from the library. Lately, though, I'd noticed that more and more of what I wanted to hear was on CDs — and my old Beemer only has a tape player.

Books, creating scrapbook pages, working with crafts. I lived my life in my head. Maybe to escape the childhood I'd had.

Maybe because that was the way I was made. Who knew?

Patricia startled me. "They're running late again."

I nodded in agreement, tucking the book under my arm. She tapped her watch, a tiny timepiece bordered in diamonds.

"I need to get Anya back home and started on her homework," I said, thinking out loud. My eyes swept the clubhouse and its privacy fence for signs our children were coming. "Hey, what's this?"

Dangling from a matching set of silver chains, the clubhouse sign said CLOSED. I hadn't noticed it when I pulled up. Had the coach changed the location of practice? Wouldn't be the first time.

"Is this the right place?" Patricia asked. We fell into step, staring at the plaque board, a shared sense of purpose bonding us. We were three feet from the sign when the clubhouse door opened. A weathered man as thin as a putter with hair a similar shade poked his head out and scanned the parking lot.

"Are you closed?" I asked.

He shook his head.

"The girls from CALA here?"

He nodded his head.

"How come your sign says CLOSED?"

I pointed with my free hand. Bellowing a mighty "hmph," he let go the door and marched up to the plaque. Never was a fellow so badgered by women. Yanking at the board, he turned it over to read OPEN, and stomped back into the building.

"That clears that up."

"Good thing we asked," Patricia laughed as we walked over and leaned against her car. Her black pants were perfectly cut and hitting her shoes just right.

I mimicked her stance by settling back onto my own bumper. I'd just gotten comfortable when my cell phone rang. After digging into my purse, I flipped it open to check the number. It was Detweiler. Not wanting to seem rude, I hit the talk button and held the phone to the ear farthest from Patricia.

"Did Connie McMahan check out?"

Patricia stared off into space, ostensibly studying a gate with hinges along the far edge of the clubhouse wall. A tiny sign bore the legend "Driving Range" in woodburned letters. When was the last time I saw a woodburning set. Back at Girl Scout camp? In arts and crafts?

"Uh, fine. We had a nice visit. She's fine."

"Anything else?"

"No, I'm waiting for Anya to finish up

here. I'll be over in time for dinner, Sheila."
I hoped using my mother-in-law's name would alert him to my plight. I didn't want Patricia to overhear or to suspect I was discussing the murder.

I waited. When Maggie had called me "Mother," I'd caught on pretty quickly. Would Detweiler see through my ruse?

"You can't talk."

"You got it," and we said our goodbyes.

Patricia turned to me slowly. "Who do you think it was?" A deep crease interrupted Patricia's forehead.

"Pardon?" I tried to seem confused. "On my phone? My mother-in-law."

"Silly. I mean, who do you think killed Sissy?"

"Beats me. This'll probably be one of those weird cases where the cops discover someone, a person we don't know about, held a grudge against her."

"You think?" Her eyes flickered with concern. "A lot of people didn't like her. You should have heard the teachers in the break room today. They're all glad she's gone."

That was awful. I shivered. I didn't want my child picking up on those attitudes. I mused out loud, "One important question is, why now? There must have been a trigger, some event that caused the killer to make his move."

The gate attached to the side of the clubhouse began to shake as one of the golfers worried the latch. The signboard bounced and threatened to flip back to CLOSED. The players' voices rose behind the fence, loud and whiny. The girls were overtired, what with two emotional days at school and these overlong golf practices. They bolted out of the doorway, jostling each other along, acting more like children than young ladies. They carried their clubs low, nearly dragging the ground, as they scanned the lot for their mothers' cars. The tension showed on their faces. All of them were more than ready for the comforts of home.

I finished my thoughts as Patricia jingled her keys. I didn't want the girls to hear us. "The police have their ways. They'll keep interviewing people, comparing stories, and checking what they learn. Sooner or later, someone will crack, someone will say something. All the cops need is a motive. Maybe Corey Johnson will give them information. Maybe that's why they let him go, because he's cooperating with them. Maybe they've found a new direction."

Anya stumbled toward us, her khaki pants

grubby around the hem and her royal blue and gold golf shirt rumpled. Tilly followed close on my daughter's heels. "You'll see. They'll catch up with the person who did it —"

"And then?" Patricia whispered right before the kids were in earshot. "What do you suppose they'll do?"

I pitched my voice low. "Missouri has the death penalty." "Where's your jacket?" It wasn't much of a greeting, but Anya had forgotten her jacket twice the week before and her backpack once. Now her clubs were in the trunk and she'd settled into the passenger's seat, her hands suspiciously free of her belongings.

In answer to my question, she shrugged, guzzled Gatorade, and wiped her face on her sleeve.

"Oh, Anya! You need to go get it!" I felt bad about my outburst, but I was also fed up with her forgetfulness.

She threw open the passenger door and exploded from the car, narrowly missing Patricia who shot me a crooked grin and then climbed into her car.

"I'll be back," and Anya was off.

Tilly was sprawled across my backseat. She sipped her own Gatorade and fingered her backpack. Geez. Maggie's kid was so much more self-reliant than mine. "That's because you do too much for Anya," Maggie once told me. She lectured, "Never do anything for them that they can do for themselves."

But for heavens' sake, then why have a kid? I wanted her, and I loved doing things for her. However, I didn't enjoy nagging her. And I especially didn't like the way I channeled my mother each time I was forced to remind Anya of her responsibilities.

Ella pulled up to take Patricia's place. I stepped out to say, "Hi." We exchanged hugs.

"You okay? You didn't seem yourself at Jennifer's." I envied her the navy-blue designer jeans and marine-blue, scoop neck tee she wore so stylishly. She'd changed clothes after the book club. I was still in the outfit I'd put on that morning. By now, I could barely stand myself. The sweat I'd worked up gardening was now making me itchy and sticky. I wanted and needed a shower desperately.

"I'm okay. Mahreeya knows how to push my buttons. Always has. And I have a lot on my mind."

"I stopped at the library and looked up the Veiled Prophet."

"Bet you got a surprise."

"What was it really like? Was it really that grand?"

She raised an eyebrow. "All cotillions involve spectacle. Remember, there are other debutante balls here in St. Louis. The Fleur de Lis for example."

"I did a scrapbook for one of the attendees. But it's only fifty years old, whereas the Veiled Prophet is 132 years old!"

"That's the point. What you saw was a history lesson. Nothing more, nothing less. The world has changed. That's what vibrant societies do — they grow and change, sometimes slowly. What was acceptable and even desirable a century ago is viewed differently today. Whatever the V.P's original mission, isn't it important to concentrate on who they are now?"

"And who are they now? I mean, I still don't know."

"It's a philanthropic association that provides community services through a number of local organizations. It supports a parade modeled after the Mardi Gras in New Orleans."

I mulled over her comments. "But its history is quite different."

"That's my point. Let me ask you this: Are you the same person you were two years ago?"

"Not even close."

"The Veiled Prophet organization has changed, too. It's less about exclusion and more about inclusion. If you look at photos in the *Ladue News* you'll see black fathers and their daughters attending the event. Let me ask you this, if Anya was invited to attend, would you let her go?"

The question caught me off guard. Suddenly, I stood face-to-face with my own hypocrisy. I could whine about privilege with the best of them, but wasn't that exactly what I wanted for my child? A chance to live a better life than I had?

I made one last clutch at my prejudices. "But isn't it a secret society?"

"The prophet's identity is a secret. Other than that, you have to be proposed for membership just like a country club."

"Then why did you protest?"

"So you saw the infamous photo?" She peered at me and tried to read the source of my interest, whether looking for dirt or simply curious.

Actually, I was in awe. "Must have taken a lot of guts to be in a march like that."

"I marched because I had to. I knew what I needed to do. Blacks had already been admitted to membership in the 1980s, but the group needed to take their concerns more seriously. Things had to change. I had my reasons. Protesting wasn't hard. I wasn't alone. The repercussions were harsh, but being involved was important. For once in my life, I followed my heart. Well, maybe not for once, maybe for the second time."

"But the cost!"

She shrugged. "You see, the Queen is actually a stand-in for her father."

"So it isn't really a beauty pageant?"

Her laugh was harsh. "Heck no. Believe me, the Queen of Love and Beauty is not about good looks. It's about your family, especially your father and his status. Having a daughter rise up against the organization, well, it hit my dad hard." She stared off toward the horizon. "He had his first stroke a week after the picture ran. A second one finished him off. Shortly afterward, my mother lost the will to live."

"Oh, Ella! I'm so sorry."

"You needn't be. They're all gone now. I've been sorry enough for two people. Or three. If I'd been more patient . . . if I'd let things take their natural course . . . things would have changed anyway . . . without my involvement." She tilted her head to the sky and studied the changing colors of the clouds. Above the tree line, the sky was crayon orange. A pink layer with maroon

streaks rose up until it faded into gray blah-
ness. The color thinned out quickly into a
neutrality. The sun was setting, and the air
was so temperate that the atmosphere
echoed the nothingness of the faded sky. We
were floating, out of time and space, and
not anchored to the earth or this moment.

"I can certainly understand why you were
upset about Corey Johnson being arrested.
That must have seemed like a throwback to
—"

"No. I had my own reasons for being
upset about Corey. He's a good coach. He's
very understanding, and Corey deserves
better."

"Mom?" The gate banged opened, and Ella's daughter Natalie walked out, with Anya
following close behind. My daughter carried her jacket tucked under her elbow.

Ella turned away suddenly.

"Great round," said Natalie, tapping my
daughter on the shoulder. I saw Anya smile
up at the older girl, a beam of pure sunshine
on her face.

Ella stepped to the kids, "Hi, Anya, how're
you? Natalie, honey, how's your new
putter?"

"Hi, Mrs. Walden," said Anya. "I'm fine.
Mom, let's go. I'm hungry. See you, Nat."

Ella's daughter was tall, blonde, and lean.

As she started toward their car, her brother Frederick jumped out to help her with her clubs. The boy made a quick nod toward Anya and me. I could see the family resemblance: his thin straight nose — what did they call it? Patrician? — his high cheek bones and his pointed chin.

Distinctive. I filed away the image of Ella and her children as she drove past me, a cloud of dust rising from the wheels of her big Mercedes SUV.

FIFTEEN

We dropped off Tilly after driving about twenty minutes to the southwestern suburb of Des Peres. Dutifully, she thanked me for the ride. I waited outside the neat, white-shingled two-story until she waved from behind the closed front door. I turned back east, backtracking.

Anya dozed as I drove. We were two feet inside the kitchen when she turned and said, "We have to go back. I forgot my backpack."

I counted to ten. Ten times. I even counted to twenty twice as I let the dogs out. Mr. Gibbes and Gracie didn't have to go. Bama must have let them out. I needed to remember to thank her.

I chided myself about us walking off without Anya's backpack. I'd reminded her about her jacket, but the backpack had slipped my mind. "You left it at the golf course, didn't you? Call them and see if they're closed."

She called the golf course only to discover it was closed. I thought about what Maggie said. I decided not to bail my child out.

Anya frowned. I could see her trying to figure out what to do. I willed myself not to butt in. She could handle this, and I knew I should let her. Besides, the hassle might, just might, make her a bit more careful about her things. Finally, she flipped open her cell phone and called Coach Bosch. After a quick give-and-take, she thrust the phone at me. "Coach Bosch's going to tell you how to get to his house."

Scrambling for a piece of scrap paper (and thinking how ironic it was that I, of all people, couldn't lay hands on a piece of paper!), I took down directions from Coach Bosch. As I said goodbye, I realized we'd been close to his home at the golf course, but I now had easily forty-five minutes of driving ahead of me. The St. Louis area is one of the most geographically spread-out in the country.

I tried not to feel cranky, but I did. Anya protested coming with me. "Moo-oom. I'm tired. Why can't I stay home and you go get my backpack? I need a nap!"

"Because I'm not the person who forgot my stuff. This was your responsibility," I said as I hustled her and the dogs into the car.

Driving counter to the flow of rush-hour traffic, I poked along the highly trafficked Kirkwood, which becomes Lindbergh, which is also Highway 67 only for the sake of totally confusing out-of-towners. Anya held Mr. Gibbes on her lap and cranked back the passenger's seat, which caused poor Gracie to hunker down in the back since there's so little room in my BMW. Everyone was uncomfortable but my daughter, who quickly dropped off to sleep.

Coach Bosch's house was a neat Cape Cod in a tiny subdivision directly north of the school. Clearly, the coach was a DIY type of guy. His was the only mailbox on the street that had been white wooden shingled to match his home. His plants were cropped as tidily as his own crew cut. I stood on his stoop and thought of the yard work I needed to get done and felt a fresh wave of irritation. My daughter needed to get her act together.

Coach Bosch answered the door, invited me inside, and retrieved the backpack, but not before he beckoned me to his mantelpiece to admire his recent 25 Years of Service gift from the Sports Boosters.

"Ella Walden dropped it by this morning.

They officially gave it to me last week, but Patricia took it home right after the sports booster meeting. She put it in this case for me. Isn't it something?"

If you get excited by a paving stone engraved with your name, it was pretty nifty. Didn't do much for me, but then you couldn't eat it, wear it, or glue it to a scrapbook page. (I reflected on what a pathetic creature I was that these three qualities determined "useful" and "useless" in my life.)

"Its twin is being laid outside of the new football stadium. The one that's going to replace the old Busch Stadium. They'll intersperse these with plain bricks to form the concourse. Isn't this great?" Coach Bosch rubbed his hands together. I made low murmurs of appreciation. I owed him that. After all, the man rescued more than $452 worth of schoolbooks.

Anya slept through the entire exchange. She lifted her head when the garage door rose at home and sprinted past me into the house. I picked up my purse, and my daughter's backpack, and went into my dirty kitchen. I started a load of laundry, let the dogs out, and fixed Anya a plate of meatloaf, veggies, and fruit.

■ ■ ■ ■

Anya had been a colicky baby. Unlike infants who cry from four to six p.m., she'd screamed around the clock. Two weeks after she was born, she cried for forty-eight hours straight, only sleeping for forty-five minutes. The pediatrician, Dr. Lee, gave us phenobarbitol drops for her.

"One drop for baby and three drops for Mama," he laughed.

"Won't Anya get addicted?" George had asked. I was so exhausted that I could barely follow the conversation.

"As baby grows, her weight goes up and she gets less and less," explained Dr. Lee. "It's okay."

On the way home, George joked, "I don't hate you enough to make you a single parent." It became one of those "catch phrases" you have as a couple, a sort of signal between you.

While we hadn't been soul mates, we had loved each other. Maybe more importantly, we were committed to being good parents for Anya. While some might argue that the most important thing a man can do for his children is to love his wife, I was willing to settle for the kind of love two friends have, not two lovers.

Days like this, I missed him. I missed having a partner. Someone to vent to. Someone to take over when our pre-teen got on my last nerve and ground her heel down. That's when my mind turned to Detweiler. Why did he have to be married? Why had fate brought him back into my life just when I was moving ahead without him?

I gave myself a stern slap, and a lecture not to be such a wimp. I got Anya started on her homework. She was sitting on the sofa, totally absorbed in a textbook, with both her feet tucked under Gracie's large body. Mr. Gibbes slept at her elbow.

"Mom? I need help with my algebra."

George? Oh, George? I shook my head. This was when I needed my husband. I couldn't do math to save my neck. Dodie had forced me to work up a budget and to balance my checkbook, but I sweat copious amounts of blood each month doing so. I gritted my teeth.

"Sweetie, you are out of luck."

"How about you drop me by Nicci's house? Stevie is really good at this. He helped me over the weekend."

Coffee and Crime, a get-together for mystery lovers, was scheduled at a nearby bookstore less then two blocks away from the Moores'. If we left now, I could be there on time.

"You need to check with Mrs. Moore."

My daughter smiled at me. "Already did. Nicci and I texted each other."

"Grab your stuff."

I watched her walk into the Moores' house, then I sped off toward the Barnes & Noble on Olive. I loved this book discussion group, although I was rarely able to attend. Unlike the CALA mothers' book club, these people really discussed what they read. Local authors often came and talked about their creative processes. How odd it seemed to hear perfectly ordinary and harmless people natter on about the ways they chose, on paper, to do bodily harm. One memorable evening, the store was packed with middle-aged women in twin sets discussing the after-effects of various poisons with the sort of thorough interest that typically accompanies church rummage sales.

A mythical murder was the very thing for taking my mind off my bad mood and my futile snooping into Sissy Gilchrist's death. I picked up a cup of gratis hot tea and pulled up a chair to listen in on a discussion already in progress. A chair scraped the floor beside me, and I turned to see Connie

McMahan cradling a tall cup of coffee. To put it bluntly, she did not look good.

"Are you all right?"

She shook her head, paying extravagant attention to the cup between her hands.

I took the hint. We concentrated on the discussion. A sprinkling of laughter followed the guest author's admission that she hoped her mother never read her manuscript. The sex scene was too realistic? (This made me put the book immediately on my "wish list." What a sales pitch!)

The group broke up, leaving Connie and me huddled over empty cups.

"Connie? What's up?"

"They've loosened the hounds of the hunt on him." Her voice was full of emotion.

I got up and refilled her coffee cup.

She took it from me gratefully. "They're all over Elliott."

"They who?"

"Old St. Louis. Blaming him. Calling him a turncoat. Siccing their lawyers on him. This afternoon he went to play golf at the club, and one of the members took him aside. Told him he wasn't welcome. Suggested he leave and not come back."

"But why?"

"The Gilchrists. They say he's ruined Sissy's reputation."

"You have to be kidding!"

"They say he's sullied her good name. They say he's the one who told the police she was sleeping around. They said he's responsible for the halls being patrolled by police. That no one is safe at school, because of him! His lack of judgment. His failure of leadership. We're getting anonymous letters. The Gilchrists have all their friends calling and canceling pledges to the development office." She turned to me, her face stricken.

Right before she spilled her coffee, she said, "He's ruined."

Sixteen

Elliott McMahan was a pompous so-and-so. When he shook your hand, he had an annoying habit of peering past you to see who he was going to greet next. He wrote long-winded letters in the school newsletter that rambled self-indulgently. He prided himself on his military bearing (back in Indiana we called it having a corn cob up your backside) and his liberal arts education. He didn't really listen, although he preached the value of it. He would nod his head during a conversation and mutter, "Uh-huh," and remain unengaged. Like my Nana would say, it was like talking to a brick wall. Once he learned I was Sheila's daughter-in-law, he treated me with more courtesy and respect, once even remarking positively on my appearance.

Okay, all he said was, "You're looking nice," but it was a big moment for me.

Strangely enough, that compliment made

me like him less, a whole lot less, because it signaled how Elliott ranked people by importance. All in all, the man was a terminal prig.

Even so, no one deserves to be hounded out of a job by an angry mob. Especially a job he's done well. And sending out letters anonymously? That was really bush league. I've gotten myself in trouble many a time by speaking my mind, but I'd never stoop to write an anonymous missive. If you believe it, if you have evidence, why not sign your name?

Elliott deserved better. He deserved the right to face his accusers. That's the American way.

For all Elliott's snobbery, he managed to increase the number of scholarships CALA offered. As Connie had reminded me, he'd launched an outreach program to bring more minority students to the school. Before his tenure, this had been a pie-in-the-sky part of a long-range plan toward a more diverse student population. But Elliott had taken the task seriously.

I didn't care for him as a person. The luckiest day of his life was the day he snagged Connie, a woman who had every quality he lacked: graciousness, sincerity, and humility. But I was mature enough to separate how I felt about Elliott (and his shortcomings) from my appreciation for the job he was doing. And although Connie said all of Old St. Louis was against him, I was confident he was being harassed by a small, vocal — but powerful — few.

The Gilchrists couldn't make up their minds. First, they used their clout to get Sissy hired. Now, they used their power to castigate Elliott for his poor judgment. They had turned on the man who gave their daughter a chance! I couldn't help but think about the signs you see in London tube stations: "Mind the gap." The Gilchrists had fallen right into the gap, the crevasse between what they wanted and what they got. In that misstep, they'd taken no responsibility at all for their part in this fiasco.

With her death, Sissy had become the saint she could never be in life. Yes, Sissy was a victim twice over. Once of her own poor choices and once of a cold-hearted killer. But now Elliott McMahan, through no fault of his own, was being made a casualty as well.

I picked up Anya and thanked Jennifer for her hospitality. To my shock, Nicci's mother gave me a warm hug. "Thank you for being so kind to me at the book club meeting."

We made it home a half an hour after Anya's day normally ended. "Time for bed, Anya-Banana," I told her. She grumbled heartily and stomped off toward our bathroom. I checked my phone and found one message. Bama had called to tell me that Dodie's tests were negative for breast cancer.

I took a long grateful breath of air.

As I snapped my phone shut, I heard Anya rustling around in her room next door. I could hear drawers being slammed as she searched for clothes to put out for the next school day. I opened my e-mail and sent a message to Maggie.

Dear Maggie: Will Coach Johnson be back at school tomorrow? K

Dear Kiki: No. He's on leave. I wish I was. Maggie

Dear Maggie: How come? Anything new? K

Dear Kiki: Can you bring me a sack lunch tomorrow? Meet at 11:15 outside the Alumni Offices on the picnic tables? Can't talk online. Maggie

I confirmed that I'd be there and took down her sandwich order. Things would have to be pretty tense for Maggie to want to talk over lunch. She usually used the noon respite for catching up on her paperwork.

As I sat staring at the screen, a message from CALA popped up.

Sure enough, Elliott McMahan indulged himself with a long and desultory attempt at the meaning of life in the wake of violent death. "Rest assured," he concluded, "all proper safeguards are in place to keep our children from harm. This administration is cooperating with law enforcement officials to the fullest extent, leaving no quarter un-examined, and supporting all staff members as they are interviewed, in a right and ap-propriate examination of the crime that happened on our grounds. Meanwhile, the condolences of our entire student body, alumni, staff, parents, and friends of CALA go to the family of Ms. Sissy Gilchrist, a dedicated instructor whose presence is sorely missed. A memorial tribute is planned. Details to follow."

Sorely missed?

Wow, and I thought Elliott didn't have a sense of humor.

SEVENTEEN

On my way back from dropping Anya at school on Wednesday morning, I called Detweiler. Hearing Connie talk about Elliott and the full court press to blame him for the murder lit a fire under me. I wanted to make progress on this situation. I wanted the suspicions to end and for the police to put a REAL suspect in custody. I also needed a better sense of where the investigation really stood.

He and I arrived simultaneously at the original Kaldi's Coffee on DeMun, nestled in a cul-de-sac in a lovely, tree-lined area. I had to talk quickly in order to be on time opening the store. I wore a pair of Ralph Lauren jeans and a V-neck sweater with turquoise detailing. His gorgeous green eyes swept up and down with appreciation, causing the back of my neck to warm.

Neither of us said anything about our feelings. Well, maybe I was the only one with feelings. Maybe he was the "victim" of my stray hormones.

A part of me longed to say, "Did you ever really care about me? Or are you a hound dog?" But I didn't. What was the use?

Instead, we leaned against my car, and both of us produced lists of names. He quickly marked off the male teachers.

"Got them covered. Pinning them down, checking them out."

"How can I help?"

"Keep talking to the moms. Someone somewhere's got to know something. There's got to be a motive out there. Maybe twisted and nonsensical to us, but not to the killer."

"Has the task force closed its investigation of Corey?"

He drummed his fingers on the door panel. I could tell he was debating what to say. He dragged his hand over his jaw as though trying to rub his face clean, but not succeeding. I noticed the bags beneath his eyes, and how gaunt he seemed.

"Not yet. But we're not learning anything to help him either. That jerk of a lawyer he has, Jim Hagg, is giving us fits."

"Jim Hagg?" I nearly choked on my coffee. Hagg was the high-priced spread, the go-to guy used by all the big money folks caught cheating on their taxes, driving while intoxicated, or looking at kiddy porn. If you did it, and everyone knew you did, Hagg was your man.

Detweiler nodded. "I know. I mean, I'm glad, don't get me wrong, but where's the money coming from?"

"Did you try asking Corey?"

"Not yet. Hagg's good. I'll give him that. He's got Corey's mouth closed tighter than bark sticks to a tree. Meantime, we've got diddly. Whatever Corey knows, he's keeping to himself. Like they say at the Ed Jones Dome, we're losing momentum."

"But I thought you two were friends."

"We are." Detweiler's shoulders drooped. "But I'm a cop. And he's the accused. You'd think I'd be used to this . . . no matter how good friends you are, when people are in trouble . . ." He sighed. "I became a policeman because I wanted to help people. But I've learned that most people don't think of cops as helpful."

I could think of nothing to say. I understood entirely how "most people" felt.

The silence between us was uncomfortable. Detweiler ducked his head down and studied the papers before us. "Doesn't matter. He and I don't need to discuss it. Corey didn't kill Sissy Gilchrist." I noticed he didn't use her courtesy title the way he did everyone else he ever mentioned in the course of an investigation. I assumed this reflected both how well he'd known her — through Corey — as well as his lack of respect for the woman.

"And what did you think about her? Did you spend time with her and him? Did you like her?"

"I . . . we . . . as couples we spent time together." His face reddened, and I averted my eyes thinking of Detweiler's wife, Brenda.

"I thought Sissy was trouble," said Detweiler as he slapped the quarter panel of his car in frustration. "I thought she was having fun with him. Payback to her controlling mom and henpecked dad, for goodness knows what. I told him he was crazy. He laughed. Didn't even get angry. Said he knew I meant well, but that I was wrong. He said I'd see how much they meant to each other. Right. I'm seeing. I'm seeing him taking a bum rap. I told him he should stay away from her. Now look what's happened."

"Were you worried about how people would react? Or worried about her flirting?"

"Both." He spit the word out.

I understood. A black man with a white

woman might not turn heads in New York City or London or Scott Air Force Base, but here in the more conservative St. Louis suburbs, it would cause a bad case of whiplash. And a mixed marriage? Oh, baby. You had to be joking. Take Sissy's loose behavior, add her flair for making people angry, and stir it with the deep-seated revulsion some portions of society felt toward miscegenation, and you were talking risky business. Deadly risky.

The thought of the two of them carrying on this torrid romance in the hallowed halls of CALA made me shiver. Maybe they were right for each other. What was it Marvin Gaye called it? Sexual healing? Maybe they'd found that in each other. I wasn't a total cynic. Deep in my heart, I hoped the right person could really make your dreams come true. Whatever clicked between them, their diverse racial backgrounds must have added yet another dimension of drama to the relationship.

And from what I'd heard, Sissy seemed addicted to drama.

"You don't have any evidence on Corey, do you?"

"I can't tell you that. But Kiki, you don't understand. Law enforcement professionals hate to be wrong. You learn to trust your gut in this business, or you don't last long. We believe where there's smoke there's fire. The members of the Major Case Squad aren't going to give up on Corey as the killer that easily. In fact, hiring Jim Hagg was a bad move. Mr. Hagg's reputation has been built on defending the guilty, on getting off rich folks who deserve to be put behind bars. Once Mr. Hagg walked into the station, the entire force became even more determined to find evidence to convict Corey. They took it as a challenge."

"Oh, no." I poked around in my cup with the wooden coffee stirrer. What I needed to say next had to be said gently. "Are you sure Corey didn't do this?"

"I had my moments, but . . ." he paused, "Corey was cool with her past. And we've already found three people who've said she changed her ways after she hooked up with him."

That jibed with Maggie's comments. "Any progress with the murder weapon?"

"No. We're still trying to talk to the folks attending the sports booster meeting." He slammed one hand into the other. "This case is like dealing with another culture. A foreign country where I don't speak the language."

It was the language of privilege, and my

daughter was becoming fluent in it.

I shook my head in agreement as I thought back to what I'd learned about the Veiled Prophet. If you would have told me a week ago that an entire city bought into a mythical figurehead — who arrived by barge on the river no less — I would have laughed. But now, I knew differently.

"But here's a way you can help. A call came in this morning from a woman who swore up and down that she knows who the killer is."

"That's good news, right?"

"The rest of the squad blew her off. What if she's on the level? See, the other guys thought she was a nut-case without a clue. A rich housewife bent on seeking attention. No one even thought it worth following up on. They heard 'mom' and her Zip Code and decided she wasn't worth listening to."

Again, I nodded. Harry Potter might need a cloak of invisibility, but for one-half the world — the female half — we didn't need a cape. We moms were already invisible. I flashed back to a dinner party I'd attended with George. The minute my companions to the left and right found out I was a SAHM (Stay-At-Home Mom), they cleared their throats and talked over my head to each other. In the space of four little words,

I became a non-entity. I spent the entire meal developing a close and personal relationship with my braised scallops, risotto, and sautéed baby vegetables.

No wonder I'd become overweight. At least food didn't diss me.

And that Zip Code thing? The private school culture would be unfamiliar territory for the majority of police. Made sense. After all, I was a product of a poor, middle-class family, and I was resigned to circling the outskirts of CALA culture, even though I looked like I should be teaching Sunday school at the Episcopal Church. (Which I might have done, had my life not followed another path.)

I closed my eyes and tried to imagine Elliott McMahan's position. He would be busy juggling two priorities, keeping the police at arm's length and finding the murderer. It was a no-win situation.

"Vicky Ventner's our caller's name. Do you know her?"

"Oh, I know her all right." I smirked. "I'll just bet she sounded confident."

"You think she knows something?"

I couldn't help it. My evil twin was trying to take over my body. I resisted, resisted, and then gave up. "Vicky Ventner knows everything, absolutely everything."

EIGHTEEN

I opened the store, found Diva Craft
Lounge Radio on the Internet, and put in a
solid hour of work while listening to the
hosts Danielle and Rayme. By creating a
repeated visual theme for the confidential
album, I could work on the pages and keep
the photos locked in the briefcase. To help
me know exactly what I had to work with,
I'd created a series of thumbnail sketches,
numbered each photo, and keyed those
numbers to my thumbnails. The store was
mostly empty. Bama finished an inventory
of our punches. She didn't ask me what I
was doing until half past nine.

"That a special project?"

"Yes."

"You owe me time," she said. Her voice
was pitched high and her eyes were sharp
and angry. Oh, crud, I realized with a start.
She was ticked off that Dodie had given this
project to me instead of her.

"I know I owe you time on the clock. Unfortunately, Dodie scheduled me to work on CALA's alumni publication. I have to go over to the school right now."

Bama made an indecipherable noise, rather like a growl. "At least take these." She gave me more flyers about upcoming workshops. "Why you? How come you get to leave the store?"

I explained how as part of our "outreach" program, Dodie had volunteered my services to CALA's alumni publication. "Put those three journalism courses you took in college to use," she'd said. Frankly, in my heart of hearts, I suspected an ulterior motive. Dodie determined that I should become part of my daughter's school community. "You're an outsider because you don't put forth the effort," my boss scolded me. "If you don't know them, don't pal around with them, you miss out. So will Anya."

I suspected Dodie and Sheila had discussed my multitudinous and manifold deficiencies, and this "lack of involvement" ranked high on their list. I faced Bama. "I'm doing what our boss told me to do."

Bama pouted. "Whatever."

"Hey, it's extra work for me."

Bama's frown deepened. "Extra pay, too."

Over summer vacation, I'd been assigned articles to run throughout the year, including profiles on CALA's prestigious alumni. After dragging my eraser butt for a week on my most recent task, I knew the research couldn't wait any longer if I was to meet my deadline.

I took the dogs around the block, penned them up, and drove into the parking area in front of the Bread Co. on Ballas. It's one of the few eating spots my daughter and I agree on. Anya hates the lunches the school serves. "Too starchy. I'll get fat," she says. Last year the middle-school nurse called and put a scare into me when my daughter quit eating and lost weight. Since then I actively looked for ways to put healthy food in front of her on the sly. I was already stopping at Bread Co. to order lunch for Maggie and me, so I decided to splurge on extra bagels for the rest of the week. Anya would never ask for them, but the smell of the dough toasting in the morning would be irresistible.

Although only 9:45 a.m., Bread Co. was crowded as usual. I ordered the baker's dozen bagels and cream cheese special to take home for later, as well as a Bistro Salad for myself and an iced Green Tea (a splurge), plus a turkey sandwich on sourdough with a bag of Kettle Chips and a Coke for Maggie.

Mr. Beacon monitored the parking lot. As I walked past, he gave me a friendly wave and a tip of his cap. The alumni office at CALA was located in Wellingham Hall just off the main corridor to all the admissions offices. As my heels clicked along the marble, I paid new attention to the glossy black and white photos of illustrious alums, which gave way to color shots of more recent vintage.

Mrs. Glazer, head of alumni services, gave me a nod and went back to her paperwork when I walked in. I'd shown up often enough to be unremarkable. During the first week, she'd stood over me. But lately, Mrs. Glazer pretty much left me alone to do my thing. I guess she figured her lecture on the confidential nature of the materials in the files had soaked in. Now she barely noticed me when I came in, and she seemed to have decided I could be trusted with whatever secrets were hidden on old sheets of paper.

She shouldn't have.

The file cabinets in a smaller, second office off of her work area held the records for each school year. I settled myself into a well-worn arm chair and pulled out my notes. In no time, I collected the rest of the information I needed for my article. Sitting around me in neat manila file folders was a cornucopia of information on the elite of St. Louis.

I ached to know more about the women I'd dubbed the Four Alumnae: Jennifer Moore, Patricia Bigler, Ella Latreau Walden, and Mahreeya Nichols. Really, it was none of my business. Actually, it was the whole reason I majored in journalism in college — being able to poke around where it wasn't my business. And wasn't nosing around how I came up with those wonderful alumni articles? You betcha.

This looked like a grand time to snoop. I started with the CALA yearbooks.

Bingo. Young and hopeful faces, bearing a vague resemblance to the women I knew, stared out from the pages. I would never have recognized Patricia Bigler without the cutline below the photo. The list of names included Jennifer's, but not Mahreeya's. I studied the photos more carefully. Where was she? I thought back to Ella's crack about Mahreeya's looks being surgically enhanced. A class photo showed Ella, Jennifer, Patricia, and a handful of other girls. Mahreeya had to be in there somewhere, hidden behind her original features and figure. The cutline only referenced the activity, May Day preparations, not the participants.

I flipped the pages back and forth reluctantly, trying to decide what to do next. I had little more than an hour until lunch with Maggie. The book I held covered the girls' freshman year. I tried to remember my high school yearbook. As the girls drew nearer to graduation, the yearbook would logically devote more pages, more images, to their class. The next annual did just that. Ella, Jennifer, and Patricia appeared on every other page. Toward the back was a group picture of the graduating class and a carefully annotated cutline. The students' names were printed as they'd appear on their diplomas: Ella Martha Latreau, Jennifer Anne Hallback, Patricia Esther Krupp, and so on.

I still couldn't puzzle out which girl was Mahreeya.

The body of the yearbook was broken down into individual photos arranged alphabetically by graduating class interrupted by student life photos featuring activities. Where was Mahreeya? I studied the photos of the girls participating in various clubs. Then I flipped to the list of graduating seniors' names.

Of course! All of the girls' names were

spelled conventionally and most of the students went by their given names, not their middle names. Mahreeya's given name was Deborah, and her middle name was Maria. There she was, with a face that could stop a Mack Truck, Deborah Maria La-Fevre. An unexpected wave of pity swept over me. What a plain, unattractive child Mahreeya had been. The poor girl had a nose like Cyrano de Bergerac, a chest as flat as Kansas, and saddlebag hips that stuck out like panniers. The harsh light of the photographer's flash highlighted a complexion marred by large abscesses from acne.

Obviously, as her outside self changed, Deborah Maria decided that her name needed to change, too. Hence, the phonetic spelling "Mahreeya." It was a sad, but understandable way of saying, "I am someone special!"

No wonder Mahreeya felt insecure. Any one of her physical challenges would have sent a teenage girl's self-esteem plummeting. I hadn't noticed her in the other photos because she was deep in the background, as though willing herself to disappear. I moved to another page and saw a stunning photo of Ella, smiling directly at the photographer, in all the glory and sensuality of budding womanhood. What a contrast the two girls made.

For kicks and grins, I made chicken scratches in my notebook to mark the number of times each girl appeared in photos. Although this meant using a highly unscientific methodology, if CALA was anything like the high school I had attended, the final tally would be an indicator of popularity among classmates.

When I counted my marks, I was surprised to discover that Ella appeared not most but least of the quartet. And yet, she'd been Queen of Love and Beauty. Apparently I'd been told the truth. The coronation was not a popularity contest.

I put the yearbooks back on the appropriate shelf and stood in the center of the room, beating a rhythm with my pencil against my teeth. Snooping around is a process of casting your net wide, then looking over your catch, sorting through the fishies, and casting your net again. Hoping eventually you'll pull up a big tuna. I decided to look up all the girls' parents and any information on the four alumnae. The files were cross-referenced and indexed. I jotted down relevant file names and made more notes on my notepaper.

A silhouette passed by the frosted window

of the office where I worked. Low voices conferred. I hurriedly shoved the files I'd pulled under a notepad and started working on notes for my article. When the voices left, I went back to poking around.

I crossed off each file as I pulled it. The folders were crammed with photos and articles. Pay dirt. Obviously, the girls' parents had played integral parts in the life of the school community. A photo showing the four girls hunched over a school project was in one of the first files I opened. From the same file came another photo showing Patricia and Maria/Mahreeya, and a young man labeled as Patricia's brother, Donald. Two of the women changed so much over the years that I wouldn't have recognized them without the cutlines. Maria/Mahreeya was pudgy, and her hawkish nose had dominated her face before she'd had it trimmed to scale. Patricia was rail thin, not nearly as tall as she was now, and so frail a stiff wind could have blown her to Kansas City. Only Ella and Jennifer looked much as they did today.

In journalism school, we were taught never to write on the back of a photo because the pressure of the pen would mar the image. Instead, we glued an identifying sheet to the back piece of the photo. On the attached paper was a cutline that listed who was in the photo, the name and date of the event. The school photographers had done exactly that, listing each person with his or her entire given name. Probably, given the amount of intermarriage expected among St. Louis' Old Families, this method facilitated tracing complicated family interrelationships. I studied the names, and the thought came to me: I might as well have been perusing the records of a dog breeder.

The clock told me I was going to have to hurry to grab lunch and get it to Maggie.

Maggie was pacing laps around a picnic table when I arrived. Her brown pants held a sharp crease, and her soft green and tan turtlenecked sweater was tucked in and held tight with a polished brown belt. Maggie wasn't one for fashion, but she did put a priority on neatness. Her face, I noticed, looked tired and pale.

"Hey, what's up?" I handed over the Bread Co. shopping bag. Maggie unwrapped her sandwich and bit into it eagerly. We ate with the abandon of our two teenagers instead of their more dignified mothers.

"I needed this. The food and the break. I'm still upset about what happened yesterday." With that prelude, Maggie explained that a new family had visited the kindergarten the day before. True to CALA's commitment to diversity, the head of the lower school had persuaded an African-American doctor and his wife to consider enrolling their son. Dr. and Mrs. Percy showed up with their little guy in tow right before snack time.

"The class was divided. Half of the children were up in the library choosing books. The other half was finishing a matching project to develop fine motor skills. Very age appropriate. Jared Percy sat down at the worktable next to the children working on the matching project. Cute kid. Big brown eyes, and a thoughtful expression. He was totally into his activity when the library group came back."

Maggie stopped. She closed her eyes and took a long sip of her Coke. "Sissy's son Christopher was one of the kids returning. All of a sudden, he stops in his tracks. He drops his library book and stares at the Percys. He begins to scream. I mean, this was a yell of pure terror.

"He's pointing at the black family. He's incoherent, blubbering. I mean, he had a major meltdown. He started to run out of the room, but I grabbed him. He started kicking me and screaming."

She pulled on her collar and for the first time, I noticed a series of claw marks on her neck and jawline.

"What did you do?"

"I remembered seeing Patricia Bigler in the halls earlier. I got my assistant to track her down."

I repeated what Connie McMahan had said about Patricia being Christopher's favorite person, and Maggie's pale face nodded. My friend reached up and massaged her temples. "I thought we'd have to call a pediatrician and have him sedated. That little boy was literally foaming at the mouth by the time Patricia arrived. She picked him up, and he grabbed onto her, screaming about his mother being killed by . . . Well, he used the 'n' word."

I hadn't heard the "n" word from a white person's mouth in years. Ever since political correctness became the unofficial law of the land, folks had wised up to the fact there are certain words you just don't say under any circumstances, unless you are a rap star or a shock radio host. Then people get paid to say horrible, ugly words in combinations most folks would never imagine. How on earth had a white kindergartener added that ugly sobriquet to his vocabulary? I was stunned. "The 'n' word?"

"You heard me."

"What on earth got into him?"

"Other than his mama dying? And his dad and grandparents fighting over him? Hmm?" She gave me a sour grimace that said volumes. I was being stupid.

"Oh. Yeah. Even so, isn't that an extreme reaction? I mean, okay, kids can feel overwhelmed. Helpless. Out of control. Especially when their lives get, um, in turmoil. But to call someone that . . ."

Maggie sighed. "Kids are great observers and poor interpreters. Who knows what he was thinking? It's not like he's never seen a black person before. Hello? How about our first family? And we have black students and black parents and black instructors here at CALA. I was wondering if he blamed Coach Johnson for his mother's death? Maybe heard his grandparents blaming the man? That's both probable and possible."

I was processing this rather slowly. "So, you think Christopher believes Corey Johnson killed his mother? Or he's been told as much?"

"That's what I wondered. See, he kept on yelling. He said black people wanted to kill him. Kill all of us white people. He said he wanted his daddy. Which is totally bizarre because his father is uninvolved. He's never been to any of our school functions that I know of. I even asked the lead teacher who's out on maternity leave, and she agreed. It just seemed so odd. I could see him asking for his grandfather because Mr. Gilchrist drops Christopher off regularly and picks him up. They seem very close. Or he could have hollered for his grandmother, she's a bit of a pill, but she dotes on him and stops in all the time as well. But his dad?"

"My friend Mert told me Sissy's ex was some kind of racist. I wonder . . ."

"If his daddy has reinforced his fear of blacks?"

"Makes sense. I doubt it was an amicable divorce —"

"Are they ever? It's always the child who gets hurt in the fight. Spoils of war. That's all they are when two people decide to go at it."

I asked Maggie how they calmed the boy down. I remembered her telling me once how an intense kid can keep on cranking up the emotional volume, even to the point of physically harming himself.

"Patricia carried him out of the classroom. I guess they went for a walk. You could hear his screams as she walked with him down the hall."

"And the Percys? I guess it's safe to assume their son won't be attending here."

"You would be assuming correctly." Maggie wadded up the trash from her lunch. A slight odor of pickle scent lingered on her hands. She smashed the cup, the wrapper, and her napkin vigorously, working the paper into a wad the size of a walnut. Her face was strained and tired.

I couldn't bring myself to ask her to reimburse me for the food.

Mrs. Glazer glared when I returned to the alumni office. She stood to face me, her body bristling in a palpable way. "Mrs. Lowenstein, it has been brought to my attention that you have overstepped your bounds."

My heart dropped. I'd really screwed up. I should have put back all the files. Now word would get around that I was untrustworthy. My actions would reflect poorly on Time in a Bottle, as well as on my daughter and myself. Crapola. I'd ruined our family rep and endangered my livelihood all in one fell swoop.

"I walked into the file room and noticed you'd been rummaging through our folders. As you are well aware, much of that information is strictly confidential." One of Mrs.

Glazer's fingers pointed at me as if aiming a gun at my chest. "You know, Mrs. Lowenstein, when I accepted your help on the alumni newsletter, I thought I made it perfectly clear that certain areas were off-limits. I trusted your integrity. Now, it seems I might have been mistaken." Her jowls shook in anger. She was so angry that her nostrils had turned white against the red glow of her cheeks.

I decided to take my lumps. "You are right. I apologize."

The woman sagged, her loose jowls flapping as she unclenched her teeth. I guess she'd expected a confrontation. But a soft answer turneth away wrath. What she hadn't expected was me being agreeable. I took advantage of her shock to continue, "I should have asked your permission. I was trying to keep a secret, and I was wrong. You see, Ella Walden's forty-fifth birthday is in a few weeks, and I was hoping to find old photos to scan for a special present. I wanted to make her an album of her years at CALA. Her family has such a history here, and the school means so much to her . . ." I let my voice trail off. When you lie, always mix a large dose of truth along with your falsehood. I don't remember where I read that. Probably in a mystery novel. I'd heard Ella talking about her upcoming birthday. I had no clue when it was, though.

"Uh. Yes. You're right. You should have asked me first," Mrs. Glazer gathered herself. "But I must admit that's a perfectly wonderful idea."

I saw my opening and sprinted toward it. From my satchel, I opened one of my more recent album projects. Mrs. Glazer's face changed from angry to astonished as she flipped through the pages. "You are so creative! Someday if you have time, I'd really, really like to learn how to scrapbook. I bought all these materials and can't seem to get started." On and on she went.

It got worse. Seems she had photos. Loads of them. In her desk.

She wanted to share every one of them with me and add commentary. The clock ticked off the seconds very slowly. Finally she said, "My, I'm a bit hungry. I'm heading down to the vending machines. Would you like something?"

I said no, and retreated happily to the alumni office, where I continued to look through the files. Something niggled at me. Something I'd seen. It was like playing that matching game Maggie talked about the kindergarteners playing. The trick was to remember what you'd seen and match it with a card lying face down. Part of the challenge was recalling placement, but even more important was recognition of sameness.

I spread the folders out on the old Formica-topped table. It wasn't until the third file that a lightbulb went on in my tiny pea-brain.

CALA files on alumni employees were here in this office. I bet these were off-limits to the cops. Heck, Mrs. Glazer had warned me against peeking in them. Was there anything of value there? Only one way to find out. I dove into the files belonging to Sissy Gilchrist and Corey Johnson.

Most of the contents were unremarkable: resumes, posed head shots, grade transcripts, letters of recommendation so mundane that the signers could have been talking about Homer Simpson and Grover Cleveland. But part of the job application process was an essay every teacher had to submit on why he (or she) wanted to teach. Those, I hoped, would give me additional insight into Corey's and Sissy's lives. I waded through the desultory details in the files. One item in Corey's caught my attention — and I jotted that down.

The essay portions were handwritten and

would take time to decipher. More than likely, they'd both written stirring stuff on the order of the standard Miss America line, "I want to be a Peace Corps volunteer," but who knew? I looked at Corey's date of birth. I did the math.

Twice.

Wow.

I stared at the photo of Corey.

I formulated a theory astonishing and disturbing, but plausible.

Mrs. Glazer stuck her head in the door. "Still at it?"

I nodded and tried not to look guilty as I slid Corey and Sissy's information under my stack of research papers. "I found great photos of the girls Ella ran around with. But I couldn't find many images of her, or any good anecdotes. It'll be hard to create a nice memory album with so few resources."

"Hm," said Mrs. Glazer. Her face didn't betray anything. Then, giving me a "just a minute" hand signal, she disappeared and then reappeared with a pale pink sheet of imprinted paper in her hand. "Why not join us? I'm sure you'll want to interview people who've known Ella since she was a student here."

The sheet was an invitation to a farewell party for Mrs. Selsner, the school nurse.

"Fifty years of service!" read the headline.

I'd forgotten how long she'd been a part of the school. She would have information on the Four Alumnae: Patricia, Ella, Jennifer, and Mahreeya.

The festivities were to be held this coming Saturday night at La Casa, an old family-owned St. Louis restaurant. Mrs. Glazer indicated I could keep the invitation.

A nasty thought presented itself: Mrs. Selsner was getting the bum's rush. Her goodbye had been instigated by Sissy Gilchrist's death.

That didn't seem right.

Wasn't the nurse a victim here? She — along with my daughter and Tilly — had stumbled over the body. Was this a punishment? If so, for what?

KIKI'S TIPS FOR USING PUNCHES

Punches are one of my favorite tools because they are incredibly versatile, plus you can use them over and over again!

1. Punch through a sheet of tinfoil when your punches get dull. If they get sticky, punch through a piece of wax paper.
2. Think of your punches as shapes. Trying making new art by combining various shapes. For example, three circle punches of increasing sizes could be stacked on top of each other to create a snowman. Add a rectangle for the body of stovepipe hat. Cut a thin slice from an oval to create the brim.
3. Buy a set of punches in the same shape, but in increasing sizes, and layer them together. This is particularly effective with circle punches. Secure them through the center with a brad. Rough up and curl the edges to make a cool flower.
4. Use a punch to create a cool border of negative spaces (holes!). Start by punching a piece of waste paper. Use this as a pattern and mark lightly with a pencil where you want

your holes to go along your border. Turning your punch upside down so you can see the mechanism, align up your punch with the penciled marks to create a perfect border.

5. Take a punch to your extra family photos and create a stockpile of mug shots. Carefully position the punches so you can frame the faces. Keep these extra portraits in an envelope marked with each person's name. Use them on pages of small albums!

6. Create dimension and interest by combining punches. For example, to green holly leaves, you can add small red circles to make the holly berries. Or put a punch art bow on top of a punched out square to make a gift wrapped package!

7. Use a foam adhesive dot or square under parts of your punch art. This will raise the art off your page. It's a cool effect.

NINETEEN

Poking around in the alumni office had given me a motive for the murder. And I didn't feel good about my hunch. In fact, all I could feel was depressed.

That weight pressed on me as I walked through the polished marble hall of the administrative building, stopping to enjoy the stately architecture, the statuary, the art, and the displays. Inside its hallowed halls, the school looked more like an art museum than an educational institution. My own school days took place in a sad concrete building with low ceilings, dark halls, and tired, worn equipment such as wooden desks studded with clods of chewing gum like cloves in an orange.

This school was rich with culture, from the poems framed on the walls, to autographs of important visitors, and cases lined with valuable gifts, such as personal memorabilia of famous alums. I always lingered here, because the ambience fed my soul. How I envied my daughter the chance to go to a place teeming with such inspiration, rich with resources, and overflowing with opportunities.

I moved through the archways outside, taking in the old trees, the fountain, and the benches. I walked into another building, noting the name on the plaque "Barlett Building," which signified a gift from the Barlett family, whoever they were. I remembered a conversation Anya and I had about a third-grader who was acting out. "Gee," I'd mused. "If he doesn't quit that, he might not get invited back." (You didn't just "go" to CALA. You were invited to be a student there, and the invitations were considered and reissued on a yearly basis.)

Anya gave me one of those looks only a kid can give her clueless parent. "Duh, Mom, his name's on a building. I don't think he's worried about getting an invitation to return." And she chuckled.

Remembering how stupid I'd felt, I stepped outside and headed toward the parking lot. My old Beemer with the crumpled right fender sat in the very farthest edge.

"Howdo, Mrs. Lowenstein."

I turned to see Mr. Beacon, the security

guard, driving a golf cart emblazoned with the seal of CALA. One hand on the wheel, he waved a red clipboard from his other.

"How are you, sir, on this lovely day?"

A slight dipping gesture of his head preceded a "fine, fine."

I noticed the papers on his clipboard were covered with writing.

"You get assigned homework?" I teased.

"No, ma'am. My job is homework. I take all type of notes. Jot down who all's in the parking lot. Who I ask to move their car. Who works late. Who loads anything and what they are loading." He tapped the papers. "It's all in here."

"That's good news about Coach Johnson being released, isn't it?" I dug around in my handbag for my keys.

"Yes, ma'am. It sure is. Guess that means they know he didn't do it."

I hated to burst his bubble, but I had to correct his assumption. His job was security, and he needed to know the truth if he were to protect our children. "Sorry, Mr. Beacon, but it only means they don't have enough evidence to charge him. They don't have another suspect. At least not that I've heard."

"Hmm. That's so?" With a gnarled hand, he reached up slowly to pull off his cap. He

226

ran his hand through his salt-and-pepper hair, his face tired and sad, in testimony to all the troubles he'd seen.

I continued, "Coach Johnson doesn't have an alibi. Sissy was killed roughly between nine-thirty and ten a.m."

Mr. Beacon's brow furrowed and he blinked thoughtfully. "From when to when?"

"From nine-thirty to ten. Staff saw her before that. Time of death is always approximate, but she dropped Christopher off in kindergarten at nine-thirty."

"I thought they knew how he couldn't have done it."

I very nearly discounted his remark. I expected to hear Mr. Beacon expand on Corey's devotion to Sissy Gilchrist. Because my mind was made up as to what I was going to hear, I nearly missed what he did say. But, thank goodness, I didn't miss it. "Come again?" I asked in embarrassment.

"Coach Johnson couldn't have killed Ms. Gilchrist because he was clear at the opposite end of the campus. I know that for a fact. See, I had to ask him to move his car that morning. He'd been unloading soccer balls from the intramural league tryouts, and he was blocking the fire lane. He was fine about that, always is, whatever I ask of him. Matter of fact, he offered me a ride up here to the north lot, 'cause the golf cart was broke, and I got arthritis. Makes that uphill climb painful. I took him up on it, and we walked into the building together. I smelled coffee coming from his office, and Coach laughed and offered me a cup — now wait —"

Mr. Beacon unclipped his papers, shuffled through the stack and began a search. He gestured with the clipboard to a paper completely filled with neat handwriting. "See here? Right here?"

I skimmed the script, but he came to my rescue, using a finger to point out the pertinent line.

"Right here, I got down that he and I ate a Krispy Kreme donut — mine was plain cake with no topping — and had coffee — mine was black and I used Splenda — over in his office." Mr. Beacon's finger pointed to a neatly written scribble on the paper.

"You sure?" My heart was going from zero to sixty. This was too good to be true. The police might think so, too. "Why would you be writing about a snack you had? Isn't this a security log?"

His eyes widened. "Yes, ma'am, yes, it is indeed a security log. But you see, first I write it here and then I copy it neat-like before I hand it in. And since I've got to copy it anyways, I write everything down. Just everything."

"Donuts? Coffee?"

A solemn expression pulled down the corners of his mouth. "Yes, ma'am. 'Cause you know what they're teaching me over at Weight Watchers. You bite it; you gotta write it, and that nice lady over at the Weight Watchers office gets real fussy with me if I don't get down every little dinky bite I take, so's I just got in the habit of putting everything down loose-like here, before recopying the security part in my official work notebook. Sure takes a lot of the fun outta eating, I tell you. I think this diet works because you get tuckered out doing all this writing stuff. Most time, it just ain't worth eating it because you got to find your notepad and write it down."

I couldn't help it. I laughed out loud. I clapped the man on the shoulder and told him, "You are a genius. How come the police don't know this? Or do they?"

He straightened up and stared at me. "I expect they don't know because they don't ask. Some police don't think much of us security folks. I guess they didn't think about talking to me. I figured they knew what they were doing and all, so I didn't go mess in their business. Besides, I didn't know exactly when Ms. Gilchrist was on her way to glory."

I told Mr. Beacon to hang on, and I flipped open my cell phone and called Detweiler. "You aren't going to believe this," I started. I was right; he thought my news amazing.

After introducing the detective to Mr. Beacon via the phone and letting them work out the details of sharing Mr. Beacon's revelation, I exited the parking lot and drove through the nearby residential area.

The city of St. Louis proper was considering a referendum allowing city police to live outside the city limits. Proponents explained that keeping good police was tough enough without mandating where they rested their heads at night. Opponents explained that police needed to understand the community, that having a policeman living next door helped stabilize a neighborhood, and that the city needed all the good citizen taxpayers it could get. This situation, overlooking Mr. Beacon as a witness, happened in part because the police were not products of the prep school system. They'd probably ridden buses to school and attended public institutions. So the cops had no idea exactly what Mr. Beacon did, or how seriously he took his mission.

The police had been blissfully unaware of the information Mr. Beacon could provide. Observing the CALA community from the outside wasn't the same as having an intimate knowledge of its inner workings. And if they had questioned Mr. Beacon in his role as parking czar, I'd just bet they'd stuck to a script which didn't include asking about his diet habits.

How lucky we'd all been that Mr. Beacon was on Weight Watchers!

I took a look at my watch and panicked. No way could I pick up Anya and get ready for our homecoming crop. If Dodie had been well, I could have asked her to help me with the setup. But Bama? Hadn't she already railed at me about the hours she'd worked in my stead?

I dialed my mother-in-law's number. Come on, come on, pick up, I mumbled to myself. "Sheila? I need to ask a big favor. Can you pick up Anya? She's over at Bellerive."

Silence greeted me. Bellerive was a golf course my late husband George had loved to play. Sheila had avoided it since her son's death. But I was in a bind. I started begging. "I know it's last minute, and I know

231

you are uncomfortable with that place, but I really, really need your help. I've been working on the alumni newsletter, and I lost track of time, and I have that homecoming crop to do. Dodie had her biopsy yesterday, so she can't help me. Please? Please, could you go get Anya?"

I shut up.

Finally she said, "I suppose you need me to keep her overnight, too?"

"That would be nice."

She hung up on me. I took that as a "yes."

My phone rang.

"Don't forget we're having dinner on Friday night here with the Novaks. I suggest you dress appropriately." And for the second time in less than five minutes, my mother-in-law hung up on me.

I closed my phone and set it next to me carefully. Sheila had made it abundantly clear she thought Ben Novak was a suitable second husband for me. She was right. Ben was sweet-tempered, well-mannered, and his family owned a local alternative newspaper, *The Muddy Waters Review.* When I'd been hurt last summer, Ben had sat by me and read to me for hours. We'd gone out to dinner many times, and I blushed to remember how compatible we'd been. I mean, I hadn't let him go very far, but he'd already

232

impressed me as a generous and gentle man.

You'd think I'd be head over heels over Ben. Dodie had said, "He's the best-looking man I've ever seen. Good Jewish boy, too. I remember his bar mitzvah."

Mert seconded that. "Whoa. If I weren't so fond of gospel singing, I'd be first in line for a hunk like him."

But I never daydreamed about Ben. Never.

I wanted to. I tried to. But it just didn't happen.

Cut it out, Kiki, I told myself. This isn't the time.

I couldn't let myself get all moony. Not when I had such an important meeting ahead. Instead, I switched my thoughts to what I'd learned examining the files in the alumni office. I had a theory. And if I was right, there might be another reason Sissy Gilchrist was murdered. Excited as I was that I might have stumbled over a clue, my elation was tinged with regret. Surely this person wouldn't have hurt Sissy.

Could I possibly be right? If I was, could this information help solve the murder? The person I had in mind had motive and opportunity. Heck, everyone within spitting distance of the school and its ton of bricks had means.

What should I do next?

I did what I always do when I need help. I dialed Detweiler.

His phone rolled immediately to voice mail.

I left a garbled message which barely made sense to me. Finally, after being cut off, I squeaked out, "Call me. Hurry, please."

I ran into my house and let the dogs out to piddle. Anya was taken care of, but I hadn't planned to run so late. Part of my responsibility was to provide treats for the crops, and I didn't have time to stop at the grocery store.

I would have to sacrifice the Bread Co. bagels and cream cheese in my trunk. That would cover the gastronomical demands of the crop.

The dogs gave me sour looks and lolly-gagged until I shooed them into their crates. A wave of guilt rolled over me, but I couldn't do much more than fill a Kong with a slice of cheese for each pooch, as I sped out the kitchen door.

At the store, Bama shouted at me. "Where have you been? The crop starts in less than a half an hour!"

I mumbled something and tossed the pre-made kits onto the table. I knew from experience that at least one if not two or three women would show up early. In fact, I could put Las Vegas odds on who would sail in through our front door ahead of the listed time, and who would then monopolize my precious pre-crop minutes.

I was right.

Twenty

Vicky Ventner made me sick. She was obnoxious and arrogant. Black holes leave more substance in the universe than Vicky after they collapse. She's an energy vampire who sucks the life-blood right out of your veins — all the while flashing a smile with as many falsehoods as teeth.

This visit was no exception.

"You aren't ready!" This was a crow of pleasure. "You need to plan your time better."

Vicky, you see, is the Empress Supreme of Unrequested Advice. She doesn't converse, she dispenses. The All-Knowing, All-Seeing, All-Wise Vicky condescends to help us mere mortals muddle through our miserable lives, secure in the knowledge she could do everything better than we can.

I nodded and ran out the back door to grab the cream cheese and bagels from my car. I dashed back inside, letting the heavy back door graze my heel and take a layer of skin off the top. The blood trickled into my shoe. I did not stop.

I set out the food, plugged in the toaster, and thanked God Above that Vicky had brought two unfortunate souls with her to the homecoming crop. This meant she had a captive audience of two poor dopes to lecture. And lecture she did. They were treated to her thoughts on albums: "Strapbound is the only way to go!" And paper: "You must buy kits or you are simply wasting your money." And tools: "Insist that one of the clerks open the package and test items for you first."

I breathed a sigh of relief. Then Bama screwed up my evening. She decided to demonstrate inking the edges of a project. When my co-worker pointedly ignored Vicky's chatty attempts to take over, Vicky wandered over to pick on me.

"I heard Anya saw Sissy's body. Have you signed her up with a good psychologist? She's going to need one or she'll be scarred for life. Here's a name," and Vicky jotted down a reference in the middle of the back of a piece of paper I'd been using for journaling boxes.

Rats. That ruined a perfectly good sheet of 8 1/2 by 11 cardstock.

"She'll probably need multiple sessions. You really can't neglect having her speak to someone. That would be criminal."

I nodded. Here we go, I thought. Vicky, the busybody, is on duty to save my life. I wondered how to maneuver the conversation so I could find out what Vicky had told the police. But I needn't have worried.

She pulled up a seat to watch me distribute the page kits. "Of course, the police have been very interested in what I have to say about the investigation. You might say I'm an invaluable resource. I belong to the Sherlockian society, you know. I've studied all the Sherlock Holmes books in depth, and I consider myself a keen observer of human nature. My father used to say, 'Vicky, no one can put anything past you.' And he was so right, dear Papa was."

Despite my aversion to rolling eyes, I fought the urge to do just that. It was hard, really hard. Instead, I crossed them and said, "So who did it, Vicky?"

She smirked prettily. "Of course you'd like to know."

"Who killed Sissy, Vicky?"

"I'm confident Jennifer Moore did it. And who could blame her? You know, that cougar Sissy made a play for Stevie. You do know what a cougar is, don't you? A vulgar older

238

woman who has the hots for a much younger man. That detective you hang around with, he's younger than you, right?"

I stifled a groan. I wanted nothing more than to run to the back and bang my head against one of our concrete walls. Instead, I smiled politely. "So you're sure Jennifer Moore is the killer?"

"Either that or Sissy Gilchrist's ex-husband did it. He's a cop, you know. It's a fact they are prone to violence. Which you should think of, Kiki. Really you should."

I made a mental note to ask Detweiler if they'd thoroughly checked out the ex. I also hid my smirk. Detweiler is not younger than I am. Bingo! Vicky was WRONG. But I couldn't tell her. Not now.

I could, however, gloat silently. Which I did.

The places around the table filled up quickly. I showed each of our guests how turning a punch upside down allowed you to perfectly position it on a piece of paper. Merrily they punched out a variety of shapes and sizes of flowers. The chatter filled the room as the women discussed the different homecoming events scheduled around the area.

I squirmed with tension. The person I wanted to confront worked quietly. I checked my cell phone. Still no return call from Detweiler. I reviewed my arguments against confronting her. The sight of her easy demeanor and her slight smile gave me pause. What if I was wrong?

Throughout the two hours, I helped clients ink the flower petals, stack the flowers, secure them with a brad and curl the petals. Customers got up and helped themselves to the food. The page I'd designed was incredibly simple. Strips of coordinated paper in different patterns were stacked on top of each other to form a wide band through the center of the page. A large matted photo went in the center. An arrow moved from the page title at the top of the page to the journaling block at the bottom. A cascade of flowers followed the arc of the arrow.

After a couple of hours, most of the women were finished. They ooohed and aaahed over their work, which was usually the best part of the crop for me. One by one they left the worktable, wandered around the store, purchased supplies, and let Bama ring them up.

"Could you stay after?" I asked my suspect. "I need help with a project for the CALA alumni newsletter."

Meanwhile Vicky Ventner proceeded to tell

everyone how to improve their lives. She corrected several customers as they worked hard to put together their pages. She explained how her son Frankie had been asked twice to consider early admission to Harvard. "They value his mental acumen. But then so does Stanford. Both have offered him scholarships, which we don't need, of course. Really, as one admittance officer told me, Frankie is an example of a superlative child, and my husband and I are to be commended. You know he had a perfect score on the SAT. Plus, he's a straight-A student. And on the school council. That's not to minimize his musical talents. Or his acting ability."

We'd all heard this ten thousand times before. Vicky had this narrow bandwidth of topics she could chat on, and she and her son's perfection were on her Top Ten List.

I'll give her this, she was a constant source of new customers to our store because no one she brought with her could stomach her for more than one visit. For the life of me, I don't know why she doesn't tape record her "my Frankie is perfect" speech and put it on an endless loop to save her voice. I was so happy to see Vicky leave I briefly considered running back to the refrigerator and breaking out the bottle of champagne Dodie keeps for special occasions. In fact, if I'd had the time, I would have, because I was that happy to see the woman go.

By nine-fifteen Bama had rung everyone up. By nine-thirty the place was empty, except for the person whose secret I had uncovered, and me.

"Ella, you have three children. Frederick, Natalie, and Corey, right? Corey Johnson is your son, isn't he?"

The newspaper photo I'd found of Ella was taken on July 4th, 1982. She and her fellow protesters were reacting to a racially motivated fight at the V.P. Fair that left two people dead. As I examined the protest picture more carefully, I noticed Ella's blouse covered an obvious bump. The records in the alumni office showed that Ella graduated from college a full year after most of her CALA classmates.

But the real giveaway had been a peculiar family trait, the very pointed chin that both Frederick Walden and Corey Johnson shared. When I held a picture of Coach Johnson right next to one of Frederick, the resemblance was unmistakable.

I'd delivered my bombshell without any preamble or subtlety. I clamped my mouth

242

shut and prayed I hadn't blown the investigation.

Detweiler still hadn't called me back. I knew I should have waited and talked with him, but I was too keyed up. After three hours of having Vicky Ventner correct me, marginalize me, and embellish my instructions, I wanted desperately to be right about something! Anything! Yes, Vicky had irritated me mightily, and now I blurted out my suspicions. I dropped a bomb on the woman I'd considered a friend.

Ella tipped her head back to stare at the layouts we'd run along the top of the wall, between display racks and the ceiling. Her arms were crossed tightly across her chest, and her fingers gripped the back of her biceps hard.

"Jim Hagg warned me people like you would come out of the woodwork like cockroaches!" said Ella. "But I didn't expect it of you, Kiki. You totally pulled the wool over my eyes. So let's put an end to the charade."

Then she reached into her handbag and rummaged around.

Oh, boy, I'd done it now.

What if she had a gun? The panicky thought blazed through my mind. My gut did an elevator slide toward my feet. Would she really shoot me here? I backed away.

She dug around in her purse a little more. "I know exactly how to fix this."

Would Bama open up tomorrow and find my bleeding body? Was Ella willing to ignore the fact the neighbors might hear the gun go off? Was she planning to shoot her way out of this? Go down in a blaze of gunfire?

My feet were rooted to the spot. I willed myself to run, but I couldn't. I was frozen. My whole innards went liquid. Except for my mouth. That was so dry I couldn't shout.

I was about to die.

With a stupid flower punch in my hand, no less.

Crud.

TWENTY-ONE

Ella's shaking hand pulled out a slim striped rectangle that matched her Kate Spade purse.

I must be coming up in the world, I thought, because I'm about to be murdered by a woman with a designer handbag.

Ella flipped open the checkbook. Her Montblanc pen paused over a blank check.

"How much?"

She should have shot me. It would have hurt less. I'd spent most of my adult life leaving behind the poverty I'd grown up in. No matter where my daughter went to school, or who I'd married, or where I'd lived, I would always be a poor kid from the wrong side of town. A vortex opened in the space time continuum, and I was propelled back to a grubby house on a scabby patch of grass bordered by a cracked and buckled sidewalk. I saw my dad and smelled the whiskey on his breath. Heard his rant,

"People are no dang good." Wondered if he'd spent his whole paycheck at the Dew Drop Inn bar, or just part of it. I watched my mom let down the hem on my best dress, leaving a faded white line that blazed a trail to our poverty. I felt the pinch of wearing shoes I'd outgrown. I recalled the worry my classmates would figure out why I brought peanut butter sandwiches from home and drank water from the fountain instead of buying a carton of milk every day as my classmates did.

The pain must have shown on my face. Ella had ripped away my protective bandages and exposed my secret self. Growing up poor never leaves you. Never.

"I don't want anything from you." I spat out the words.

Ella gulped. Slowly, she closed the checkbook and put it away. With a trembling hand, said, "Sorry. Old habits die hard." Turning away from me, her body sagged. "I've had a bad week." She pivoted to face me, her eyes wet and red-rimmed. "Sorry."

My heart eased its way out of my throat. "So . . . did you kill her?"

A hurt expression crossed her face. A slow shake of her head, "No," followed. "How could you think that?" Her eyes filled with tears. One coursed down her elegant cheekbones. Her lower lip quivered.

"Sorry." My turn to apologize. During the crop I'd been distracted. I'd practiced all sorts of elegant ways to pop the question of Corey's parentage. I'd skirted around the question of whether Ella might have killed Sissy. But then she hurt me, and I struck back. I was ashamed of myself.

"Guess we're even," she said.

"I guess so."

Neither of us spoke for a few minutes. The lump in my throat positively ached. I'd lost a friend. In my eagerness to solve a crime, to feel important and powerful, I'd put two and two together and come up with three. Still, what else could I have done? I knew that by talking to her here, catching her off-guard, I would get an honest response. No, I reprimanded myself, you got a costly response. A response that cost you a friend.

Next time, I'd leave the questioning to the police.

Ella stepped closer to me. A long fingered hand plucked at my sleeve. "I can see why you'd think I did it. You thought I was protecting my son. You probably heard about Jim Hagg and figured out I hired him. If I were you, I'd have thought I was guilty too. But I'm not. I understand why you asked what you did."

"Why didn't you tell me Corey was your son? That night we did the family trees. You left a tag blank for him."

"Actually, I planned to tell you about Corey. I just couldn't find the right time. He'd only agreed to meet with me a few months ago, and for a while, a delicious while, he was my secret, and I didn't want to share. Do you remember when you first learned you were pregnant?"

I did.

"It was a lot like that. That sense of feeling such a private joy. He was lost to me for years. My dad and mom promised to place him with a good family and watch over him. Then Dad had the strokes and Mom's health failed. I buried Dad first and Mom soon after, and I discovered my baby had been adopted but that the records were sealed. I thought I was being punished for giving him up. But I tried to do what was best for him! You have to believe me! Back then, experts said that black children needed black families to form their sense of identity. So I sort of gave up on the idea of raising him. And I gave up on the hope of ever finding him. Walter urged me to hire an investigator. My husband saw how it preyed on me, wondering what happened to my first-born. But I care about Corey, and I wanted to go slow. It took him years to forgive me. And more years to understand that I . . ." and she choked, "I gave him up, but I never gave up loving him."

She went on to explain that it took time to wade through the Department of Social Services documents to find out where Corey was placed. After her first private investigator died of a heart attack, Ella had to start over. Once Corey was located, he refused to talk to his birth mother. He wanted nothing to do with her. He refused to meet with her.

Then there was the issue of Corey's father, who had been killed in a drive-by shooting shortly after his son was born. Like many adopted kids, Corey was angry. He never wanted to meet the white woman who'd given birth to him and, in his mind, forgotten him. Meanwhile, Ella had worked behind the scenes to get Corey the college scholarship. She claimed she'd done nothing to help him win a job at CALA as basketball coach. "He did that all on his own," she said proudly. In fact, Ella had backed off of all attempts at communication after Corey was hired. The investigator she hired would contact Corey twice a year repeating an offer for him to meet his birth mother. Only recently had Corey decided to forgive and meet the woman who'd given him up for adoption.

I marveled at Ella's story. Some women would have only felt guilt, some would have worried about lost reputations. But all along, Ella had tried to improve her son's life — even while he was rejecting her. She had managed the hardest of all parenting tricks, waiting patiently. And when Corey decided to give her a chance, she took it. Her eyes brightened as she told me the story. Clearly she gloried in finding the child once lost to her. She'd accepted that he would have to move ahead at his own pace rather than hers.

"Ella, I am happy for you. This will go away and —"

"And Corey will leave town."

"No!"

"Yes. I wouldn't want him to stay here and put up with all the whispering. But he didn't kill Sissy. I didn't either. After he was lost to me for all those years, do you think I'd care who he married? Once he accepted her — with her checkered past — he softened toward me. I didn't have the right to say anything to him about his choices. Sure, I would have liked someone better for him, but what right would I have to tell him what to do? After all the mistakes I'd made? After getting a second chance? I would have turned myself in, I would have confessed to a crime I didn't commit, to absolve myself, but where would that leave Natalie and Frederick?" A long sigh floated from her. "And my husband? I couldn't do that to Walter. He's known about my lost boy from the beginning and supported me in my search. I couldn't do that to him."

I could see what she meant. I could also tell she'd given this a lot of thought.

Then she surprised me.

"Besides, I was desperately happy to be a grandmother."

"You mean to say —"

"Sissy was pregnant."

TWENTY-TWO

I drove home in silence, mulling over what I'd learned. Of course, it was entirely possible that Ella was lying to me. But I doubted it. Her explanation made too much sense. At the end of our conversation, she promised to talk with Jim Hagg about letting Detweiler speak to Corey. I explained that the detective was on her son's side. I couldn't be sure Detweiler would talk to Corey — or even if that was a good idea, given the politics of the police department. But now that the coach was out of jail, maybe it wasn't a problem. Besides, according to Ella, Corey needed all the support he could get. The chances of him going back to work at CALA were slim and none. The poor man would have to rebuild his life while a felony hung over his head.

"These past few days have really done a number on him. He's lost weight. Hasn't slept. It didn't seem to matter that they arrested him. He's devastated by Sissy's death. He's tried to communicate to the Gilchrists through Jim Hagg, but their attorney won't hear of it. He's worried about Christopher. Evidently Christopher's father Danny Gartner filled his head full of nonsense about how blacks kill white people. What a jerk. Corey thinks Danny poisoned Christopher's mind just to make life more difficult for Sissy. He knew Christopher would meet all sorts of people at CALA," and here Ella shook her head. "I can't fathom that kind of hate."

"Be glad you can't," I added.

This explained the boy's reaction in kindergarten. I briefly considered telling Ella about the scene Christopher had caused, but I figured it would only upset her.

"The empty tag on my tree was for Corey. I've found him. I don't want to lose him." Ella's eyes shone with moisture. "But at least we'll be able to stay in touch when he moves."

I longed to ask how the kids were accepting their new brother, but Ella clearly teetered on the edge of exhaustion. We hugged goodbye and drove off in separate directions.

After I got home and let the dogs out, I

dialed Detweiler's cell phone, and still no one answered. The voice mail didn't even pick up. This was unusual. He checked his personal cell frequently.

Maybe, I thought, he's out having fun with his wife.

I noticed Ben had called me. He left a message which sounded somewhere between urgent and ticked.

I didn't phone him back. I couldn't handle any more drama. Instead, I crawled into bed in my underwear and fell asleep.

While the dogs watered and fertilized my fenced-in backyard on Thursday morning, I depressed the plunger on my French press and turned my radio to a local talk show, sniffing the air appreciatively as the robust fragrance of coffee filled my small kitchen. In my last house, I'd decorated this space with white second-hand curtains, but they didn't fit the windows here. I'd also framed art from fruit crates, but that proved too small for the walls, and the images floated aimlessly about in the space. I'd found a pair of curtains I'd liked, put them up, and came home to find Sheila tearing them down. "These look cheap," she said. "I'll have a decorator come in and measure."

Unfortunately, since she'd loaned me the

rental deposit, she now acted like my house was an annex to hers. I bristled at the invasion, but I also had to hold my temper. She had, after all, given me the money to make this place affordable. Her taste was more upscale than mine. I really didn't have a good reason to complain about her bringing in a decorator.

Or did I?

I'd dodged the interior designer's phone calls. (She'd quickly corrected me when I called her a "decorator," and let me know none too subtly that the term was offensive.) Maybe if I held off long enough, I could gussy up this place myself. I was due a little money from the settlement of my husband's old company, Dimont Development. Nearly six thousand dollars was coming my way. Maybe, with some of it, I could repay Sheila and decorate my home on my own terms.

I had hoped to claim a reward for clearing up a mystery last spring involving a dead scrapbooker. But, that didn't happen. I lived on the Missouri side of the Mississippi, and the reward was offered by a company on the Illinois side. Since the Illinois police carted the killer away, they were the ones in charge of closing the case. Local politics being what they were, money tended to stay on one side of the Mississippi River or the other. I hailed from "the other."

As if she knew I was sitting in my kitchen thinking of ways to outwit her, Sheila called. "Ben has been trying to get in touch with you. You're being very rude, Kiki, and I wouldn't blame him if he lost interest."

I groaned. "I've been working really hard. You know, that CALA alumni paper takes up my time, and Dodie —"

But Sheila wasn't having any of it. "Get your act together," she said and hung up on me.

There was no help for it, but to make the most of every waking minute. If I hurried while getting dressed, I could put in a solid two hours on my confidential project. As I pulled on a yellow cotton sweater over a paler yellow cotton tee, I listened to the local news.

"Repeating our top story, police are investigating a suspected suicide attempt by Corey Johnson, a basketball coach at CALA, the private school rocked last week by the murder of one of their teachers, Sissy Gilchrist. The Major Case Squad confirms that Johnson was a person of interest in the investigation. However, Commander Steve Fenders said, 'The investigation into the Gilchrist murder is ongoing.' Unnamed sources mentioned an uncooperative attitude by school administration as hampering progress in the murder investigation. Officials at Barnheart Hospital say Johnson is in serious, but stable condition."

Stable condition.

That was promising, wasn't it? I mean, it was a step up from critical. I didn't know much hospital lingo, but it sounded to me like Corey was out of danger. I dialed Detweiler and Ella alternately and listened to busy signals. My helplessness consumed me. What could I do? How could I help? I paced my kitchen, and the dogs marched back and forth with me, Mr. Gibbes jumping up and down, convinced this was all a fine game.

Finally, I did the only thing I knew to do: I lit a candle and I prayed. "Dear God, please hold Detweiler and Ella in the palm of your hand. Give them strength and courage and succor. Please be with Corey Johnson. Let him see how much he is loved. Please God, please help all of them."

I set it in the enamel sink where it wouldn't burn down the house. As I pulled out of my driveway, I noticed the reflection of the flame dancing in my kitchen window.

At least I'd done something.

I'd been working on the confidential album

for about an hour, and sipping coffee, when I made a run to the bathroom. I was zipping my jeans back up when I heard a pounding on the back door. I dithered. I couldn't let anyone see the album. I ran to my work area and shoved my stuff back into the briefcase. By the time I made it back to the rear of the store, the pounding became frantic. The dogs barked with a vengeance like Lassie always did when Timmy was in trouble. I threw open the back door and caught Detweiler mid-thump. His eyes were red-rimmed and blurry, and he hadn't shaved. His normally crisp shirt sported wrinkles and damp spots under the pits. A distinct odor of alcohol formed an aura around him.

"I've been trying to call you," I said. "What's happening with Corey?"

The detective looked — and smelled — like a guy who'd been on a bender. He crumpled. I grabbed a chair and shoved it behind his knees.

"Corey. He's gone."

"Gone? Gone where?"

"Dead." Detweiler sank into the chair, lowering his head onto his hands. I pulled over a folding chair and joined him. For what seemed like forever, we sat there side by side, shoulder to shoulder, saying nothing.

My arms ached to hold him, to reach for him. I knew it was a bad idea. But for all he'd done, he was still my friend, and even if he hadn't been, I'd have comforted a stranger in pain. And oh, the pain. It came off him like the heat around an incinerator. Finally, gingerly, I slid my arms around him in a loose hug. For a moment he stiffened, then relaxed. He buried his face in the crook of my neck, resting himself against me in a semi-embrace. I held him tight. I patted him and murmured soothing noises. We rocked together, back and forth in that comforting rhythm every mother knows. I'd never felt closer to any human being.

This was dangerous. For both of us. And we knew it.

Finally, he pulled away and reached into the pocket of his khakis to retrieve a white cotton square so he could blow his nose.

In spits and spurts, he told me a revolver bullet had entered Corey's left temple on an odd angle, and tunneled around his skull, traveling under the skin and exiting at the back of the head. He named a surgeon — a name I recognized as one of the best in the city — who operated on Corey. The procedure went as well as could be expected, but since brain swelling would follow, Corey was put into a chemically induced light coma. The plan was to bring him up and out slowly this morning after monitoring his vital functions.

Detweiler was surprised when he saw Ella Walden take a seat next to his friend's bed, but a nurse explained she was his next-of-kin. That was how the detective learned about his friend's ties to Old St. Louis, and the identity of Corey's birth mother.

Ella sat beside her son all night. Detweiler slept on the sofa in the family lounge. He had his phone turned to vibrate, but as he tried to get comfortable on the couch, it fell out of his pocket. At six, he'd risen to the beeping of the alarm on his watch, grabbed his phone, and wandered back into the Intensive Care bullpen area, hoping to at least wave to his friend before going to work. Everything went as planned. Corey was floating back to consciousness. "Mrs. Walden stroked his face. She talked to him, told him she was there. His eyes didn't focus, but he sort of looked at her, sideways, through all those bandages. I stood outside. They got those cubicles. And there's stuff like shower curtains? Around them? I wasn't family, but my badge got me close. I didn't want to push it. So I stood there, and I heard . . ."

His voice cracked. His Adam's apple bobbled furiously as he swallowed over and over. He stopped, got control of himself, and spoke in a rasp. "I heard him say, 'Mom.' Clear as could be. Just that. Just one word. Then she said, 'Love you.' And the alarms started ringing. All heck broke loose. Nurses came running. The doc on duty came barreling around the corner. I moved over, but I tried to see, and they threw Mrs. Walden out, I mean threw her. I grabbed her because she nearly toppled over. All these bells and alarms kept going. They called, 'Code Blue,' and more and more nurses and equipment showed up. A big man in scrubs came round the corner with a cart. I pulled Mrs. Walden back — and she fought me — because she wanted to see what was happening. A voice yelled for a drug, stat. Then for another drug. Someone said defibrillator. They called for paddles. I heard a man yell, 'Stand back . . .' "

His breath caught in his chest with a rattle. He covered his face with his hands. I could smell sweat, overnight sweat, the kind of tired body odor that comes when a meticulously clean person doesn't shower for a day. I stared down at the back of his neck with all those fresh hairs, filling in after a haircut, vulnerable and new. He leaned against me and took my hand in his. After a bit, he raised his head and began again.

"It didn't stop. Over and over, they shocked him. Mrs. Walden just . . . just let go. She was howling. She yelled, 'No, no! Not my son!' and then, then there was nothing. No sound but the beeping and the alarms. A voice said, 'Call it.' Another said, 'That's all we can do. Must have been a blood clot. They break loose like that.' But they didn't leave. They were cleaning him up. Making his body presentable —" caught on those words, Detweiler jumped up, knocking over the lightweight folding chair. He ran for the bathroom.

I listened to gagging noises and the sound of the toilet flushed repeatedly. Water ran, and splashing followed. I rummaged around in the refrigerator, retrieved a bottle of Coke, opened it, and handed it to him when he stepped out.

He downed it in two long swallows. "I don't get it. It doesn't make sense. We corroborated his alibi with Mr. Beacon." Detweiler rubbed his eyes miserably. "Corey'd told Hagg that he wanted to talk. He was coming in today. Yeah, Hagg — that pit viper — told him not to, but he was going to anyway. Then I hear he's shot himself and left a typed message saying he can't live with the guilt! What guilt? For what?"

"So it's over," I said. "Case closed." Now Anya was safe. Now I wouldn't have an excuse for seeing Detweiler. Now life would go back to normal, or at least the "new" normal.

"I can't accept that he lied. What did Mrs. Ventner say?"

"Back up a minute. You never told me Sissy was pregnant."

He had the good sense to look embarrassed. "Doesn't make any difference."

I sighed. "Vicky Ventner suggested that Jennifer Moore killed Sissy because Sissy came on to her son. We both know that's nonsense. Vicky also thought Danny Gartner was worth investigating for his temper. But, none of this makes any difference now. Corey is dead. Sissy is dead. Corey as much as admitted he was involved in her murder."

The back door flew open. Bama froze, half in and half out, and stared as we jumped apart. "Am I interrupting something?"

Detweiler and I both reddened. "No," I said. "The detective came by to update me on the, um, murder that Anya stumbled onto. We were finishing up."

Bama nodded. Her eyes moved from the

detective to me and back again. The "gotcha" look I'd feared wasn't there, though. I braced myself. Something was up. She stepped inside, and paused as she stood with her back against the door. "I heard. It's all over the radio. The guy committed suicide, right? Well, sorry about that, but it's a good thing that's over, because we have a new problem. I tried to get through to you earlier, Kiki. Dodie has cancer of the larynx. It showed up in some of the tests after her biopsy."

TWENTY-THREE

"That's a shame about Dodie," said Sheila. "I suppose you need me to pick up my granddaughter, right?"

"Yes, please."

"I'll keep her overnight, too. Have you called Ben yet?"

I squirmed. "I was planning to call him next."

"See that you do. I hope you've chosen a nice outfit to wear tomorrow night. That blue suit I bought you would be appropriate."

I sighed. Ugh. I hated that blue suit. Yes, it was expensive and fit me well, but as Mert said when she saw the outfit, "That's SO not you." Every time I wore it, I broke out in hives. I'd have to pop a Benadryl before I took off for Sheila's place. That would cause me to nod like a daffodil over my meal. Oh, joy. I'd be a real stimulating conversationalist, and Sheila would have a new complaint.

"I'm sure you've forgotten that CALA has early dismissal tomorrow. The afternoon is when families gather for the bonfire and pep rally."

"Right," I said as if I had any idea what she was talking about. Bonfire? Pep rally?

"You need to go to the pep rally. It's a tradition."

"I have to work. I already owe the store a ton of hours."

"Part of being a member of the school community means attending special functions. I pay for the tuition. The least you could do is show up once in awhile." And she hung up.

I spent a very, very long day at Time in a Bottle.

Friday morning I drove through McDonald's and treated myself to a sausage-egg burrito. Plus an orange juice. At this rate, I'd eat away — literally and figuratively — at the money coming to me from Dimont Development. Still, as the cheese and spices melted in my mouth, I reflected that this was the only way I could fortify myself for what lay ahead: a massively crummy day. The "confidential" project was coming along, but slowly. Horace and I had talked the night before. Dodie would begin her treatments this upcoming Monday. "My zaftig sweetheart is in good shape with her weight. They tell me she will suffer from terrible burning in her throat and sores in her mouth. They do believe they can kill her cancer, but they warn me she may not feel like eating."

I shivered. The whole routine of tattooing her so they could precisely aim the radiation and having her sit for hours while toxic chemicals dripped into her veins struck me as horrid. But if it would save her life, we would all stand up and cheer for modern medicine. Although I suspected that someday these methods of curing cancer would seem as antiquated and barbaric as bloodletting.

"I have dropped off more photos for your project. They are in the bottom drawer of Dodie's desk," said my boss's husband. "Kiki, you are keeping your silence, yes?"

I assured him I was.

"This is good, very good."

I got the dogs settled and dipped into my new batch of confidential photos. These were of jewelry. Whoever my client was, she obviously had a lot to lose. The photos of her travel had evoked jealousy in me, more so than any pictures of her home and wardrobe. Someday, I promised myself, I would see the world.

I put in a good two hours on the secret album, before starting on what would be the centerpiece of our Saturday night crop. Bama came in shortly before lunch. I was shading punch art of pinecones and cutting paper to resemble pine needles when Patricia Bigler walked in carrying a thin grocery bag from which a corner of her album protruded. I managed to introduce her to Bama without falling prey to a mnemonic mistake of saying "Patricia Bigger." I cleared the punches away and settled into helping her select a few nice journaling stamps and suitable ink.

After she'd stamped a few lined embellishments, I encouraged her to write her thoughts about the sports booster event. "Here's a photo of Ella giving Coach Bosch the commemorative stone," she said. "What else can I write? I wasn't able to attend. They needed me in the kindergarten."

Most folks have problems with journaling. I excused myself and retrieved a journaling handout I'd put together.

Patricia accepted it sweetly. "This is great. Hmm. I think I'll make a list of everyone who was there."

My heart slammed about in my chest. That was the information Detweiler had needed desperately. Then I remembered: Corey Johnson is dead.

And I sank down into my chair like a quickly deflated balloon. "Using the list of attendees is a great idea. It will help round out your pages. You may want to copy the names in pencil first to be sure you have the right amount of room. I always do that. Otherwise you can have a word squished or have to re-do the whole project."

Patricia grabbed a pencil and printed her journaling in perfect block lettering. I ran to the back to get us both a cold cola. "I do this three days a week with kindergarteners. I help out at CALA," she said, popping the top and slurping quietly. "I love children, I really do."

I nodded and reflected on her miscarriages. Life wasn't fair. Here was a woman who had the means and the desire for a house full of babies, but only able to have one child. I noticed Patricia was staring at me expectantly.

"I like kids a lot, too. I wish . . ." and I stopped.

"Elizabeth loves golf. Does Anya?"

"She does."

From what I'd heard, Elizabeth couldn't connect with a golf ball if they replaced it with a baseball on her tee.

"Is Anya going to the field hockey game tomorrow?"

"No, she's spending the night at Jennifer Moore's house. The girls usually wake up late. I'm glad. It gives me time to myself."

"You and Maggie are good friends, aren't you? She talks about you a lot. I did a good job, didn't I?" Patricia held up the copied names. She was trying to recover a bit of pride. I'd seen this before: people both wanted guidance and resented it. I understood.

"You're already well on your way. See how that journaling box adds to the page? How about another cola?" I still wanted to get a copy of that list. Maybe, maybe if I filled her bladder with cola, she'd be forced to leave her project and I could photocopy it.

Leave it alone, Kiki, I castigated myself. It's over. Sissy is dead, and so is her killer.

I sighed. Now I'd have no reason to stay in communication with Detweiler.

Ben Novak is a gorgeous, eligible man, and he's interested in you, said a voice in my head.

Maybe the problem was I wanted what I couldn't have. I sighed again. Patricia tapped my elbow. "That Coke? Could you get one for me?"

I retrieved another drink from the back. I

270

put a little check mark on the tally Bama had "thoughtfully" suggested to our boss. Thus, we could each be called upon to "repay" the cola bank. I sighed as I shut the refrigerator door. I was tired of being broke. I wanted my old life back. The one where I didn't have to think twice about the money I spent.

A pox on you, George, I groused and shook my fist at the sky. On second thought, I bent over and repeated my curse to the Underworld. That's where he belonged after all he'd done to Anya and me!

I served the cold beverage and settled into finishing the paper table ornament we'd be doing for our Saturday night crop.

Saturday night! Crud. That was the night of the party for Nurse Selsner.

Bama, I'd noticed, was in a particularly good mood when she came in. "Good news. Horace talked to the specialist. Dodie's prognosis is great. Sure, we'll both have to work a lot of extra hours, but I can use the money with the holidays coming up, can't you?" She stepped away humming and ticked off boxes as part of a new order for our paper. "Mert can help with some of the hours we'll need. But we could really use part-time help. Sis and I wanted to see a movie next Friday, but I'm scheduled to work."

Bama had occasionally mentioned her sister, Katie, a single mom with kids. I had the impression they all lived in one house, but Bama had never been forthcoming.

I had an idea. I left the table and Patricia, who was laboring over her printing.

"Bama? I know I owe you a bunch of hours, but how about if I give them to you in a lump sum? If I could have this afternoon, tomorrow, and Sunday off, I'd work the next two weekends for you. How would that be?"

Bama stared at me. I willed my face to be still. If she knew how badly I wanted tomorrow night off, she'd probably shut me down. On the other hand, a full weekend off, much less two, would be a rarity. I held my breath. Would she go for it?

"Okay."

Patricia squinted up at me, with the Sakura pen clutched in her hand. "Are you going to the bonfire later today? It's tradition for parents to come. Your daughter will be so disappointed if you don't." She was carefully recopying the list of names she'd penciled in.

"Another Coke?" I offered Patricia a beverage.

"The whole school can go back to normal now that Sissy's murder has been solved." She started recopying her printing.

"I don't know. I can't help but wonder if Coach Johnson really shot himself."

Her head jerked up. "He couldn't live with the guilt."

"But he'd been cleared. Mr. Beacon was drinking coffee with him at the time the murder must have occurred."

Patricia cocked her head. "That so? Where's your restroom?"

I pointed Patricia in the right direction.

Her list sat there, staring at me. Not that it really mattered now. Still, it couldn't hurt to copy it. I took it over to the scanner and made a quick duplicate. I put the paper back carefully exactly where I'd found it. Then I noticed, I'd replaced it upside down.

I reached to rotate the sheet counterclockwise 180 degrees when the door minder rang. Detweiler came striding in, his long legs leading the way. He pulled me outside so we could speak privately. His face wore a jumble of emotions. "Corey didn't kill himself. The coroner found a partial fingerprint on a bullet in the magazine, and the angle of the entry wound was all wrong. Corey was murdered!"

TWENTY-FOUR

The bonfire was terrific as far as bonfires go. The flames licked at a September sky, vivid tongues of orange and yellow lapping up the blue. A chill settled over Ladue. I couldn't get warm, and when I neared the blaze, I was equally uncomfortable and too hot. Anya and her friends ran, squealed, and jumped like nimble goats, playing a form of tag and generally showing off for the boys who stood in clutches with their bored, slumping posture. An ash drifted my way and I flicked it off my sleeve. A gaggle of cheerleaders in school colors — royal blue and gold — chanted their way to the center of the quad, where they stopped and screamed for the incoming team as they ran through the middle of the crowd.

Around me, voices roared approval. Men wearing bright blue sweaters, and no doubt carrying their AARP cards, yelled and clapped. Women old enough to need walkers raised withered fists and squawked, causing their bright corsages of mums festooned with ribbons to quiver on drooping bosoms.

Verily and truly, I was in a black funk because normally I would have taken a zillion photos. The combination of old and young, raising their voices and praising the team, reminded me of the send-off Romans gave their troops going into battle.

Detweiler's announcement worried me. The news wasn't public yet, and I feared that whoever killed Sissy and shot Corey was wandering among the gathered throng and enjoying being an invisible part of the festivities.

Meanwhile, I could only stand on the sidelines and fear for my daughter's life.

Next up was dinner at Sheila's. I knew I should be looking forward to formally meeting Ben Novak's parents — we'd bumped into each other a couple of times as services let out in temple — but I simply couldn't muster up the energy. This was a look-see. They'd evaluate me, give me a thumbs-up or a thumbs-down, and on the basis of their appraisal Ben would continue to see me or dump me.

Not that he'd said as much. He had assured me that I would love his parents and that they were already pre-disposed to like me.

I'd heard that before and wound up having a mother-in-law who was my sworn enemy.

I swallowed the Benadryl and changed quickly at my house, all the while shouting to Anya to "hurry up." Her presence was requested — no, demanded, by my mother-in-law — so that my darling offspring could be shown off, I presume as proof I could make pretty babies.

"Why are you so grouchy?" My lithesome child asked as she ran a brush through her hair.

"Do you have everything you need for the sock hop and to spend the night at the Moores'?" I had shifted from scurrying about on my behalf to running around like a squirrel chased by a cat on hers. I grabbed her usual overnight bag, a Tumi on wheels which Sheila had insisted Anya needed, and which Anya and I both loathed, and piled clothes, iPod, pre-braces retainer, and toiletries inside. "When were you planning to do your homework? Remember, there's the homecoming game Saturday night, and I expect you'll be really tired and sleep late Sunday —"

"Mo-om. Quit nagging me!" sniped my darling. She turned and fixed me with a beaming smile. "But could you get my social studies book from my backpack, please? And the notebook? I wasn't really paying attention in class, and Nicci always takes good notes."

I laughed. Welcome to Hormone Heaven. One minute it was "go away" and the next it was "come snuggle." I remembered she dropped her backpack on the floor of the kitchen, despite every effort I made to get her to hang it on the hook. We'd gone back and forth about it, and finally I threw up my hands in surrender.

With a grunt, I lifted it onto the kitchen table, pulled out everything, and rummaged through.

That's when I found a bright pink sheet of paper with a stick-figure person. The eyes were Xed out, clearly proclaiming the character was dead. Curly hair covered the figure's head. Underneath was a handwritten scrawl: "Tell your mom to back off, or she'll be next."

I was positive Anya hadn't seen the paper. If she had, she would have told me. Ever since what happened to George, Anya knows better than to keep secrets. But I needed to know. I gulped air. Took a long drink of water. Returned to her bedroom.

"Anya, did you happen to see a bright pink note in your backpack? It had a cartoon drawing and a note about me?"

"Nope."

"Did you have your backpack with you all day?"

"Mom! You saw me at the bonfire. We all left our backpacks in a pile by the auditorium door. A couple of parents offered to watch them for us."

"Which parents?"

"I dunno. There were a bunch of them standing around. I didn't take roll." She gave me an elaborate shrug. "Parents are parents. Why? Did someone steal something from my backpack? That never happens at CALA. Never."

It never happens because no one at CALA goes without. So they don't need to steal.

I willed myself to stay calm. "Okay, just wondering. You ready to go?"

With wobbling knees I led the way to my car.

I'd met Leah and Alvin Novak at temple several times, but only long enough to say, "How do," as my nana would put it. Leah's eyes, bright as a wren's and sharply focused, swept me up and down. The creases at the corners smiled even as her mouth curved generously. Leah was nobody's fool. We studied each other quietly, each wondering if we'd get along long-term. Alvin, clearly, took a backseat to his wife, but that didn't mean he was a weak man. I knew that in some marriages, the husband deferred to his wife's judgment of, uh, horseflesh. Especially mares.

I thought about opening my mouth and pulling my lips back so they could get a better look. I was thinking all this when Leah shamed me. "Kiki, I've seen a few of your scrapbooks. Your talent amazes me. Rabbi Sarah says you positively glow with spirituality. And of course, Dodie Goldfader thinks you are terrific. I'm glad to have the chance to get to know you better."

Okay, I'm a jerk.

Chief Holmes walked in and Sheila introduced him around. While everyone else discussed the upcoming High Holy Days, I managed to catch his eye. I said, "I need a glass of water, anyone want anything?" He followed me into the kitchen. With shaking hands, I pulled the nasty note from my pocket. He surveyed it and harrumphed. "Detweiler is right. This isn't over. Mr. Johnson was killed with a service revolver," and with that he rubbed the back of his neck. "I have a bad feeling about all this. I guess I don't need to tell you to keep this quiet."

At sundown we lit the candles and said our prayers. Sheila took the lead, which I expected. I've never caught the hang of the glottal "ch" sound that ends the first word of the prayers, "baruch." It comes out "ba-rook," and as often as she's corrected me, my pronunciation simply gets worse over time. We sat down to an elegantly prepared roasted chicken. My daughter fidgeted in her seat, finally asking to be excused so she could call Nicci Moore and get a ride to her friend's house. Chief Holmes walked Anya to Jennifer's car and talked briefly with the woman, out of hearing of the girls. He'd called backup to double-check the Moore's house, but they already had a high-level security system.

I tried to make sparkling conversation, I really did. The Benadryl made me so drowsy, I struggled just to keep awake. Ben slipped his hand into mine, and I turned to see those bronze eyes, steady and ready to love me.

"You sure seem tired. But then you've had a rough week, haven't you? I noticed Anya seemed to be doing well, considering."

I agreed. Considering.

I wished I could tell him about my fears, but I couldn't. They seemed to mark me as a weirdo. I understood this was my choice — not to open up. With Chief Holmes nearby, he'd back up my worries and concerns, but everything I'd been tackling over the last week seemed wildly out-of-place in the tapestry-filled, needle-pointed-pillow-plumped living room that belonged to my mother-in-law, and the cozy, protected life she loved.

A protected life that did not extend to me.

TWENTY-FIVE

Do NOT Park Here! Parking for La Casa is across the street! Parking for Cici's Pizza only!

Like Topsy, La Casa had grown and grown, and as it grew, the parking space became increasingly insufficient. I drove up and down Manchester, alternatively named Manslaughter Road by those who've witnessed its dangers, hawking vainly for an open spot. On my third pass, I got lucky. A car was pulling out of the La Casa lot, and I had slowed to let it leave like a good scout, so I scooted in to the tight space.

Because I was late getting out of my house on this Saturday evening, the party was already in full swing when I arrived. A trio of mothers was leaving. Connie and Elliott McMahan were saying their goodbyes to Mrs. Selsner. Elliott looked like he'd aged ten years. His graying hair now flecked with white. Connie gave me a tiny "thumbs up" that made me smile. Somehow she'd put starch back into her backbone, and I was glad for her. An empty bucket with Corona printed on the side sat in the middle of the table. In front of many of the guests were margarita glasses with only a few crumbles of ice in the bottoms. Half-eaten plates of food littered the tabletop.

As I walked up, another woman I didn't know planted kisses on Mrs. Selsner's cheek, leaving a vacant seat next to Mahreeya, Patricia, and Ella for me to slip into. "I don't deserve this," I heard the nurse say. A small Tiffany's box sat in front of Mrs. Selsner, and she examined it as though it were the source of physical pain.

Mahreeya made some noise about how of course she did, how this gift was only a token, and so on.

I caught Ella's eye, and she made a motion of her head in the direction of the restrooms. We walked silently side by side until the door closed behind us.

"Ella, I am so, so sor—"

She threw up her hands in a "stop it" signal. Tears threatened to spill from her eyes. "Don't. I'll start crying and never get a hold of myself."

I settled for putting my hand on her shoulder and giving it a squeeze.

She gripped the sink and held on tight. "I have to keep going. The body won't be released for a while. They need to do tests. Like on television, you know? But it's much slower in real life. Or so they tell me. I know I shouldn't be here, but Mrs. Selsner was like a second mother to us." Ella stood up, rolled back her shoulders and stared into the mirror. "The show must go on. Stiff upper lip and all that."

Ella wasn't alone in her warm feelings for Mrs. Selsner. A continuous flow of well-wishers came to say their goodbyes. I placed an order for La Casa's famous vegetable dip and a glass of Diet Coke. I really wished I could be ordering a margarita but I had a considerable drive home. The last thing I needed was an encounter with the local police.

The Diet Coke came before I had the chance to decide whom I'd call in such a pickle. Dodie was resting up, readying herself for her round of chemo and radiation. Mert had a habit of ticking off authority figures. Detweiler was, well, off-limits. Ben? He'd kissed me tenderly and urgently, backing me up against my car door before I'd pushed him away last night. He didn't offer to follow me home. Poor Ben. He wasn't comfortable around the dogs, and while he'd never been unkind to Gracie, he did give her a wide berth. And Johnny? Asking him to come rescue me if I was picked up for a DUI would be out of the question. He'd served time as a felon. While Clancy was so far on the other side of the Mississippi, it'd take her hours to come to my aid. Besides, she'd been taking a class at the Lewis & Clark Community College and was busy most evenings. Too busy to spend time with me it seemed.

While the waiter delivered my order, the group shifted to a smaller table to accommodate our intimate number. I'd arrived on the tail end of an "in progress" revisiting of memories by the Alumnae Four and didn't want to interrupt. Instead I dug into the dip and chips with gusto. I picked up a word here and there, realizing the girls were laughing about eating marijuana brownies before being crowned by the Veiled Prophet. Patricia looked extremely uncomfortable and changed the subject. I was having trouble following Mrs. Selsner. After straining for a while, it dawned on me that I couldn't understand her because she was rip-roaring drunk. Drunk as a skunk, as Nana used to say.

"I don't deserve this . . ." Mrs. Selsner was pawing at Patricia's arm. Patricia's face was pale. She sat frozen, not returning any of Bromo's gestures, her body tilted away from the overwrought school nurse.

"Of course, you do." Ella spoke to the older woman in a kind but firm tone of voice. She was wearing a frilly white blouse and a pair of tight, dark-washed jeans. Even with the glowing plum-colored circles under her eyes, the woman was gorgeous.

Mahreeya held up her wrist watch conspicuously, "Look at the time." She had on a turquoise blouse with a stand-up collar and matching capris topped with a wide leather belt sporting a Virgin Mary hand-painted on the enamel buckle. I'd seen a similar one in a fashion magazine for $350.

Mrs. Selsner stood up — and then every bit as quickly, sat back down.

Our waiter passed behind my chair. I thrust a bill at him and instructed him to keep the change. This was not looking good. Ella made a wild "come here" gesture with her hand, and I left my seat to come to her aid.

"She's in no shape to drive," Ella whispered to me over Mrs. Selsner's head. Patricia and Mahreeya began gathering their purses. Neither woman looked interested or sympathetic. A small mound of spittle sat on the corner of Mrs. Selsner's lips and a big green stain — guacamole, I'd guess — marred her white polyester blouse.

Ella's eyes entreated her school chums to help. Mahreeya turned away in disgust. Patricia took a turn glancing at her watch and said, "I really need to run."

I spoke up. "Tell you what. I'm almost out of gas. What if I drive Mrs. Selsner home in her car, and you follow me, Ella? You can bring me back here to pick up my car." Hey, any friend of my friend is my friend, right? Besides, the good deed would give me the chance to talk with Mrs. Selsner alone.

Mahreeya gave me general directions to Mrs. Selsner's house in Olivette, and Ella promised to lead the way by driving slowly on ahead. With a deft combination of coaxing and cajoling, Mahreeya talked Mrs. Selsner out of her keys.

"I'm not drunk," said Mrs. Selsner obstinately, clutching the robin's egg blue gift box to her bosom where it made a colorful counterpoint to the big green stain. "I'm upset. Upset about Sissy and Corey. That's all." The phrase came out "thash all," but it was clear what she meant.

Ella shored up the left side, and I took the woman's right, inhaling a snogful of Youth Dew, that most fragrant oxymoron. Nobody under sixty wears Youth Dew. Nobody. We left Mahreeya and Patricia to cover the bill. Mrs. Selsner muttered a vague protest, blinking up at me unsteadily with bleary eyes. "I don't need you. I can drive."

I ignored her. "Isn't it a lovely night?"

Ella loaded the woman into her car, an old Pontiac. I walked around and settled into the driver's seat, adjusting the rearview mirror before backing out slowly. I glanced over and noticed the nurse's seat belt wasn't on. I pulled back into our parking spot and fumbled around, embarrassingly reaching over the woman's flaccid gut. It took a bit of fiddling around until Mrs. Selsner was secure. Ella's car waited for me across the street in front of Cici's Pizza.

"I'm so sorry. Should have followed my instincts . . . should have . . . known . . ." Mrs. Selsner's face was mashed against the passenger side door but that didn't stop her from talking.

"Known what?"

"Sissy was in trouble . . . again . . . thought the Twelve Step . . . thought she was straightened out." Suddenly Mrs. Selsner sat bolt up and slammed her fist against the dash. Scared the guacamole out of me. Good thing we were stopped at a light or I'd have veered right off Manchester Road. Spotting a Wendy's, I pulled into the drive up and ordered their largest size of coffee. Ella must have figured out what I was doing because she paused at the drive-through exit until we were served.

The java had a sobering effect on Mrs. Selsner.

"Sissy was in a Twelve Step program?" I tried to sound nonchalant.

"Yes. Sexual Addiction Rehab. Out of Minnesota. Lots of women members. She needed help."

I thought such programs were the stuff of urban legends. I mulled this over. We drove along silently for a while. Mrs. Selsner said, "It's no surprise. Not really. You know what happened to her, right?"

Mrs. Selsner filled in the details of the story my mother-in-law had related. When Sissy was fourteen, a family friend heard of her love for horses and offered to let her come out to his ranch to ride his Arabians. The man owned a spread out on Wildhorse Creek Road on the way to St. Albans. Soon after, Sissy began taking equestrian lessons. Her parents investigated buying a horse, but Sissy couldn't settle on one. Until the decision was made, the family friend offered to let her come and ride as often as she wished. Her parents began dropping her off at the stables and leaving her there for hours after school and all day on weekends.

One day, while Sissy was grooming her horse, the family "friend" dragged her into a stall and raped her.

"By the time Mrs. Gilchrist arrived, Sissy was hysterical. There was . . . ah . . . internal damage," Mrs. Selsner drained her cup of coffee. "The Gilchrists talked to a lawyer. He advised against pressing charges. As did the family doctor. Agreed the whole experience would be demeaning and . . . embarrassing. In the end, the family decided that pursuing the matter . . . would make it worse."

"But what did Sissy think?"

"Her parents let her down. She never forgave them." The slurring nearly gone, the coffee had done its job. "She got in the habit of dropping by the office to talk. She said her parents treated her like a . . . well . . . She said, 'Everybody knows I'm not a virgin anymore.' That's how she justified her loose behavior. She punished herself. Blamed herself. Said she should have fought him. She said, 'Maybe he was right. Maybe I wanted it.' "

My stomach gurgled as I imagined Anya in a similar situation. I wouldn't have let the matter drop. I'd have killed the man with my own two hands.

Ella led us to a neighborhood of older homes with front lawns as even and smooth as squares of felt. Ragged borders of flowers and shadowy pots with uneven topknots of plants edged concrete walkways. The front doors were all solid wood, devoid of fancy glass side windows that burglars could use to gain entry. I guessed the residents were mainly older, probably retired.

"But Sissy turned her life around."

"She said she found Mr. Right. He was good for her and to her. She seemed happy."

"Corey Johnson?"

"Yes. They wanted a fresh start. He had a job offer in Raleigh, North Carolina, as an assistant coach."

"And her son?"

"I told her to take it slow. Baby steps. Have you seen Christopher? He's adorable, but he's . . . troubled. Doesn't adjust well." Her corduroy veined hands rubbed her eyes. "And now this . . ."

Ella rolled down her window and pointed to a brick bungalow with monogrammed awnings over the front door and windows. Ella helped Mrs. Selsner into her house while I parked the car. At the last minute, I remembered the box from Tiffany's. Making our way through the house took a bit of maneuvering because Mrs. Selsner never met a piece of furniture she didn't like. The place was chockablock with armchairs, straight-back chairs, end tables, scattered plant stands, and ètagéres. Without discussion, we headed the older woman toward the back and after a series of wrong turns, we stumbled into a bedroom. I set down the gift and withdrew leaving Ella to help the woman undress. The front door had a simple push button lock but that didn't seem very secure to me. While Ella was putting Mrs. Selsner to bed, I turned on the front light and began a systematic check under flower pots and welcome mat and along the upper sill of the door. Ella came to my rescue, holding up a silver key marked Yale on a State Farm insurance key ring with a paper label: house key. "Dug through her purse," she said.

As we drove away, I realized someone would have to drop by the next day, Sunday, and return her key. Probably me. Ella had held up remarkably well, but as the shock of Corey's death wore off, she would have to face her grief. And her guilt.

"I doubt that Mrs. Selsner's going to be up and at 'em early," I said as Ella handed me the house key. The grooved metal felt cool and weighty in my hand.

"Gee, and wasn't that a memorable retirement party?"

"What set her off?"

"The gift."

"Didn't see it."

"A cut glass flower vase. Patricia's in charge of all gifts for all parent-faculty events because she's the Parent Guild's faculty liaison committee chair. She picked it out. Just like she picked out Coach Bosch's gift and was there to give it to him. Too bad it isn't light outside. Mrs. Selsner's backyard is full of roses. She'll be able to keep the vase full. I guess she'd never had a gift from Tiffany's before. Sort of overwhelmed her. That and the pitcher of margaritas."

Ella hit the sunroof button, and we purred along under alternating patches of light and dark, a duality played out by streetlights and trees.

"I wish you'd known him. My son."

"I wish I had, too."

"He forgave me. At the end. I just don't know if I can forgive myself."

TWENTY-SIX

Too keyed up to go to bed, I worked awhile on the confidential album, sorting through photos of jewelry and clothing. I'd prepared the background pages. All I needed was to adhere the photos in their places. But that was a job I wanted to tackle in one go.

Finally, I decided reading Sissy's and Corey's files would be a good use of my excess energy.

Corey had a surprisingly good command of the English language. His forms were filled in with a neat, almost prissy hand. He'd struggled as a student in elementary and middle school, but clearly he'd picked up speed as time went on, graduating with a high B average. Most of the information was unremarkable. His foster family was listed as his next-of-kin.

His employment essay might easily have been the most bland document I'd ever seen until he answered the question, "What special skills, talents, or insights can you bring to the job of teacher at CALA?" Obviously, this touched a nerve. He wrote:

"Because of my background, I know what it's like not to belong. I know how it feels to be an outsider. My birth mother gave me away, and I have always wondered what was wrong with me that made her do that. Now that I'm an adult, I understand that people do things for all kinds of reasons. Some might even seem like good reasons at the time. So I think that when a student is troubled, I can relate to him. The one thing every person wants is acceptance. I can give a student that. I can tell him that his future happiness is up to him, and he has more control over his life than he thinks — on and off the basketball court. Even if it seems no one loves him, someday if he's lucky and a good person, he will find people who will care about him, I know it. It has happened to me."

I closed the file and looked at my own hands for a long, long time, thinking about my own fight to feel good about myself. It hadn't been easy.

I was sure Ella hadn't read Corey's file, and I was glad. You could tell Corey was struggling to forgive her. First, he had to believe he was not abandoned by an uncaring woman. Then he fought to accept himself and his situation. I thought back to what I'd heard about Corey before the murder. He'd led the basketball team to a string of victories. The alumni newsletter bragged about his warm relationship with his athletes, his ability to "get the best" from all his players. Of course, Anya had told me how much the kids thought of him. To be successful like that, he must have found a measure of peace and acceptance. And he must have brought those qualities to his relationship with Sissy.

Sissy's file held cursory particulars in a rounded, childish script. Grade transcripts mingled with an information sheet detailing biographical data. The line at the bottom listing her "call in an emergency" number, struck me as particularly poignant. She was a low-B, high-C student except for her grades in math which were all A's. At the very back of the stack was her personal essay. Skimming over the opening paragraphs, it was obvious why she wasn't an English major. Her thinking on paper was trite and repetitious. She had numerous usage problems. At first glance, the work seemed more on the level of a high school freshman than a college graduate.

Buried at the back were a few lines worth

reading. Like many writers, as she went on, Sissy warmed to her subject:

"If I'm excepted as a teacher there's one thing you can count on. I won't lie to my students. Adults like to tell kids they are doing this or that for there own good when really they are protecting themselves. Adults are very good at slanting things so they come out looking good. They can create the allusion that they really care when they don't. Mostly they care about themselves and how they look to there friends. I know from personal experience.

"Honestly, I'd like to work here because of my son, Christopher. He's the most important person in the world to me, and I love him with all my heart. I want to be around to protect him. He's all I have in this world that is true and good."

I put down the paper and brushed away my tears.

TWENTY-SEVEN

Sunday morning very early, Detweiler listened over the phone to the tale of Sissy Gilchrist's rape with an attitude of restrained outrage. He promised to check old police reports. "Maybe the Gilchrists reported it before they decided not to press charges. That's common. Tomorrow I'll call them. I hate having to bring up old hurts, but I can't overlook a possible connection. Maybe the man who raped Sissy felt threatened. Maybe she decided to confront him before she moved away. Maybe he and Corey had words."

I hung up feeling incredibly lonely. I really missed George. Maybe I should encourage Ben's attentions. His parents liked me. Sheila would be thrilled. I could love him. Even if, right now, my loyalties were divided because I still had the hots for Detweiler, perhaps Ben would light a fire inside me, and my fantasies would revolve around the journalist instead of the cop. After all, Ben was a good man. And I'd had practice being a partner to a good man who wasn't my soul mate. I could have that sort of relationship again. I knew I could.

I could have a "settle for" existence. Perhaps the emptiness of my life would be filled up with a new husband. Maybe even a new baby. Wouldn't that be lovely? Surely holding a baby would cause my heart to overflow, and whatever empty spaces were left in my soul would fill up . . . and I'd love Ben. Yes, of course, I would. Hadn't I loved George in part for his love of Anya?

Weren't arranged marriages like this? Initial attraction was unimportant, and a different sort of love flourished? A love made more secure because the "lovers" were surrounded by a family unit showering them with positive encouragement?

Putting one hand on the windowsill, I stared out into the empty backyard. The weather was turning colder. Trees shivered in the early fall chill, and parchment-dry leaves blew about like so much trash. A few leaves tumbled end over end, caught on a bare branch and waved like brown flags. Winter would come soon, sending its painful cold drilling deep into my pores. I could offer no resistance. The chambers of my heart were empty voids. How long could I hold up with this vacuum in my life? This echoing vastness within me? Was this exactly why people — even those in bad marriages — married on the rebound? Even when I suspected George was being unfaithful, a part of me knew he wouldn't walk away from our family. How I missed having someone to share my life with!

I wanted someone to grieve with me over what had happened to poor Sissy Gilchrist. I wanted someone to sorrow with me about the horrible injustice that must have haunted her. I wanted to talk over how I — how we — would handle a situation like that, if God forbid, it happened in our family. My thoughts returned again and again to Corey. To thoughts of how he forgave Ella just in time.

The worst part of being a parent is knowing you'll make mistakes, and fearing them, and feeling the pain that accompanies the inevitability of letting your child down. But two people can better strategize. Two people can talk through the process. Two people can bear the disappointments more fully and comfort each other with the reminder "we did our best."

But there wasn't anybody in my house to talk to. My house was empty.

I fell back on routine. I followed our typical Sunday morning ritual, but without Anya. After all, sometime in the near future, she'd naturally choose time with her friends over time with me. I might as well get used to this.

I headed directly for a park, choosing Tilles because I rarely went there.

After our third round of chasing squirrels — who are much smarter than you'd guess and twice as fast — I decided to tell the dogs about Sissy's essay. They were good listeners. The dogs frolicked through two quick runs, before the chill in the morning air was too much for me. We headed home for breakfast. I spilled my (coffee) beans to Gracie — complaining about missing Anya — as the big dog gobbled the biscuit and the two tablespoons of canned food on top of her kibble in two gulps. Mr. Gibbes licked his meal tentatively, teasing my big girl with his slow consumption.

For the first time, I noticed the gray hairs sprinkled in the black in Gracie's muzzle.

Danes don't live long. Seven years is normal. The vet had estimated her age as three when we got her. Maybe even four. Now she was five. What would I do without my dear dog? I got all weepy again; I'd cried a little this morning as I dressed.

I rummaged through my cabinet and pulled out a box of Prilosec that I hadn't needed in months. I knocked it back with a slug of cold water and hoped my ulcer wasn't flaring up. It had been full-blown off and on when George was alive. The pain had seared my gut now and then since, but now it nearly doubled me over.

I needed to get my mind off my troubles.

This would be a good day to work on the confidential album. I had time until Anya got home. But I couldn't settle into my work. I had a key to return.

Showing up early, unannounced and empty-handed at Mrs. Selsner's seemed awkward, so I ran into a nearby Starbucks first and bought another hit of caffeine for me, a coffee and a bag of bakery items for her. Okay, I lied. If she wanted both the low-fat cinnamon coffee cake and the blueberry muffin, she'd have to arm wrestle me. I gulped the tall skinny vanilla latte as I drove. The houses in her neighborhood seemed more shopworn in the daylight, but the area was neatly tended.

My first stab at the doorbell did not produce Mrs. Selsner. I stood patiently, reflecting on the hangover she no doubt was nursing. The second ring brought a scuffling noise from within. Standing on the doorstep was tedious, but dropping a key labeled "house key" in her mailbox would expose an old woman to unnecessary risk. Besides, I had more questions to ask. My forefinger pushed the glowing doorbell button for the third time.

The doorknob jumped to life with a rattle. "Who is it?" she called in a quavery voice.

"Hi, Mrs. Selsner. Kiki Lowenstein. I have your house key. From last night." Come on, lady, I thought, don't make me explain to your door that you were in no condition to lock up last night.

What seemed like five minutes went by, then the knob turned slowly, and Mrs. Selsner glared at me. Her watery eyes gave me the once over. She struggled to place me, considered, reconsidered, and then mumbled, "Oh, you."

Oh, you, indeed. That fell a little short of the thanks I deserved, but what the hey?

"I stopped by Starbucks and brought you a coffee and a cinnamon coffee cake." That blueberry muffin had my name on it. Holding the bag up in the manner of a peace offering, I continued, "Last night Ella and I locked your door for you, so I came to return the key." This I dangled before her in my other hand.

"This early? Don't be standing there telling the whole world my business," she snipped, waving me inside.

I followed the figure wearing grubby beige house slippers and a faded floral smock that my mother used to call a housecoat. The Youth Dew had worn off and was replaced with the smell of dirty hair. Putting the coffee and the bag on the imitation Early American table, I took a seat behind a vinyl placemat covered with yellow daisies. Seeing as how Mrs. Selsner obviously wasn't interested in acting like a good hostess, I asked if I could help myself to a glass of water, and received a go-ahead grunt. As I waited for the tap water to run cool, she drank the coffee and devoured the crumb cake. I returned to the seat I'd vacated, and we sat in awkward silence.

"Anya's your daughter?"

I nodded.

"Has problems eating?"

"Occasionally."

"You keep an eye on it. Hear? These girls get the silliest ideas." Mrs. Selsner fingered the paper napkin I'd provided her along with her breakfast. "She's a good child. Sensible."

A clock ticked above our heads. We sat silently. Most people are afraid of silence. Try this: sit and stare at another person for

304

fifteen seconds. Time yourself. It's nearly impossible to do without laughing or saying something, anything.

"You know, I found Sissy."

"You mean . . . her body?" Of course, I knew this.

"Yes. She wasn't the only one who snuck around in that balcony. I caught others. Two teachers. A couple of freshmen. A parent and a teacher. Told Mr. McMahan we needed to get that changed right smart. He wanted names. Heavens, if I'd turned in every person I'd stumbled over in the past thirty years . . . well, I could fill all the seats in the Latreau Theatre. That was hardly the point.

"In this day and age of people suing each other for one fool thing or another, I said, 'Why don't we keep the balcony locked?' Mr. McMahan agreed. Still, the lock was one of those flimsy do-hickeys you could pop wide open with a credit card. Mr. Mc-Mahan doesn't always follow through like he should. Bringing in money, he's a regular Speed Racer, but spending it's another story."

"How'd you happen to discover the . . . uh . . ."

"Sissy had been in the hall reading a note right before the first class period. Her room

305

is on the other end of the campus. She would have already dropped Christopher off at kindergarten. I'm pretty sharp, you know." Mrs. Selsner tapped the side of her head with a finger.

"She had no business being at the south end of the school . . . no business except monkey business. I kept getting up from my desk and looking into the hall, wondering if she'd popped the lock. Planned to catch her in the act. I'd broken up a little powwow between her and Coach Johnson the week before. Then I took a call from a mother about whether fifth's disease is contagious. Which it is. And I thought I heard a noise. I keep a radio on in my office so I can hear the weather bulletins. I wasn't sure, but something told me to go and check."

Mrs. Selsner stopped abruptly. With a grubby finger, she mashed crumbs and brought them to her mouth.

To string out the conversation, I stepped to the faucet and poured myself another glass of water. I needn't have worried; Mrs. Selsner started up again.

"First I opened the door and saw a foot. The shoe was silver — one of those Aigner loafers they sell at Dillard's? — it was on the floor. Figured someone had fainted. The lights were off, so I hit the switch. The police said I smeared the fingerprints. How could I know? At the time, that wasn't my concern. The light came on. I could tell she was gone, but still . . . you have to . . . I felt for a pulse."

"Could you tell right away what happened to her?"

Mrs. Selsner blanched. "My Lord, yes."

"Any ideas who did it?" I took my glass to the sink. I rinsed it out and set it next to a similar glass and an empty packet of Meta-mucil.

Mrs. Selsner folded the paper wrapper from her cake and stuffed it into the Star-bucks bag. She took a searching drag from her paper coffee cup, popped off the lid, and ran her tongue along the rolled rim try-ing to chase down any last drops. "Told the police to check out her ex-husband. They'd fought in the hallway last week, yelling and cursing, loud enough that the nearby teach-ers called security. I ran out of my office when I heard the commotion. He had her by the arms and was shaking her so hard her head was snapping back and forth. A security guard separated them, and her ex stormed out into the parking lot."

"Then a lot of people saw and heard the fight?"

"Even their son."

■ ■ ■ ■

"Questioning Danny Gartner has been . . . uh . . . less than productive," said Detweiler when I called him on my cell phone as I drove home from the nurse's house. "The man's a cop in a small town. We got the runaround for a day and a half from his boss. Commander Fender sent down a detective, who just happened to be an old friend of Gartner's family. You know, I've heard it said that St. Louis is a big small town, but now I think the whole state of Missouri is a big small town as well."

I thought about the connections between families at CALA and concurred.

"It's on our list to go down and talk with Gartner again, but the detective who went down there says Gartner has an alibi, so it's not been a top priority." Papers rustled in the background. "Here it is. His dad says Danny was at a conference. Sounds pretty weak, but other than the fact most divorced people seem to hate each other, we've got nothing on him. Besides the usual bad feelings, we don't have a motive. And timing's an issue."

"Maybe it was her engagement to Corey Johnson."

"That would make sense. I'll re-examine his statement. If Danny did go to a conference somewhere, Spock didn't beam him there. There have to be plane tickets, gas receipts, whatever."

I closed the phone. I'd fiddled around enough. I needed to finish my confidential album.

TWENTY-EIGHT

I spent an hour before lunch mounting the photos. I left large spaces and marked them with yellow sticky-notes as "journaling goes here." I included a title page in the front, which I had to leave uncomfortably blank. To the second page, I added a table of contents: home, travel, events, clothing, and jewelry. I paused, thought about my work, and did another flip through.

One of the pieces of jewelry on the page was familiar, a diamond and emerald pin. I knew I'd seen it on someone, but who?

Feeling good about my progress, I decided to take a break and research Danny Gartner.

Time to brainstorm. My work generated his name and a short list: KKK, Roma P. D., Missouri, and policeman. When my Dogpile search pulled up the computer equivalent of a small hill of poop, I sat back and stared at the screen, tapping my front teeth with a pencil. How could I find out more about this man?

Again I turned to the Internet, and this time, I cast my net wider. In no time, I was ready to make a phone call. For safety's sake, I hopped in the car and drove to a store in a local grocery chain. I then dropped coins in a pay phone.

"Hello, I'm looking for Douglas Gartner." My voice was cool and professional.

"Who's this?"

"Kay Collins from the student newspaper over at the state college." No lie, that's exactly what it said on my old press pass from my days as a journalism student. My teacher refused to believe my name was really "Kiki Collins."

"What's this about?"

"Mr. Gartner, we're coming up on the August anniversary of the death of Lieutenant Commander George Lincoln Rockwell."

"Commander," Gartner echoed, making me glad I'd done my research. "As fine a man as ever led our troops."

"Yes, sir, in Korea." Steady girl, I told myself. Don't let the fish know you've got him. Set the hook. "As you might be aware, over in Illinois, the city of Bloomington does its best to deny Lieutenant Commander Rockwell's Midwest roots. Recently a less-

311

informed reporter noted that the Rockwell family had no ties there. But anyone who reads Lieutenant Commander Rockwell's stirring autobiography would know the family owned a business in Bloomington, a theatre actually."

"That's right."

"All this makes him of particular interest to our Midwest readership."

"So?"

"I have a class project due. I thought it would be a good idea to take a new look at Lieutenant Commander Rockwell in light of the recent denial of freedom of speech to Knights of the Ku Klux Klan here in Missouri."

"And why are you calling me?" The voice was raspy and he paused long enough to hock up a loogie in that liquid cough smokers never seem to shake.

"My research shows you were one of a group of people who petitioned the State of Missouri to allow the KKK to participate in the highway cleanup program." We hit a long patch of quiet. Either I was right, and I'd done my research correctly, or I was about to be hung up on.

"You do know what happened to that there stretch of road, don't you?"

Gotcha! "Yes, sir, I am well aware that the

312

state legislature denied your right to participate in the cleanup."

"But the Supreme Court ruled that Missouri can't discriminate against us. Then, those blankety-blank so-and-so's went and named that there stretch of road for that black woman. Rosa-Park-Your-Butt."

Hang in there, I told myself. Obviously this man is not a listener to our local public radio station.

"Sir, that's exactly what I'd like to discuss with you. You and anyone else in your group. I'm especially curious about how any of your family members might feel about this."

"You free tonight? A bunch of us is having a barbecue." He pronounced the word "bar-bee-cue" with a long emphasis on the last syllable. In a wink, he rattled off directions and a time and I ended the call with my thanks.

I set down the receiver of the pay phone at the grocery store. Around me was a hub-bub of activity. Bet no one else in spitting distance was crafty enough to wrangle an invite to a meeting of the local fans of anti-Semitism and white supremacy. Or dumb enough. Take your pick.

I struggled into the kitchen, dragging plastic

313

bags of groceries. Putting them away was one of my least favorite jobs. When the phone rang, I happily took a break.

Ben said, "Kiki, I was wondering if we could get together."

I stalled. I wasn't sure I wanted this relationship to move along any faster than the cold honey pace we'd established. But my good manners won out. "Um, when?"

"How about dinner tonight? We could go see a movie at Frontenac and have dinner — before or after — at Brio."

"I'd love to, but I have a previous engagement."

A long cold silence followed. I squirmed. On one hand, I didn't want him to think I was dating anyone else. On the other, such a thought could keep him at bay a little longer. Maybe long enough for me to get off the fence and fall in love.

But with him? I wasn't sure about that.

"I see."

Somehow we said "goodbye," but I don't know how.

I closed my phone and pondered a really pressing question: What exactly does one wear to a party hosted by bigots?

TWENTY-NINE

Mert phoned immediately after, and I spilled my guts to her — including how sickened I felt after viewing the ugly note in my daughter's backpack.

She was very quiet for a few minutes. "I told you not to get involved."

"But Anya is in danger."

"You are too! And you're gonna make everything worse!"

"Mert, they haven't made progress on Sissy's murder. Or on Corey's fake suicide. I can't expect them to check out a silly threatening note."

Mert sighed. "I know. You're right. Listen here, girl, you and I need to have a talk when this is all over. I've been thinking we got to get you hitched. You ain't safe on your own."

Yeah, yeah, yeah. Blah, blah, blah. I couldn't go there. Being surrounded didn't work for Custer, and it wasn't looking good for me either.

My phone rang again, right after I said goodbye to Mert.

"I wanted to apologize for being so mealy mouthed the other night at Coffee and Crime," said Connie. "I shouldn't have said those things. Even though we're friendly, I still have to remember you are a member of the school community. Sharing my husband's problems was wrong. Please forget what I said." Her voice had an edge to it, the raw sound of panic. She wasn't asking me to forget our conversation. She was begging.

Whoa. What caused this dramatic change of heart? "How is Elliott?"

"Things are . . . fine."

Oh, yeah, like I totally believed that. "Even though a teacher and a coach from CALA are dead."

The steel emerged within the magnolia. "You better back off. I'm telling you. You're in for a world of trouble, Kiki."

What was happening here?

"Is this a threat?" I was shocked by the abrupt change of tone in her voice.

"It's a friendly warning. Look, I like you. You've had a hard time of it, but things are turning around. Just go on about your business."

"Corey Johnson was shot. Sissy Gilchrist had her head bashed in. A killer is running around my daughter's school. Oh, and let's review, Connie. Your husband hired her. You were angry with her. Shouldn't you want this investigation closed? Shouldn't you — of all people — want the killer found?"

"Of course I do. Don't act all ignorant on me. But I don't want anybody else hurt. You're making waves. You're riling folks up," she paused. "I'm not threatening. I'm just asking. See, it wasn't just my husband who was acting stupid. He had plenty of company. Let this go. You're causing more pain than you can guess. And there will be repercussions. You count on it."

With that, she hung up.

I had a couple hours to waste before the barbecue. I also had to figure out where to park my child. I needed a safe place. I could ask my mother-in-law, but she was in constant contact with Ben's parents. What if he'd told his folks about me turning down his dinner invitation? Well, shoot. Sheila would keel-haul me.

Instead, I needed a clean getaway. I tapped my front teeth with a pencil and thought hard. Then, I picked up the phone and asked Jennifer Moore if Anya could stay for another night. I offered to take her kids and my child to school the next morning. I explained I needed a long bike ride to clear my head.

Jennifer was happy to oblige. Evidently, I'd caught her in the midst of a visit with one of the other moms, but Jennifer insisted she didn't mind my interruption. "Anya can wear something of Nicci's to school tomorrow. Stevie can drop the girls off at school in the morning. Where are you planning to ride? Should I meet you somewhere or just call you if nothing fits Anya?"

I said I'd be out on the access road by Highway 40 until dusk. Jennifer repeated my coordinates, but the tone of her voice told me she was out of her league. For a lot of folks in Ladue, anything west of 270 and they act like they're personally mounting the Lewis and Clark expedition. Next up, she'd be asking, "What should I pack in the canoes?"

But she didn't. Instead, she called my daughter to the phone.

Predictably, Anya was thrilled with my decision to let her stay one more night. "Mom, you're the best."

Boy, did I ever feel guilty. She had no idea

I was dumping her off at her friend's so I could snoop around.

I changed into a pair of bike shorts, an exercise bra, and one of those cool bike shirts that wicks away moisture. I was hooking my bike onto the rack at the back of my car when Detweiler called. The ballistics tests showed unusually large, elliptical traces of gunpowder on the front of Corey Johnson's skull. Clearly, the gun had been fired at a severe angle.

"Suicides eat their guns. Or screw them into their temples," Detweiler mused. "This sure isn't a suicide. No one holds a gun twelve inches away from his head and squeezes. There was only a trace of residue on his hand."

"Meaning the gun might have been shoved into his hand after the shooting."

"That's right."

We were quiet. Being right wasn't much fun when it meant a killer had stepped up the action.

"I can't," Maggie sounded weary. "It's been a terrible week."

"All the more reason for you to come riding with me. Fall will turn rainy and cold soon. Come on, Maggie." In the distance, I heard a tiny shriek.

"Christopher, Christopher, honey, please calm down."

"You're babysitting!"

"Yes. His grandmother asked if I'd watch him. They're making funeral arrangements with Sissy. I guess those goons at the lab are finally done with her body."

I wanted to tell her the news about Corey Johnson being murdered, but I couldn't. Detweiler had sworn me to silence. Instead, I asked, "How's the family doing?"

"Good. No thanks to you."

I gulped. "Excuse me?"

"Don't think I haven't heard about your snooping around, Kiki. Everyone's talking about it. You even got that cop friend of yours to dredge up ancient history. Paula and Quentin Gilchrist are beside themselves over your accusations."

"Accusations? What are you talking about? Mrs. Selsner told me about Sissy being molested. The Gilchrists did nothing about it, Maggie. Nothing. Would you have sat by if something happened to Tilly?"

"That's a very, very personal decision. You have no right to question them. You don't know what you'd do under the circumstances."

"The heck I do. I'd go after the man with my own two hands."

"Right — and smear Anya's name and face over all the media? Huh? Have her be a laughing stock? Have everyone point at her? Have her be embarrassed at school? Have everyone ask her if she could still wear a white gown on her wedding day? Call her a . . . a . . ."

I stood there with my mouth open and my heart pounding. My calm, cool, collected ever-so-proper school marm friend let loose with a list of swear words like you wouldn't believe. All of them were euphemisms for loose women.

This was a kindergarten teacher? This was my meek pal? I waited until she ran out of steam. When the silence was so long you could have run a football along it and shouted "Touchdown!" I finally said, "I have no idea where you are coming from, Maggie. None. And lest you forget, our daughters may have seen a murderer. A killer who is still out there."

"You stupid fool! You are so bullheaded. Coach Johnson killed Sissy. Get that through your thick skull, Kiki. When the guilt got to him, he shot himself. You can't use our daughters as an excuse. Hello! You are just full of yourself. And you've got the hots for that married detective so you'll do anything, and I mean anything, to get his attention."

THIRTY

I was still shaking by the time I pulled off the access road. It seemed so weird to be here alone without Maggie. Sure, we hadn't been close long, but I thought we were good friends.

I already missed her company. We'd talked a lot as we rode. We'd covered all that early friendship jazz like our early lives, our natal families, our hopes and dreams, and our hurts. I sniffled as I ran our conversation over and over in my mind. Was she right? I knew information that she didn't. I knew Corey Johnson hadn't committed suicide. But was it true? Did everyone think I was that awful? Was I really so driven that I'd hurt my own daughter? Was I that transparent? Was I more interested in chasing a married man than protecting my child?

I put all my angst into my ride.

I have a love-hate relationship with bike riding alone. I mean, I love being alone with my bike rimming the edge of the fields. Watching red-wing blackbirds light on the fences, hearing the brittle click that passes for a birdsong with cardinals, and having quiet time with open spaces suits me fine — which is one reason I don't mind driving out here rather than riding closer to my home. As the spokes turn, there's a meditative feeling to biking. The motion is rhythmic, and your breathing falls in line. The sights, the sounds, the feel all work in harmony and produce a soothing experience.

But when you are alone, perched on the top of a slender, thin set of metal tubes, you would be a fool not to feel vulnerable. A blown tire could send you flying. A crevice in the pavement could lock up your wheels and throw you to the ground. A rock, hit the wrong way by a one-inch-wide tire, could send you sprawling. Being alone meant accepting responsibility for a more dangerous ride, but it also meant freedom from having to communicate with another human being.

This afternoon, especially, I welcomed the quiet because I wanted to think.

I adjusted my helmet, pulled on my gloves, and climbed on my Trek. After the initial pedal stroke provided me with momentum,

I settled into a cadence. The shoulder of the access road was uneven enough to demand a modicum of concentration. I picked up speed. My bike was a wedge, creating a slipstream, slicing the air around me in half. One of the joys of biking as a form of exercise is that you create your own breeze, your own cooling system. Feeling surer with each stroke, I picked up my pace, and my mind moved into another zone.

I built a partition and put Maggie and her accusations behind it.

I thought about Dodie. She'd been a lifesaver after George died. She taught me so much. She'd given me my self-esteem by offering me the job at Time in a Bottle. I would do anything I could to help her and Horace. But what? I didn't want to be intrusive. I picked up my pace. I'd have to wait and see. Surely he'd tell me and Bama what we could do. He'd have to. How else could we run the store?

I took those worries and packaged them up in a box marked, "Get well soon."

I navigated the turn at the end of the access road and doubled back. I thought about the week ahead. The Gilchrists were planning Sissy's funeral, but when would Corey's body be released? I'd have to attend his services. Ella. Poor, poor Ella. The image of her in a militant stance floated to the surface of my consciousness. What would it have been like to be both Old St. Louis and a civil rights protester? How would her peers have responded? Did her actions cause the rift between her and Mahreeya? Or was their tension a throwback to when Mahreeya was the proverbial ugly duckling and Ella a swan?

Even though the world had come to agree with Ella in the decades that followed her protest, it would be a mistake to overlook the impact of her gesture. Here was the daughter of an outstanding businessman with a membership in a secret organization originally intended — if you were to believe one historian — to keep minorities in their place, and she'd been shouting activist slogans in a state that still harbored a deep-seated ambivalence about issues of race.

What would she say when she heard Corey had been murdered? That her suspicions had been confirmed? That her son had been targeted and killed and for what? For loving a white woman? To cover up a murder? Because of what he knew?

What we needed was a motive for Sissy's murder, a motive that made sense in view of the murder's timing. That would help us figure out why Corey had been shot. The method of the violence, grabbing the nearest object to hand, a brick from the nearby construction site, suggested the murder was not premeditated. A lot of people had reason to want Sissy dead. But Sissy had changed. And she'd changed for the better. So why kill her now? After she'd turned in her resignation? What irritant became intolerable? And why now? Our only hope seemed to be to keep turning over rocks, so to speak, to continue talking to anyone and everyone, while eliminating possible suspects. Given time, surely the police would discern a clue within the detritus of Sissy's final days.

After eight miles, I stopped for a drink from my water bottle. I downed most of the contents and readied myself for another eight miles. I clicked my right bike shoe into the same side pedal while holding the brake lever firmly so I didn't roll.

I rose to my seat with the downstroke and felt along the left pedal with the ball of my left foot until I could click and lock in my shoe. The noise from Highway 40 started to fade. The gap between one flotilla of cars and the next left room for the calls and cries of one red-wing blackbird to another. The blue bachelor buttons along the access road waved as I went by. A curious rabbit observed me from behind a fencepost and thought how clumsy I was. My computer said thirteen mph, but I knew that once I warmed up, I'd be hovering around fifteen mph. My goal was to work up to sixteen mph, but with my chronic asthma and my erratic biking schedule, I wasn't making much progress.

I thought back to the list of suspects. Initially Sissy's behavior moved Connie Mc-Mahan to want to strangle her husband. But Connie was among the first to know Sissy was leaving the school. So the timing of the attack didn't make sense.

Who else might have come unhinged by Sissy's flirtations? Someone with less self-control than Connie? I'd fallen into the habit of calling the murderer "he" when I talked with Detweiler, but I knew better than to limit our search. Was another mother behind the brick that smashed Sissy's head?

Another woman who didn't like Sissy's flirtatious ways? Another mom whose son was heeding the siren call of the CALA temptress? Another wife whose husband had been involved with Sissy?

A woman like my confidential scrapbook client?

Maggie suggested the murderer was some-one sick of Sissy's interference in her child's education. A woman whose child had been belittled by Sissy? A parent who felt Sissy jeopardized his child's academic career? I thought of all those bumper stickers that proudly proclaimed, "My child is an honor student." Parents who sent their kids to CALA were overachievers who expected a lot from the school and from their offspring. On one hand it seemed a pretty weak motive . . . and yet there was that case in Texas where a mom plotted to kill her daughter's competitor on the cheerleading squad. And what about that dad who killed his son's soccer coach? Or was it hockey? It wouldn't be prudent to discount Sissy's classroom antics too readily.

And what if Sissy really had seduced students? How would a parent respond? How would I respond? I wasn't rational when it came to my daughter. Would a mother kill a teacher who trifled with her son? Considering the double standard in sentences for female and male pedophiles, this could go either way. The movie *Summer of '42* portrayed sex between a boy and an older woman as romantic. Now that I was the mother of a preteen, I'd call it creepy. Ugh.

What about Sissy's ex-husband? Could he have hired a killer? Or slipped in and done the deed himself? He knew the layout of the school. Did Sissy have life insurance? Did the school offer employees a policy? Did the Gilchrists have money problems? They wouldn't be the first family in Ladue who were living over their heads.

Or maybe Sissy decided to tattle on her abuser. The statute of limitations might have run out, but she could still point fingers, name names, and make the man pay — at least with his reputation.

All these thoughts were chasing each other round and round in my brain. My concentration was so intense, that I was on the last leg of my second lap before I realized it. Ahead was the overpass, Boone's Crossing, named in honor of Daniel's homestead down the road a piece in Defiance, Missouri.

A slight sheen had sprung up on my forehead, and it felt darn good. I pulled up on my pedals, enjoying the power in my hamstrings and buttocks. The intersection linking access roads north and south of 40 was clear. My cadence slowed as I worked my way up the slight incline. I heard a car approaching from a distance, but I made clear my intended direction, heading straight down the road, by staying to the right-hand side, away from the turn lane.

The car engine grew louder. Dipping my left shoulder, I turned my head. The passenger door was immediately to my left. The car accelerated and — to my shock — the side mirror nearly brushed my shoulder. I edged my bike as far right as possible. I gripped the handles hard, straining to keep myself balanced as I bumped along the uneven surface. I hit a tiny rock, adjusted for the response of my tires, and managed to stay upright.

All this happened in seconds, but the natural time-space relationship had changed. Everything was now going slo-mo. I held my breath. Any minute now, the car would pull past me.

But it didn't.

Instead, the mirror nudged my shoulder again. Then it withdrew. The car sped up. Testing me. Testing its options. Testing how to do me in.

I breathed again. I swallowed and tried to control my shaking. Out of my peripheral vision, I saw the car pull ahead. I was even with the back bumper. I squeezed my brakes, slowly, evenly so the bike wouldn't throw me. There was no room on my right. No place for me to put down a foot to steady myself. The drop-off was steep. Cars whizzed by below. I concentrated on my balance. I stared down at the shoulder, trying to anticipate rocks and debris that might knock me off the bike.

I can do this, I told myself. I know I can.

Then, the car started to make a right turn into my path.

All I could see was car — black shiny metal — and I was headed straight for it.

I couldn't stop. I squeezed the brakes as hard as I could. The bike tires seized but I kept moving. Gravel acted like ball bearings, rolling under me, pushing me forward. The car panel filled my vision. Closer, closer. I kept moving, propelled straight into the black side panel. My back tire skidded on the gravel. I couldn't stop. I had one option.

I could make my own turn. I could tumble down the hill. I might be able to stop my descent. But right now, I couldn't stop my path toward the car. I was skidding without control, like a skater on ice. Beneath me my wheels locked up. I couldn't get traction. A sharp right would send me parallel instead of slamming into the car.

This was really bad. Really, really bad.

Maybe I picked the wrong hobby. Maybe I should have taken up spinning, where you ride a stationary bike inside.

If I didn't turn, if I couldn't stop my slide,

there was the very real possibility I would wind up under the tires.

I jerked the handlebars as hard as I could. My back tire started sliding, sliding away from me.

THIRTY-ONE

I muscled the bike. I gave it all I had. I wrenched it. I yanked it. I careened into a right turn just as the car zoomed past me. But I wasn't out of the woods yet.

I was totally off balance. My back wheel left the pavement. It came back down. It bumped hard, rattling my teeth. I saw sky. I saw grass. I saw the black car. I saw the road.

I pitched sharply forward. The power of my turn sent me careening down the hill. My clip-on cycling shoes held me onto the bike. I bounced over the drainage ditch and continued down the landscaped verge of the overpass. At the foot of my grassy knoll was Highway 40. And on Highway 40 there were cars. Cars and trucks.

I struggled to stay upright. I held on to the bike with all my might, but I had to stop. I couldn't keep going downhill. If I rolled onto the highway . . . if I rolled into the oncoming cars . . . they were going 70 mph

334

in a 60 zone. Everyone did. But not everyone was on a stupid bicycle. They were safe and snug.

I flew through the air. My feet were clipped on. The bike and I were one, but the bike was moving without my permission.

I had to stop myself. I had to end the downhill tumble. And I had to do it fast.

The roar of cars deafened me. The smell of exhaust clenched my throat. The slap of tires chilled me. I shifted all my weight to the left. I threw my head there first, hoping my shoulders would follow. I watched the sky, the overpass, the tops of trees, the grass go by.

I crashed into the ground. My hands still locked onto the Trek. Instinct kept me holding on. I tasted blood in my mouth. I was on my side, sliding, sliding down the embankment. My forearms burned, my legs burned, as flesh was ground away. I kept clutching my bike, now bumping along on my side, headed for the traffic.

I thought of Anya and Gracie.

Of Mert's warning. Of Connie's threat. Of Maggie's anger.

And Detweiler's eyes.

I thought about Sheila.

She'd want to know if I was wearing clean

underwear.

Mert would stand over my coffin and yell, "I told you to be more careful!"

Then I got lucky.

I banged right into one of the maple saplings planted by the City of Chesterfield. My feet tangled between bike frame and tree trunk. My arm and leg were on fire. Blood gushed into my mouth. My elbow dug into a hollow in the ground. But I quit my downward slide.

I rested there on my side.

I was alive. Alive!

THIRTY-TWO

Voices all around me were speaking Spanish. I didn't exactly black out. I just lost track of reality for a few minutes. (Actually, I later learned it was more like ten. But who cares?) A brace of hands helped me struggle to my feet. The calloused palms were rough, but the touch was gentle. I swayed and a strong arm held me. The wind had been knocked out of me. I was having trouble breathing.

A crew from the landscaping business at the end of the access road had seen my wild ride and stopped to help. With the rush of business, and the demands of fall planting, they worked seven days a week. While I was busy trying to kill myself on the access road, they'd been returning for another round of trees to plant.

"Okay? *Señora,* okay?" An anxious man in a clean but tattered T-shirt waved his hands in front of my face. He stuck his face close

337

to mine as he tried to determine how with-it I was. I focused on his eyes, liquid brown like Hershey's syrup.

"I'm . . . okay." I unbuckled my helmet and took it off gingerly with my right hand. My *amigo* grabbed it and indicated he'd carry it for me.

A second man braced me on my left. His face was as leathery as a dog's chew toy. His lips were pursed in concentration. He was careful to use his arms as a ledge so I could balance my weight on him without putting pressure on the raw strip of exposed flesh on my arm.

I took a step. My hip felt stiff. My calf stung where I'd lost another patch of skin. My head felt like it was splitting.

I took another step. I didn't think anything was broken. My Latino saviors half-carried, half-walked me up the hill, cooing over me and clucking over my bike. One of them opened the tiny knapsack under my bike seat. He ran off with my keys in his hand, and it occurred to me for one wild moment that I was about to be the victim of a car hijacking as well as a bike wreck survivor. Then I felt ashamed of myself.

My new friends made me sit in their truck as they dabbed my arm with clean bandanas soaked in water. They emptied the entire contents of their thermal jugs onto me, a little at a time. They alternated between arguing among themselves and asking repeatedly, "Okay? Okay? Hospital?"

I shook my head no and saw my own car coming up and pulling in behind us. Bless that guy's heart, he'd run all the way down the road for my BMW. He threw open the passenger door and gestured to his friends.

The fellows loaded me into my car and gently set my mangled bike on the rack. Their workday was over and while they had been kind enough to help, now they were eager to go home.

I made it as far as the parking lot of the large office building at the intersection of the access road and 40. My head was spinning. I wasn't sure I could drive safely.

I started to whimper. I didn't want Detweiler to see me like this. Maggie wouldn't be sympathetic. Dodie and Horace had enough on their plate. Bama was running the store. I couldn't deal with telling Ben what I'd done — after I'd turned him down for a date. Sheila would throw a hizzy and I'd never make it out of the hospital. Or her home. Johnny worked at a construction site on the weekends until dark. He was making money to pay Mert back for his legal defense of years ago. I opened my cell phone and scanned the directory.

"Mert? I've had an accident. Could you come get me? Please?"

Mert was across the road with a friend shopping at the super Walmart. That store was bigger than the footprint of the Arch and needed its own Zip Code.

I don't know how she managed to get me out of my car, back into the passenger side and home, but she did. Her friend — whose name I never did catch — followed behind in Mert's truck as sort of a hillbilly caravan. Mert stopped at a Walgreens, ran in and bought a huge bag of Epsom Salts. She shoved a bottle of water my way. I swigged it gratefully. Once she got me home, she insisted on drawing a bath for me. I swear she poured in two cups of the salts. I'd been peeled like a banana. My exposed flesh stung like it was on fire. I held myself above the stew and went down slowly. Then I reasoned it would be best to get it over with, and I plunged in. My raw, denuded skin stung like a mother. I now have new sympathy for a pork chop being brined. Bruises were beginning to show up on my shins, my thighs, and my ribs. In addition, my one shin still bore the scab from a previous bad job of shaving. Plus there was that skinned heel. It smarted along with my new owwies.

Mert stood back and surveyed me. "Better cancel that nude photo shoot for *Playboy*. 'Less of course it's their annual S & M edition."

"Ha, ha, ha." I sank lower in the water. "They have an S & M edition?"

"Beats me." She snickered. "Get it? Beats me? I'll be back."

She returned with a glass of ice water in one hand and a cup of hot tea in the other. She handed over the cool drink and a small pill.

"What's this?"

"Illegal drugs. It's Bextra. They took it off the market, remember? It's dang good stuff and I only have ten of 'em left, but I'm willing to share. Where's the kid?"

I groaned. "At Jennifer Moore's house." I made a move to get out of the tub. Everything hurt. I moaned.

"You might want to give that Bextra a chance." Mert motioned me to sit while she perched on the edge of my tub and put the tea on my bathroom counter. She was wearing a T-shirt with the logo of Cheers, a south county bar. Five gold earrings marched up the outside of each of her ears, and I wondered idly if she was pierced in other parts of her body as well. I knew she had a butterfly tattoo on her right ankle and an angel on her lower back. She also had a degree in history from Southern Missouri. Go figger.

"Why the tea?"

"Don't know. They always drink it in those English novels when a body's had a shock. How come you didn't have on any panties?"

While I thought this a bit personal, heck, I was sitting here naked as a jay bird and sprouting black and blue marks before her very eyes. Didn't seem like the time to complain.

"You don't wear panties with bike shorts. They make the seams real flat. No chafing."

"Huh." Mert snorted as she scooped up my bike shorts, bra, and jersey and tossed them into my dirty clothes basket. "Never been chafed in my life. Won't happen if you wear your undies inside out. Put the smooth side next to your girlie bits. My momma taught me that."

You learn something every day.

She studied me critically. "You got that Angelina Jolie thing going on with your lips. Puffy? Whoowee. Forget collagen, girl. Of course, you're moving like the Tin Man before they oiled him, so I guess you won't be strolling down the catwalk any time soon. You still planning to go to that meeting with the Gartners?"

She gave me a long, appraising look, and said, "If you're wanting to do that, we better trade my truck for your car. A fancy-shmancy convertible won't fit in with that crowd." I allowed as how she was probably right. I rose out of the tub and the water that had turned cold. Mert said nothing as she watched me towel off.

InStyle Magazine doesn't offer fashion suggestions for white supremacist gatherings. I was on my own. I figured Walmart chic was my best bet. I positioned large gauze bandages over my oozing patches of flesh with Mert's help before I pulled on a long-sleeved button-up blouse and a below-the-knee jeans skirt. I slid my arms into a navy hoodie by Hanes. Even though the temperature outside was on the high side of seventy, a testimony to the Indian summer we were having this fall, I shivered and my teeth chattered. A delayed sense of shock was settling in, my bravado was quickly being replaced by nerves.

I had nearly died. If I'd continued my descent toward Highway 40, I might have wound up under the wheels of a motorist busy on his cell phone. I could have been hauled off in a body bag. I swallowed hard to keep from retching.

Mert watched me, her head tilted to one side the way a cat does when regarding a bird outside the window. I half-expected her to reach up and paw at me.

"You stop to consider that weren't no accident?"

I froze. Okay, yes, the thought had flitted through my addled brain. Primarily as I hobbled around the back of my car and got a gander at my bike. It was a crumpled mess. Bloody, too.

This was the second time a big black car had nearly done me in.

Coincidence?

I didn't think so.

THIRTY-THREE

I'd managed an invitation to the inner sanctum, sort of, of the local white supremists. All my journalism training told me this was a "once-in-a-lifetime" opportunity.

Once-in-a-lifetime because I might not live through it.

After I cleared Danny Gartner as a potential killer, I could tell Detweiler about Mrs. Toad's Wild Ride. If I told him now, he'd lock me up rather than let me go to the barbecue. If he locked me up, I'd never have the chance to study up close the people who hated my late husband and daughter for no reason at all.

There was no time for second thoughts. I had a murderer to catch. Or a party to attend. Whichever. I was a bit unsure. (Maybe that Bextra was kicking in.)

On my feet were simple, scuffed-up flats. My clothes were drab and modest. I flicked a layer of mascara on my lashes, rubbed in a dot of blush, and slicked lip gloss on my mouth. I looked like a woman who'd been beaten by her husband. Bet I'd fit right in.

Mert studied me critically. "I got half a mind to call that detective and tell him what you're up to."

"Don't you dare. Mert, do you think I'm chasing him? I mean, is it that obvious?"

"I think you're confused as a polecat raising a black and white kitten. I know this thing with Dodie's got you all het up." She sighed. "I know how much that Detweiler means to you. And I can see why. He's got a good heart. I'd like to slap him silly for leading you on, though. Hon, I know you two were made for each other. I can see it in your faces. But I also know you can't have him. It's hard to stay away from candy, especially when you're on a diet, in't it?"

I nodded. Time to change the channel. "I am worried about what Anya saw. Really, I am. I'm not just chasing after Detweiler. It's bad enough that goon who killed my husband is still out there. I can't live with the worry that another someone's out there. I can't stand the idea that two different people might want to hurt Anya."

Mert nodded. "I hear you. I know you think you're doing what's right. But I ain't sure why you're doing this. Sissy Gilchrist Gartner was low-count. Nobody's sad she's gone. Somehow she managed to take a good man with her when Coach Johnson died. If I knew what you were thinking, I'd feel a heap better about this whole thing. I mean, I think whoever done her in, well, he or she ain't after your kid. You know? Besides, it weren't only your daughter. There was two of them, right? So your kid has a one-in-two chance of being picked on."

Yeah, I'd thought of that. And I'd asked myself in those crucial moments as I waited for Mert to come rescue me, why did I care so much?

Well, actually I had several reasons. But I knew one of them would totally explain why I thought Sissy Gilchrist deserved justice.

I went over to the pile of papers I'd tucked in a folder. I withdrew Sissy Gilchrist's essay. Mert read it slowly. Out loud she read Sissy's explanation for wanting to work at CALA. Her voice cracked and grew husky as she spoke Sissy's words: "Honestly, I'd like to work here because of my son, Christopher. He's the most important person in the world to me, and I love him with all my heart. I want to be around to protect him. He's all I have in this world that is true and good."

Mert handed the papers back to me. "And now she's gone."

"Yes. Now she's gone."

"And you think Danny Gartner's behind this?"

"Detweiler and the Major Case Squad can't get good information about his whereabouts. You can see why: It's small-town cops protecting their own against big-city cops. If I can find out where Danny was, Detweiler can take it from there."

"But they say that coach shot himself. Don't you see? You're wasting your time, girl. He killed himself because he felt guilty."

I couldn't take having yet another friend angry with me. I told her about Detweiler's news. "Corey Johnson was shot with a revolver. It wasn't a suicide. The ballistics came back. Cops favor revolvers. They never jam."

"I know that about them guns."

"So who's the best suspect? Danny Gartner. Danny who might not have an alibi. Danny who hated blacks."

"How'd he get into the school?"

"I'm betting he was disguised as one of the workers laying bricks for the new cafeteria. We still don't have an accurate list of who attended the sports booster meeting. Lots of people roamed that hall, but the kids were accustomed to seeing the workers. You know how it is. You see people all the time. But if they are in service —"

"Like me when I'm cleaning."

I wasn't going to say that, but she was right. "Like you when you're cleaning. You become invisible. In fact, I remember reading about a hospital CEO. He paid all this money to trainers to teach teambuilding. To test the results, he dressed as a housekeeper for a week. Not one of his management team ever spoke to him."

Mert snorted. "I could've told him that'd happen."

"At CALA, the cops ignored Mr. Beacon. They didn't even interview him. Why? Because he's a worker bee. So, logically, anyone who was dressed to blend in, could have. Just like I'll do tonight. But the person with a motive — revenge — and a weapon — a revolver — would be Danny Gartner."

Mert's eyes swept over me. "You need a touch-up on that bruise on your face." She dabbed a bit of cover-up on my temple and tamped it with her ring finger. Now she studied me. "Something's missing. Here," she reached behind her head and unclasped her crucifix.

"I couldn't —"

She latched the clasp and adjusted the

gold cross with the dying Jesus right below my throat. With cool fingers, she reached inside my collar and pulled up the Star of David I wore under my clothes. Once she unclasped it, she folded the Jewish symbol into my hand. "You put this away. That cross has seen me through a lifetime of troubles. I'll send it with prayers for you."

"I appreciate the sentiment. But I'm not sure it's right. I mean, it's been a long time since I wore a cross. Since I promised George we'd have a Jewish household. I don't want to be disrespectful. I mean, it's one thing to borrow your truck and another to take something that's sacred to you."

"Ain't nothing as sacred as our love for our friends. Love thy neighbor as thyself, right? Besides, this here's my philosophy: Jews, Christians, Muslims. As long as we all believe in Jesus, what's the difference?"

My sentiments exactly.

THIRTY-FOUR

Mert's goodbye hug did wonders for my mood. At least I still had one friend left in this world. Okay, scratch that. Two friends. Gracie gave me a soulful look and a big slurpy kiss. But I suspect part of her affection was relief that Mr. Gibbes was leaving with Mert.

I let my dog out, gave her a treat, and checked MapQuest. My hand was on the front door knob when I heard a sharp rap.

"Ben! What a surprise."

I moved aside to let him in, but the motion caused a sharp gasp of pain.

Yes, well, he was more shocked than I. His jaw dropped. "What happened to you?"

"I had an accident on my bike." It was the truth, wasn't it?

"But good grief, Kiki, did you go to the hospital? Come on. I'll take you." He gingerly grabbed my elbow. "Are you okay?"

I pulled away. "I'm fine." I had to admit,

he was really upset. I thought back to all the weeks he'd been by my bed when I was recovering from my last entanglement with a criminal. He'd been the most patient of visitors. He showed up regularly with bouquets of mixed flowers and books on tape. He'd brought me fast food and Godiva chocolates.

And now I was lying to him.

"Believe me, Ben, I'm okay."

"If you're sure. I'd be happy to drive you. I only want a moment of your time," he said.

I didn't have much to spare. Still, I could read the misery on his face. "I've got a few minutes. But I'll have to hurry or I'll be late." I led him into my living room. I eased myself down onto a wingback chair that Sheila had brought over last week. It was covered in a heavy floral tapestry, far too fussy for my taste, but she'd pressed it on me. I had needed another chair. Right now I was happy this one was hard so I didn't sink down.

He stood, leaning against my front door, his hands deep in his jacket pockets. "This won't take long. Kiki, I've never been very clear with you about my intentions. I've sort of been spoiled. I don't know how to put this, but usually women chase me."

I laughed. "No doubt." He was a really,

really good-looking man.

"I'm more accustomed to avoiding them, than . . . being the person who gets . . ."

"Avoided? Is that what it seems like?" A part of me wanted to explain. Another part, thankfully, knew I needed to shut up.

"Yes. Maybe." His laugh was hoarse. "I'm not sure. So I thought maybe if I was up-front with you, you'd understand where I'm heading with all this."

Heading with all this? Huh? I was lost. Of course, I was also on Bextra and feeling fine.

"Look, I'm going about this all wrong," said Ben. "I'd intended to take you out and have a romantic dinner. Maybe ply you with nice wine. Kiki, I'd like to marry you."

Punch me in the gut. Oh, doggies, I had no idea this was coming. I must have looked horrified because the words gushed out of Ben.

"You don't have to tell me 'yes' or 'no.' I had to let you know I'm serious. I didn't want you to think I wasn't. We have plenty of time. And I'm not pushing you. I wanted you to know. Those are my plans. I'm crazy about you." He ran his hand through his hair and blushed.

I have to admit he was the most adorable man I'd ever seen. Suddenly, my hormones did a happy dance. In fact, they were doing a jig.

He kept on talking, almost as though he couldn't shut up. "Sounds pretty juvenile, I know. That part about being crazy about you. I mean, it's like something you'd say in high school. I guess. Kind of. But there it is." He spread his hands wide.

"Uh, wow." That was the best I could do. I had no idea what to say next. I'd never been proposed to. I mean, I thought it was a proposal. I wasn't exactly sure how to check. It was awful nice to be asked. Even at this late date. After learning I was pregnant, my late husband George had simply said, "I guess we'd better get married." That was it.

And now this. I was thirty-three years old. Nearly thirty-four. Widowed. Mother of a preteen daughter overwrought with emotions, occasional acne, and smart comments. Did this man have any idea what he was letting himself in for? Surely he jested. He must be drunk or dumb or . . . in love? With me?

It didn't seem possible.

Me?

He wanted to marry me?

Nobody married me unless they had to.

But here he was. And I wasn't pregnant.

354

"Like I said. I don't expect an answer. I mean, I don't have a ring for you. Not yet. I have some ideas. I think I know what you like. I figure I might have to speak to Anya, too. I know you're a package deal. That's fine. She's a sweet kid."

A sweet kid? Was he high? She was nearly as tall as I, and on the brink of young womanhood.

But he kept on going, "So, maybe I should check with Anya? And we could let her be involved. I mean, whatever you think. And I'm willing to wait. I'm not saying you have to make a decision right away. Or even soon. Not soon. Not soon at all." The poor man was stammering.

I simply sat there on the wingback chair like one of those gaudy yard gnomes. I was flash-frozen with shock. I could have been wearing one of those pointy red hats. I mean, after this, nothing would shock me ever again.

"I know you have to take off. You have a previous engagement."

How incredibly phony that sounded when he said it. Had it sounded that fake when I'd used it on him? I groaned.

Ben said, "If I could talk you out of where you're going," and suddenly he noticed my clothes. He squinted. "New look for you, right? Are you thinking of becoming an Orthodox Jew? Like trying it on? Converting to Reform is a stroll through the temple compared to that. I mean keeping kosher is practically a full time job. But if that's what you want, we can talk about it."

His eyes were big as Hanukkah gold coins as he mumbled, "I guess we need to find a rabbi to perform the conversion. This is going to be really intense."

For a really smart man, it was a pretty weird thing to say. I could barely manage one set of dishes let alone two. The thought of learning how to keep kosher completely boggled my mind.

But hey, it had been that kind of day.

THIRTY-FIVE

Mert's candy-apple-red Chevy S10 pickup looked right at home as I pulled up next to an older and bigger version of the same vehicle with a gun rack mounted across the back window. If the shifter had been on the floor instead of the column, I would have stayed stuck in drive. Every part of my body was stiffening up. I climbed out as slowly as an octogenarian walks on glare ice. The Bextra had kept the pain at bay, but my muscles were crying foul, tightening up and making moving difficult.

I shoved my hands deep into the pockets of my hoodie to keep myself from shaking. I found a piece of gum in the bottom of my purse and stuck it in my mouth. Chewing like an antsy teenager seemed preferable to hearing my teeth chatter. Danger, Will Robinson. It was all around me. I had to get this wrapped up, and soon.

Assuming I made it back alive.

Gartner's party was up in Roma, the methane capital of the world, which was nearer to Mark Twain's fabled home, Hannibal, than to St. Louis. One thing you gotta give Roma: lots of kids there sign up for chemistry. The local fire department spends most of their time hosing down idiots whose makeshift labs cause their double-wides to blow up. And forget trying to buy Sudafed if you've got a cold. A new law in Missouri made that illegal without signing in with your pharmacist after we'd achieved the dubious honor of being number one in the nation for methamphetamine production.

I could tell I was straying from civilization as we know it by the billboards. On one a baby stared at me in surprise as he floated over the slogan: Is it yours? Call 1-800-DNA-SURE. Another promised dentures the same day for $99. A place called Chubby's advertised BIG burgers.

The music drifted over a well-lit house backing up to a field of corn stubble as I picked my way through the tire ruts in what was the Gartner family's side yard.

A growling sound and the rattling of cyclone fencing startled me. I froze, peered around another pickup truck and saw two pit bulls hurling themselves at a six-foot-high silver screen around a concrete run.

The broad chests on the dogs rippled with muscles. Their tiny pig eyes gleamed at me malevolently. I decided on an alternate route around and behind more parked trucks. The best part of coming late to the Gartner's Sunday night get-together was that with any luck no one could block my way out.

My pupils adjusted to the dark, and I found myself in the midst of what seemed like any other friendly gathering. Three smiling women in aprons removed burgers and hotdogs from open kettle drums filled with burning coals. Kids and adults lined up like ants feeding on bread crumbs. Picnic tables covered with oilcloth bent under the weight of dishes of potato salad, brownies, Jell-O molds, baked beans, three bean salad, sliced tomatoes, pasta salad, seven-layer salad, and sheet cakes. My mouth was watering when an electronic tap-tap-tap drew my attention to a raised platform with a mike on a stand. Twin girls with full, juvenile faces and dressed in blue jeans and ruffled floral blouses were standing side by side, each holding a mike and staring out onto the crowd. Their hair skinned back, pulled into fat Heidi-type braids.

A man stepped out of the shadows. His burr haircut thinned as it moved away from his forehead. He waved toward the waiting pair. "These here girls don't need no introduction. They've come all the way from a recording studio in Wisconsin. What we need is to get their message into every schoolyard in the USA. If there ever was a reason to keep them black people and Jews from raping our women folk, it's standing here afore you. Welcome Tammy and Pammy!"

Only he didn't call them "black people." He used the n-word.

Raping their womenfolk? I did a slow panorama view of my surroundings. I stood in the midst of women who'd been rode hard and put away wet. A second glance told me that these ladies fell into two camps — conservatively dressed like me and come-on queens wearing too-short shorts and too-low tops that displayed grubby-looking bras. Most of the flashy females sported the kind of tattoos done at home with an ink pen and a sewing needle. For the life of me, I couldn't imagine any man I'd ever met wanting to exchange body fluids with one of these, um, ladies.

But then, I could be wrong.

The men were all buff and manly men with the exception of the half of the group I thought of as Dunlaps, their bellies done

360

lapped over their belts. It was a veritable butt-crack love-in with jeans hanging off hairy, pale cheeks. Somehow most of those fellows had managed to waylay the laws of gravity — at least temporarily.

The girls counted out loud and started, their young voices sweet and pure. The vocals rose and mingled with moths dancing in the illumination of the high-wattage security lights. I noticed the fencing behind the girls was rimmed with barbed wire.

On a hunch, I threaded my way through the crowd, pausing along my way, closing in on the guy who'd done the announcing. A word or two of the girls' song broke my concentration. As best I could figure, the tune was a plea that "Daddy keep me safe and Daddy keep me pure" from, well, I can't even repeat the rest.

"Mr. Gartner?" I flashed my press pass. "A real honor to meet you, sir." My guts turned to liquid. Suddenly, the import of my visit hit me squarely. I was alone, in the dark, among people who'd turn very ugly if they knew my purpose.

"I'm so nervous," I confessed to him, ducking and blinking. "I've never interviewed anyone as powerful as you before."

That much at least was true. I flashed Gartner senior my most winsome smile and quickly slipped my press pass into my skirt pocket. Four or five brawny men encircled me. A pair of hands yanked at my notebook. Fortunately, I'd locked my purse and my current driver's license in the truck's glove compartment or I'd have been roasted right along with the other weenies.

"It's okay. I tole her to come. She's giving me an interview." Gartner gestured over the crowd and emitted an earpiercing whistle. He leaned close to my ear. A fetid puff of beer and garlic engulfed me and I tried not to wince as I followed the direction of his pointed finger. "That's my boy, Danny."

A hand gripped my shoulder. It was a squeeze calculated to hurt a little, but with my recent bike wreck, it caused a tidal wave of pain to rip through my upper arm. I gulped and tried not to let my discomfort show. A bodyguard steered me onto a patio, up a short flight of concrete stairs, and into a spotless kitchen, dispatching me inside with a rough shove. Danny came in and slammed the door behind him. "So you're the media? Little squirt of a thing, ain't you? Let me get you a beer," said the newcomer as he rubbed his gut. "You know, one of my friends told me that if my belly was on a woman, she'd be pregnant. I told him it was, and she is!"

How quaint.

I managed what I hoped looked like a shy smile. Danny Gartner dipped into a cooler and cracked a Bud and shoved it my way. His father fished one out for himself. I raised the can and saluted two men each a foot taller and a hundred pounds heavier than I. I wasn't sure about mixing beer and Bextra, but I figured it was better to take my chances with the interaction between pharmaceuticals and alcohol, than between fists and my face. I lifted my can right along as they toasted "Love Our Race" and took a long drink. I nodded and smiled what I hoped was a simpleton's grin. The fizzy bubbles hit me hard. And I needed it.

I was surrounded by the sort of animals who thought my daughter had no right to live.

Thirty-Six

"Ben, I have a great news tip for you." Both hands on the clock in Mert's truck pointed to twelve. Maybe midnight was late to be calling.

He sounded a bit sleepy when he answered the phone, but when I repeated the words "Crusaders for Racial Purity," he was all ears.

"This coming Monday the Crusaders plan to hand out free CDs to kids in the Roma Middle School. A sympathetic local businessman who's a school board member got permission. The CDs are packaged to look like harmless music, like what kids would listen to on the radio, but the songs are just hateful. Plus, they encourage kids to become warriors and fight for white supremacy. These CDs are designed to cause all sorts of problems."

Ben sputtered, "You have to be kidding."

"Nope. This has worked well in other

towns. They've spent a lot of money getting these CDs produced and packaged, hoping to fly under the radar."

"I'll get one of our reporters right on this. We've got the perfect person for the job. She'll be at the school first thing with a CD player and a photographer. The minute that first disk is pressed into a kid's hand, we'll post the news on our website. Then we'll do an in-depth follow-up for our weekly addition. I'll even call one of the local television affiliates to cover it. In fact, I'll round up a lawyer I know. He'll slap them with a hate-crimes suit so quickly their heads will spin."

I smiled with relief. The publicity would put a quick halt to the Crusaders for Racial Purity's planned infiltration of the Roma schools with ugly messages. It would also expose their accomplices, like the sympathetic school board member, to uncomfortable public scrutiny.

"Kiki, how do you know all this?"

"That prior engagement? I was at a barbecue in Roma with the local leader of the Crusaders for Racial Purity."

"You were where?"

I repeated myself.

Finally, I asked, "You there? Hello?"

"Kiki, you sure know how to live life on the edge. I mean, I thought you were courageous, but this . . . this borders on . . ."

"Stupid?"

"Reckless. This isn't the sort of thing a housewife should stick her nose into."

Housewife? I didn't remember exchanging vows with a building.

"You're the person who said he admired me because I confronted my husband's killer. And when I tracked down that person who caused the death of a woman at our crop!"

Ben sighed. "That was different. You were thrust into those circumstances. You can't go chasing trouble. I can't have my future wife involved in dangerous pastimes."

"But you are sending out a female reporter!"

"She has a degree in journalism."

Now I really saw red. I'd been a journalism student when I'd gotten pregnant and had to quit school. I sputtered and drove with one hand, weaving around on the highway. My lack of education was yet another sore spot on my bruised and battered body, and he'd landed on it with both feet.

"Kiki? Where are you?"

"On the road. About fifty miles outside of St. Louis. In Mert's truck."

"You need to get home! You can't be out

at all hours of the night! And putting yourself in situations like this! How can I protect you?"

"I don't need protecting!" I yelled. "I'm not a child. I'm an adult!"

"Then act like one! Think about the consequences of your actions!"

I screamed into the phone, "You're not the boss of me!" and then I hung up on him. I drove for forty more minutes spewing and stewing my way along life's highway.

There goes the shortest engagement in the world, I thought. Shoot, I didn't even get to toss the ring in his face. I ground my teeth and screamed some more as I drove along.

I did, however, have one more phone call to make. I dialed Detweiler. I'm not even sure what I said to him.

"I'll be right there," he promised.

I pulled into my driveway.

I waited for him. I must have put my head on my kitchen table and dozed off, because next thing I knew, I awakened to him banging on my back door. I ushered him in and told him where I'd been. A glance at the clock told me he must have set a new land speed record getting to my house.

Detweiler sank down onto a kitchen chair and blinked at me with bloodshot eyes the size of Frisbees. Gracie moaned and set her big head down on his lap. His hand idly worked the tender spot behind her ears.

"You do realize a woman from Oklahoma was shot in Louisiana because she asked to leave an Aryan initiation ceremony. Right? Her only crime was wanting to go home. She was an innocent guest."

The words "unlike YOU" hung in the air. I didn't respond.

He shook his head. "I couldn't have heard you right. You couldn't have said you attended a KKK gathering. Tell me you didn't."

"I didn't." I took a deep breath.

"Okay. No KKK rally. Good."

"Huh uh. It was a meeting of the Crusaders for Racial Purity."

"Good Lord! Are you all right? Did anyone follow you home?"

I explained the Gartners thought I worked for a campus newspaper. My mouth tasted like I'd licked the floormats of Mert's truck. I pushed back my chair to start a pot of coffee. The Bextra and beer were wearing off. I winced in pain as I stood.

"Did they hurt you?" He grabbed my arm. I yelped because he'd pressed on a bruise. He pulled back to stare at me, looking me over, his face a swarm of conflicting emotions. I rubbed my upper arm tentatively.

"Did they hurt you?" His voice was louder and angrier.

"I got run off the road by a car this afternoon."

"Who did that to you? Did you get a license plate? Why didn't you call me?"

"There wasn't time. I soaked in a tub, but I needed to get going. Douglas Gartner was expecting me." For emphasis I rolled back my sleeves and pulled up the jeans skirt to show off my bruises. It was a bad move. They'd colored up in the intervening hours, and I looked like I'd been dumped in a tie-dye vat and left to soak too long.

"That close call in Ladue . . ." his voice trailed off. "Someone is trying to kill you!"

"I didn't see the plates. On either car. This time I was busy trying not to roll down the access road and onto Highway 40. Besides I had to get over to Roma. And I wasn't in any real danger at the meeting. Hey, it was pretty much like any other barbecue."

"What if someone you knew had been there?"

I shrugged. "Didn't think about that."

He took the French press from me and started measuring coffee. Gracie leaned against him, her eyes following his every move. Once he had the hot water in the pot, he squatted down and put his arms around her. He hugged my big dog so tightly she made a little "oof" sound.

Then I realized. He'd lost one person he cared about only a few days ago. Now he was thinking about what might have happened to me. I went over and tapped him on the shoulder. "Go sit down," I said. I turned on the oven and popped open a Pillsbury tube of cinnamon rolls. When the timer went off, I was pretty well finished explaining how Danny Gartner had admitted poisoning his son's mind against minorities.

"The rationale behind the Crusaders for Racial Purity is the natural physical superiority of the non-Jewish white race. If you look up their teachings, you'll see that abortion is considered a positive alternative to having a mixed-race child. Everything in Danny Gartner's upbringing led up to his warning his son about how dangerous blacks are. Suffice it to say, Danny made Christopher scared of blacks and . . ."

"Other minorities," volunteered Detweiler to spare me.

"Gays, too. On purpose. Danny sees this as building the next generation of white supremacists, but it was also a way to get back at his wife for leaving him."

"Tough guy. Roughing up blacks and

migrants. You'd think he'd go after meth labs. They ought to strip him of his badge."

"Exactly what the world needs, another jerk posing as a cop. Which is kind of amusing, considering that George Lincoln Rockwell specifically praised police in one of his speeches."

"Come again?"

"Never mind." I really didn't feel like going into the research I'd done. Downloading it made me nauseated. Cooties, it's only cooties, I told myself as I looked up one anti-Semitic, venom-spewing site after another. This is worth it, I reminded myself, if it brings one of these bad boys wearing the Black Sun, another name for the Nazi swastika, to justice. When this was over, I planned to pay a computer expert to make sure I hadn't picked up any cookies in my cyber travels. I also needed to take my bike in for repairs. Kiss that six grand goodbye, Kiki. Oh, well. As far as I was concerned, my foray into white supremacy was done and done.

"Did you see anything we can haul Gartner junior in for? Man, would I love to put him behind bars."

I had anticipated this. I'd managed to listen very carefully as different groups of people chatted. I blended in by helping clean up the Gartner's kitchen, which was a hub of activity. "They did say they were planning a big rally in Bloomington. The birthplace of George Lincoln Rockwell is now part of the campus of a hospital there. Every year a few of the faithful gather and put down a wreath. Typically the floral tribute disappears minutes after the crowd disperses. Understandably, the city and the hospital don't want that sort of attention. This year the boys are planning to hang around all day to babysit the wreath. That could get ugly."

"Rockwell? Isn't he a painter? *The Saturday Evening Post*?" Detweiler scratched his head.

"That's the uncle, Norman Rockwell. This Rockwell was the founder of the American Nazi Party. He's still a central figure in white supremacy movements."

"Maybe we can run him in."

"He's dead. He was assassinated years ago."

"Promise you won't ever contact these yahoos again. Please?" It was the pleading tone of his request that twisted my gut. That and the expression of concern in his face.

"Don't worry. I have no desire to ever see any of them again. Ever. It was . . . creepy."

"And if one of them calls you, you let me

know pronto. Meanwhile, I'll double-check Danny's and his father's alibis."

That was easy. I promised. We both had a couple of rolls and a cup of coffee.

The sky was lightening up when he stood to go. "We can take it from here. Boy, can you imagine what old Danny thought when his wife took up with a black guy?"

I didn't want to think about it. It was too ugly.

THIRTY-SEVEN

My come-uppance for cheating death and partying with white supremacists came a few hours later when my alarm went off on Monday morning. I was so sore from my biking accident that I couldn't lift my legs without pain. The muscles in my shoulder and upper back felt frozen, and I could barely turn my head. Mert let herself in the back door. She'd stopped by to trade my BMW for her pickup truck.

"You look like crap," she said conversationally.

"Thanks," I answered. "Got any drugs?"

She palmed me a Bextra. We were sitting at my kitchen table sipping coffee when my cell phone rang. I got up slowly and tripped over Gracie's tail. She gave me an indignant look, but didn't move.

"You —" and then the curses started. It was Danny Gartner screaming in my ear. "I had a friend in the campus police check you out. I've a half a mind to drive on up there to La-Jew and come teach you —" I stood stunned, unable to move. He was hurling insults and threats to my life into the phone.

Mert pushed past me and snatched the phone out of my hands, "Danny Gartner? That you? What kind of a Christian are you? Shame on you! Shame! This is Mert. You ever threaten my friend again and I'll come ram my Tony Lama's so far up your butt you'll have to pick your eyeballs up off the ground. You hear me? Now you back off 'fore I call your mama on you. This here lady's a Christian and whiter'n your undies on wash day."

Then she hung up on him.

I was speechless.

"You mean you know him? I mean, really know him?"

"Used to babysit the ugly snot. I'm only a couple years older'n him, but still. His mama didn't trust him to stay home alone. Not a lick of common sense. Heck, his stupid pit bulls got more brains than he does, and they're dumber than a box full of night crawlers."

Mert gave me a long appraising look. "You okay? Still sore from your biking accident? I'll leave you another couple of Bextras. If you're worried about Danny, don't be. I got me a squirrel gun. You can borrow it. Durn squirrels kept chewing through the electric lines to my hot tub."

"And you take a gun to them? Isn't that a tad drastic?"

"First I tried trapping 'em."

"And?"

"All I caught was two bunny rabbits and the neighbor's cat. She was mighty huffy about it."

" 'She' being the cat or the neighbor?"

"Both of 'em. That's when I bought me a squirrel gun. I'll show you how to use it. I wouldn't recommend shooting old Danny, but you can put a scare into him."

"Thanks, but I think I'll just call Detweiler instead."

"I was afraid you'd say that."

THIRTY-EIGHT

Detweiler knocked on my door minutes after Mert left. I swear he'd aged ten years over the past few hours. Air carriers would have charged him the extra baggage fee for the circles under his eyes. He harrumphed as he hit my kitchen chair with his entire weight. One fist held up his sagging head. "Did you save the message?" the detective asked when I called him about Danny Gartner's threats.

I watched my hand shake as I poured him a cup of coffee and passed the non-fat milk carton. I carefully placed the sugar bowl and a spoon at his side, taking care not to let our skin touch. "No."

"I suppose lecturing you about how dangerous this was would be a waste of breath."

"Probably. I'm not your problem, anyway." Suddenly I felt unaccountably ticked off — and irritable. I was tired of the men in my life giving me grief. Every inch of my body ached from my bike crash, and my head throbbed from the ill-considered combination of Bextra and beer. The words slipped out before I could think about them: "I'm engaged."

"In what?"

"The usual."

"Snooping?"

"No . . . engaged to be married."

"With someone from the rally?"

"Of course not!"

"Or Johnny?"

"No. It's Ben Novak, his family owns *The Muddy Waters Review.* The alternative newspaper."

"This happened last night?" His voice rasped. Gracie came over, licked his hand and made a yodeling noise. I think she was saying in Danish, "Don't worry. I still love you."

"Yep." I preened with pleasure. "He told me he wants to get married."

Detweiler looked miserable.

I knew I had upset him. But didn't he deserve it? I mean, if he didn't care about me — at all — he wouldn't care about me being engaged, right?

I liked knowing he was shocked. I liked the idea he was suffering over me. Hadn't I suffered because of him? Hadn't I faced humiliation when I met Brenda, his wife? Hadn't I gone through agony when I faced Sheila, Mert, and Dodie and they knew he'd been married before I did? Hadn't I been in pain when I told Anya about his status? And all those sleepless nights since? Call me mean. Call me a horrible person, but wasn't I entitled to a little revenge?

"You managed to crash your bike, attend a Crusaders for Racial Purity rally, suss out their upcoming promotions, and get engaged all in one night?" He scrubbed his face with his hand. "I'm having trouble keeping track here. Now you're telling me you're getting married? Married?" His voice rose an octave.

I reached in my pocket and showed him a Bextra. "I'm also taking drugs."

"oh." It was a very lower-case sort of sound. His hand stroked Gracie absent-mindedly. He stared down at my floor. Then, "Is Anya okay? Where is she?"

That's when I fell totally, irrevocably, in love with the man.

Forget three little words. He'd used six and I was a total goner over Chad Detweiler. Whatever happened next in my life, I'd have to cope with the fact I loved him. Maybe we'd never get together. Maybe I was destined to marry someone else, someone I could love but not be "in love" with. But whatever the future held, he'd found a place in my heart forever because even when I'd rejected him, he still worried about my daughter.

"This is as good a time as any to explain my behavior to you." He sat back, rubbed his face hard enough to leave red streaks. "I never meant to mislead you. I wasn't trying to trick you. Shortly before your husband died, Brenda and I had separated. She moved out. I couldn't — I can't and I won't — tell you the particulars. That's between her and me."

"You never told me your situation."

"I meant to. I couldn't find the right words. I know guys pull that 'my wife doesn't understand me' crap, and I prided myself on not being like that."

I nodded.

"The longer I went, the more difficult it became to find the right words. The day before that Opera Theatre Event, she called. She wanted to move back home. To try again." He shrugged. "I owe her that." He cleared his throat. He straightened as though he was remembering himself, himself and a vow he'd made. "It would be disloyal and disrespectful to talk about what's been happening between Brenda and me."

"oh." My turn to use the lower case.

"She's a good person, Kiki. Honest. You'd like her." He paused. "Well, maybe you would."

That explained his visits. His distance and his closeness all in one. He hadn't moved forward. He'd treated me as more than a friend but never made a move — except that one frustrated kiss. The one that kept me hoping and hanging on.

"I told myself I was keeping an eye on you and Anya. That's true, you know. I still worry about your husband's killer. I guess I lied to myself. I guess I lied to you by my actions. You know, I'm kind of a 'by the rules' type of guy. Which is why you fascinate the heck out of me. You worry about the rules. Worry a lot. But you never let them get in the way of doing what you think is right. I let myself down by not being up-front with you. I kept practicing what to say, but I couldn't make it come out right. Every time I tried, I felt like I either wasn't being fair to you, or fair to Brenda. And I admit, I had my own selfish interests at heart."

I couldn't take it any more. "I was engaged, and now I'm disengaged."

"You can do that? Get engaged and disengaged that fast? And this all happened last night? Before or after you went to Roma?"

"Before and after."

"Wow. You sure had a busy schedule."

"I got disengaged this morning on my way back home. I phoned him. He told me I was stupid for going to Roma. Tried to boss me around."

"Obviously, he doesn't know you every well."

I shrugged. "He was just being protective, but I got mad at him."

"I can't fault him for worrying about you. I do, too. And I should have guessed someone would come along. You're young and beautiful and talented and wonderful." Detweiler nodded slowly. "I guess this had to happen. I couldn't expect . . . I mean . . . why would you wait . . ."

"Are you asking me to wait?" The kitchen clock ticked, ticked, ticked as I held my breath.

"I owe it to my wife to try . . ." And he stopped.

He had offered me the tiniest sliver, the smallest crescent, the faintest glimmer of hope.

It was nearly eleven when Gracie and I

walked through the back door of Time in a Bottle. Immediately, the hairs stood up on my arms. Horace stood in the doorway of Dodie's office. The expression on his face was of a man lost. The slump of his shoulders and the vacancy sign in his eyes told me more than I wanted to know. I bit my lower lip to keep from bursting into tears. "How is she?"

"Ach! My poor darling girl. She is so brave. I sat beside her this morning as they pushed those poisons into her system. And you know, she never cried. Never complained. Not once. She held my hand to comfort me! What a woman!" He gave me a trembling smile. "They say this is cumulative. At first, not so bad. Later, much more taxing. Still, she is in good spirits and that is something good, eh? Better than spitting in your face."

He drew himself up to his full height of nearly five feet so we were practically eye-to-eye. "We must talk. You come to her office, okay? Get yourself whatever you need first."

How like Horace to think of me and my needs before blurting out that the store would have to close and my job was kaput.

His face softened as his gaze dropped to the furry figure at my side. "I forgot." Stepping closer, he cuffed Gracie around the ears. "My darling girl says to give you a big smooch. Miss Gracie, you are a blessing. You make my wife so very happy."

My dog thumped her tail at him. I think Gracie knew exactly what Horace was saying. I settled into one of the office chairs across from the desk. Horace said, "Let's begin with the confidential album. It is done, right?"

I nodded.

"Good! The owner asks that you bring it and the briefcase to Café Napoli in Clayton at noon today."

He must have read the concern on my face. "Don't worry about covering the store. Our daughter Rebekkah will be here soon. She's at home with her mother now."

"Rebekkah? But isn't she at college?"

"She wanted to see for herself that her *em* was all right."

I nodded. He'd slipped into calling Dodie "em" which is Hebrew for "mother." In the Hebrew language "mother" and "father" are descriptive of action, with "em" meaning "one who binds the family together." "Father" is "av" or "one who gives the family strength." I settled back in the chair and steeled myself for being let go. A sharp rap on the doorsill startled me. Bama stuck her head in. "May I join you?"

Taking the chair next to mine, my co-worker sat stiffly. Although we were close in the small confines of the office, neither of us brushed against the other. It was as if we were holding onto our physical selves for dear life. Maybe, in a way, we were. I had no idea what this job meant to Bama, if indeed it meant anything at all. But it meant all the world to me. I'd never been central to any enterprise. Never felt I was special. Never learned as much, given as much, been depended upon like I was here. I tried not to get all weepy, but I knew Horace was going to tell us all this had come to an end.

Time in a Bottle would close its doors.

THIRTY-NINE

But Horace surprised me. The last thing he wanted was for Time in a Bottle to go out of business. "My darling would have nothing to live for. Except our daughter, of course, and me. But she needs this. I talked with the doctors. She can come in and sit. Maybe not do so much."

There was one caveat: Bama and I would need to buy in.

"I hope you will not think I am being too concerned with numbers," began our boss's husband. "But I have noticed this: When people have a stake in a business, they work harder. My darling girl says no one could work so hard as you two. Still if you buy in, you would see yourselves differently. As owners, not just employees. I think this is good, right?"

He didn't mention they needed the money. Bama and I knew he'd been out of work. Their resources were tapped out until his former employers quit appealing the court-ordered settlement.

"We could do it," I told Bama after he left, and I'd fielded a call from Patricia Bigler offering to take both our daughters to their golf match. "I know we could."

She bobbed her head in agreement. Her finger ran along the printed-out schedule we'd been studying. "We'd need two part-timers. My sister Katie could use the work. Especially with the holidays coming up." She shifted her weight. "Would you mind if her kids played in the backroom?"

"You're asking me? The person who babysits dogs?"

She snickered. "Well, yeah. I have to ask you. Horace said we needed to work this out with each other and come back with a proposal. I figure we need to talk over everything if we're going to be successful. That includes who does what. Who works when. Who's in charge of ordering. Who does the books. And the schedule. Who talks to vendors. Who does classes. Who writes the paychecks. While we're on the subject, you got any money?"

"I'm supposed to get some from Dimont Development. Sort of a payment on what I'm owed." I turned my hands out. "How much you suppose we're looking at?"

Her head cocked, she said, "If my math is right, each of us need to put in five grand."

"You got that?"

"I can raise maybe four. That's it. But Katie might help me."

"With the holidays coming up, we'll have monster hours. You should make part of that investment back. And there's that class we discussed."

"I know. If Katie can spare it, she will. I think we can do it. We're practically running the place now. Besides, how often do you get the chance to be an owner? Not to mention, I'd do it for Dodie. She's the best boss I've ever had."

The only one I'd had. But I didn't go there.

Rebekkah popped in at half past eleven. She was a shrinky-dink version of her mom, but a lot less hairy. Also, Rebekkah used makeup to best advantage. While she wasn't what you'd call typically pretty, she was an attractive young woman who exuded a sort of strength and self-confidence. She didn't follow anyone else's fashion drummer, either. She paired an oversized plaid flannel shirt with a slouchy pair of jeans. The rolled up cuffs of her sleeves and pants added a jaunty, sporty look.

"What's up? Tell me what I need to do."

"How's your mom?" Bama and I said in unison.

Rebekkah grinned. "Better'n my dad. Whew, he's like, totally, so upset. She keeps telling him to chill."

I knew Café Napoli well. George and I often met at the tiny restaurant on a corner in bustling downtown Clayton, a St. Louis suburb. He could walk there from his office at Dimont, and I could drive there from our big house in Ladue in minutes. We loved the menu and the ambience. The people-watching couldn't be beat. George and I made a habit of lunching to discuss Anya's progress, our upcoming plans, and whatever was on our minds.

With a big lump in my throat, I found a spot a few blocks down from the restaurant and walked past where the Library Ltd., once one of the best independent bookstores in town, used to be. That had been a special treat — after meeting with George, I'd walk over and browse the stacks, often finding a new favorite author. Today, I passed the new occupant of that space and moved briskly. I pushed away the fond memories. I didn't want to keep my confidential scrapbook client waiting.

I wasn't totally surprised to see Mahreeya

waving to me as she talked loudly into her cell phone.

I did fight the urge to bolt.

I had wondered if she was my "confidential" client. Yuck. A series of images created a collage in my brain. I eventually recognized a few of the outfits photographed from her closet. I recalled vacations she'd bragged about. There was that big diamond and emerald pin she wore.

Funny, the more Mahreeya tried to push her success on people, the more we resisted. The louder and more obvious she became, the more we ignored her. The harder she tried, the more she failed. There was a lesson in there, somewhere. I remembered George saying, "In America, sex is like money. Those who really have it don't need to talk about it."

I guess Mahreeya's grasp was precarious.

I steeled myself, willed myself not to recoil, and took a seat at her table. She continued talking loudly, ignoring the anguish in the eyes of her fellow patrons. "Yes, darling, tell the ambassador we have room for his friend the CEO. And the cabinet member. Is that right? Oh, we'd be delighted!"

Finally, she clapped the phone shut and turned a triumphant smile on me. "Everything is going so well for this party launching my husband's campaign. He's planning to run for senator next year."

"Guess he's got a surprise coming."

She pointed at the briefcase. "My timing is impeccable."

"You sure you're going through with this?"

She snorted. "He'll have a choice. Divorce and a fat settlement plus the embarrassment of his affairs being made very, very public, or an alternative proposal."

I didn't ask. I figured she'd tell me. And she did.

"He can choose to make a significant monthly deposit in my personal bank account. That's his option."

"So this wasn't really about maintaining your lifestyle."

"Of course it is! And he is — and has been — cheating on me. Unlike you, I don't intend to sit by idly while he messes around."

"Like he did with Sissy."

She lifted a corner of her mouth in what could best be called a sneer. "Like he did with Sissy."

Mahreeya interrupted the waiter taking lunch orders from the table next to us. "Bring me a glass of Norton. She'll have the same." Turning to me, she said, "It's the only Missouri grape that rivals imported wines. It's the best, you know. Otherwise, I wouldn't drink it."

I said nothing. Mahreeya thoroughly enjoyed being top dog — especially when sitting across from a mutt ready to roll over and play dead.

Still, I didn't much care for exposing my jugular and lying there like roadkill.

"What are you eating?" She pressed on. Since I hadn't opened the menu, I demurred.

She pushed me. "Hurry up. I have another appointment. You're buying. Or the store is. Whichever."

How incredibly gracious!

Before the waiter returned, Mahreeya reached toward me. "The briefcase please."

I handed it over.

She didn't even open it to look. All those hours, all that work, and she didn't even care.

I pinched my thigh to hold back my emotions. That was dumb. Now I had yet another bruise to add to my collection. I swallowed the entire glass of wine in one gulp. The waiter poured another.

"Did you kill Sissy?" I blurted.

She threw back her head and laughed. "I wouldn't waste the effort. I don't care where my husband's playing around, or with whom, as long as I get to be the wife."

I didn't respond. I simply stared at her. We knew what she was. An ugly word formed in the space between us. We both could see it. We could read it the way we knew the green sky that preceded a tornado. It was a Midwestern thing. You had to live here to understand.

She broke the stare first. In a whisper devoid of bravado she said, "You know how it is, Kiki. Of all people, you have to know. He's good with the kids. And if he's happy getting it somewhere else, what can I do? I still love him. At least now I'll have security."

She sniffed. "After all, he and I are both Old St. Louis."

"Oh, really? Mah-ree-ya?" and I strung out the name syllable by syllable. I exploded. "Old St. Louis, Old St. Louis. I am sick to death of that term. What exactly does it mean? Hmm? Didn't exactly come over with the pilgrims, did you and your ilk? You're all just a bunch of second-generation fur trappers and beer brewers. And your manners? Huh. You wouldn't pass for old money in any other part of the country."

I was on a tear. "You ask me to come here so you can lord your money over me? And abuse me? You make a rude and condescending remark about the stupid wine! Now you play the better breeding trump card? Hey, I don't know what passes for manners in your neck of the woods, but as my nana would say, this dog won't hunt. Nice people, well-bred people don't trumpet their social life on the cell phone for everyone to hear. They don't brag. They don't intimidate people. They are courteous to those who are in service positions. When they ask people to join them for lunch, they treat them as guests and pick up the tab!"

I realized at the end of my tirade that I'd raised my voice and attracted several onlookers.

"So ix-nay with the Old St. Louis baloney. Indians were here before you. They had a cultured and advanced civilization. But you and your kind pushed them out. They, not you and your hillbilly fur-trapping, beer-guzzling ancestors, are Old St. Louis. Not you."

Two or three other tables were staring at me with undisguised interest.

Then they broke into applause.

I decided not to acknowledge their approbation. I downed the rest of my wine fully aware that I'd probably ruined Dodie's business — the one I had hoped to buy into just this morning! Gosh, I was setting new records for ruining my life! I'd been engaged and unengaged, a business owner and a non-owner, an employee and probably fired, all in the space of less than twenty-four hours.

Of course the Crusaders for Racial Purity were busy printing up WANTED posters with my photo on them.

I could imagine my horoscope: Your stars and planets will careen into the sun and explode. Welcome to the black hole. That noise you hear is your life sucking.

Without looking up, I focused my eyes on the blank tablecloth in front of me. I braced myself for what would come next. I fully expected Mahreeya to punish me. To bring the full weight of her social standing and her checkbook down hard on my shoulders. I'd spoken out of turn to a customer. To another mom. I was in for it now.

And I'd asked for it.

FORTY

Mahreeya picked up her glass, swirled the dregs of her wine, and downed it. "I guess I deserved that, huh? Sorry. I get that way sometimes. I guess you noticed." A wry half-smile played around her lips. "My husband tells me I'm his biggest asset and his worst problem."

Smart man. Even if he was a cheat.

"My dreams are coming true, Kiki. I always wanted to be somebody. You don't know what it's like to be a wallflower growing up, and to work so hard, and well, I guess since you know what I went through to look like this. A lot of surgery. A lot of pain. And at a very young age. Then there were the revisions as cosmetic surgery advanced. They make it seem so fun on *Nip/Tuck*. Everyone gets better quickly. But that's not how it is. It's been awful."

I didn't know but I could guess. I'd never given much thought to procedures. How could you hate yourself so much? At some point, didn't enhancement turn into self-mutilation?

"Is that what he wanted? Your husband?"

"This was before he came along. Let's see; I had my nose done first. A boob job. Then lipo on my hips and butt. I had braces and veneers. Injections. Peels. He did cast his vote for the second boob job after the kids. And a tummy tuck. Lately, I've had Restylane, Juvederm, Botox, and Thermage. I'm scheduled for an eye lift and more. My psychiatrist says I have a self-image problem. All I know is, I couldn't stand to look at myself. People talk about that reality show, *The Swan?* They wonder how women could do all that. Well, I know how they can. You see, you're willing to do that because you want to be admired. Not pitied or ignored. That's it. Pure and simple. And you believe you won't be unless you are perfect. It's awful to avoid the mirror, to walk into a room and feel all eyes are on you because you don't measure up to their standards."

"Hey," I touched her fist with a tentative finger. "I get it. I wasn't much to look at in high school either. I asked eight boys to the Sadie Hawkins girls ask boys dance and they all turned me down. So, we're late bloomers, right?"

The first real smile I'd ever seen flowered on Mahreeya's face. "I can't believe this happened to you. You're so pretty."

The compliment shocked and pleased me. "I had braces and glasses and a bad haircut."

"Here's to us." She raised her water glass, and I did the same.

Our waiter set down two large salads and sparingly poured on a house vinaigrette at our command. Mahreeya checked with me, noted my agreement, and sent the bread basket back to the kitchen. Eating like this all the time would be far too boring for me, but I had to admit that she was a good influence.

"What was it like for you growing up? I mean, tell me about your friendship with Patricia, Jennifer, and Ella."

Between tiny sips and small bites, she explained how cloistered the Alumnae Four were. Patricia's parents, it seemed, kept the shortest rein on their daughter.

Ella, on the other hand, must have been a real challenge. "They could never keep track of her. She was the original wild thing. She brought up civil rights issues so often in our classes that one teacher banned her outright from talking about them. When CALA played Vashon High School in basketball, she took one look at the boy who was their star center, and woosh, it was over. She dumped Jennifer's brother and away she went." A thin shoulder came up in a half-hearted shrug, "And it frightened all our parents. You know, part of the reason for sending us there was to keep us . . ."

"Pure?" I continued, "But go back a second. I guess I didn't realize Jennifer had a brother."

"Jennifer and Patricia both have — or had — brothers. Jennifer's brother Phil is dead. See, after he broke up with Ella, he signed up to go into the army. Didn't last three months. He was killed in a training accident. It was heartbreaking. He was the only son and destined to carry on the family name and business. Like how Patricia's brother carries on the family law firm. The Hallbacks owned a large talent agency. Jennifer runs it now. She inherited her brother's shares, and her husband actually works for her."

This was news to me. I didn't even know Jennifer worked!

Then I got to thinking. If Ella's breakup with Jennifer's brother was the cause of his death, even indirectly, was that a motive for murder? Could Jennifer have killed Sissy and framed Corey to punish Ella? And later killed Corey to misdirect the police? It certainly was worth considering. Mahreeya waved down our waiter and indicated she wanted another glass of wine. By my count, it was her third. The booze worked wonders; she was downright chatty. "Of course, we've all had our share of heartbreak. My older sister died in a car crash in California. Patricia had one miscarriage after another, was it four or five? I can't remember. I lost track. Then a hysterectomy after Elizabeth was born. She sort of went bonkers. Ella's father's two strokes, his death, and then her mother dying so soon after."

"But Ella has always been her own person."

"Exactly. And always upsetting the apple cart. Remember, the times were different. Her romance was dangerous. Not only did it put her father's business at risk, but it brought the boy she was dating — and I use the term 'dating' loosely because they were so young all they could do was sneak around — into a part of town where he didn't belong. He stuck out like a . . . well, he stuck out.

"Her poor parents wanted to take that eighteen-foot satin train and wrap it around her neck."

FORTY-ONE

"How's Mrs. Goldfader? Wait . . . have you been drinking?" Detweiler regarded me with wide eyes. He ran a hand through his hair. "Take my coffee, too. What's up with you? Drugs, alcohol, engagements. I need a scorecard to keep up."

"Dodie's doing pretty well considering." I updated him on my boss and launched a capsulized version of my meeting with Mahreeya as we sat on the bench outside of Kaldi's Coffee in DeMun. I could give him only ten minutes before I had to get back to the store.

"What am I going to do with you?" He sighed before he checked his Steno notepad. "Danny Gartner came up with an airtight alibi. In fact, it's unimpeachable. Testified before the Supreme Court in that KKK dispute. About the Adopt-A-Highway program."

Detweiler continued, "He even referred

me to their attorney, some guy named Krupp. I guess Danny testified they want to be good citizens. Keep the highways clean."

"Yes, I'm sure that's their goal. They're big on clean. The Crusaders for Racial Purity told me at the rally that AIDS is God's way of cleansing the earth of filth."

The detective sighed and gave me an oblique look. "Moving on. Besides the multitude of men enticed by Ms. Gilchrist's charms, got any ideas who done it? The gun used on Corey came back as stolen years ago. We didn't collect forensic evidence because it looked like a suicide. We're still moving bricks."

"I did uncover one possibility. A long shot." I explained how Jennifer Moore's brother had died after being dumped by Ella. Since Corey was Ella's son, and most likely to take the fall for killing Sissy, perhaps Jennifer had set him up.

I did not add that Anya had spent the night at the Moore house. That twisted my gut hard. In fact, after I pieced these new facts together, and realized Jennifer — who I'd previously dismissed — might be our culprit.

I rambled, but I did manage to cover the basics. "Maggie never mentioned Jennifer working in various classrooms as a volunteer. But she could have been one of those drop-in type helpers. Jennifer offered to meet up after work and give me the clothes Anya left at their house. She spent the night there."

"I don't know what's worse. The thought of Anya being exposed to a bunch of rabid racists or having her spend the night at the home of a murderer," Detweiler said.

The detective and I sat far away from each other. We avoided eye contact. I wanted to talk more about his marriage, but I needed to stay clear of Detweiler's nuptial problems. If his marriage didn't work out, fine. We might have a chance of a future together. But only a stupid woman — and an immoral one — would count on that. Much less encourage it.

As wonderful as my daydreams were, as much as I wanted to reach out to Detweiler, I couldn't. I knew myself. I couldn't live with the guilt. I couldn't risk my integrity. I couldn't live every day regretting my actions. So I shut down.

Because if I did follow my desires, wouldn't he have reason to wonder about me? About whether I could be faithful to him? And whether he'd really left Brenda of his own accord? Or whether I'd caused a breakup? Wouldn't I lower my worth in his eyes?

I knew what I had to do. How I had to act. His words had given me hope, but realistically, I needed to continue to live my own life.

Which hurt. Really hurt. A dull ache started inside me. Maybe I'd have been better off never hearing that they were "working" on their marriage.

Even as all this ran through my mind, I chastised myself for not having been more honest with Ben. I'd been avoiding the messages he'd left on my phone.

What should I do about him?

I drained the second cup of coffee. "We're going nowhere," I said.

Detweiler narrowed his eyes. He knew exactly what I meant.

FORTY-TWO

Rebekkah was happy for me to relieve her. "I didn't realize how tiring it can be to have to wait on people all day."

I agreed. "Hey, take your mom these pastries, okay? I know she probably won't feel much like eating." I glanced over at my co-worker and added, "Tell her they're from Bama and me."

Bama's eyes followed Rebekkah out the door. "She's sweet but she's helpless. I tried to get her to put together page kits? She ruined ten pieces of paper. Jammed the die cut machine. Which means we need part-timers fast. I put an ad on Craigslist, and I'll talk with Katie tonight. Think we can count on Mert to help us?"

"Not much. Usually around the holidays I work part-time for her, cleaning. People have family coming in. Give parties." I offered Bama an iced sugar cookie. "We'll have to do the best we can. Maybe one of our customers would like holiday hours."

She nodded. "If we hired a customer, we'd know if the person was any good with crafts."

"Yes, but we could also lose a customer if we fired her."

"We'd have to be very selective."

"Right. How about we say the job is for a very limited time? Say it's temporary? That way we could take a new employee for a test run without hurting anyone's feelings."

She smiled. "Good thinking."

We agreed that the next morning we'd meet early and go over details of running the store. She asked me briefly how handing over the confidential album went. I wasn't sure how long the legal agreement was in force for, so I didn't name names. I simply said, "Fine. If I could tell you more, I would. And maybe I can. But please let me ask Horace first. I sure don't want any trouble after I managed to keep a secret as long as I did. Besides, I'll have to make sure he billed the client."

"You deserve a fat bonus for that. You put in early and late hours."

I glowed. Bama didn't pass out compliments often.

She left and I worked until closing. Promptly at ten after, I bugged out to meet

Jennifer at Bread Co. on Olive. Try as I might, I still couldn't see her as our murderer. I wanted to eliminate her from our list of suspects. Maybe I could clear her.

Besides, what was she going to do? Shoot me at the deli counter?

Doubtful.

"I'm buying," she pushed a twenty toward the cashier.

"But I owe you for taking care of Anya!"

"I'm celebrating. Please let me," said Jennifer, pulling a moue.

Hey, it wasn't like I was rolling in the dough. I gave in. We found a booth, and no sooner had we set down our Diet Cokes than she blurted, "Good news. Best ever. My husband was definitely having an affair! Isn't that terrific?"

Not where I come from, but then I grew up in the middle of a cornfield in Indiana. I must have looked as shocked as I felt. I was stunned, hearing this right after my meeting with Mahreeya. What was it with these people? After learning George was cheating on me, I did research. According to one survey, twenty-two percent of married men admitted to straying. Fourteen percent of married women did. But how on earth did they all manage to buy real estate in one Zip Code?

"Before you ask, yes, he was involved with Sissy. But after her, he moved on to another younger woman in his office."

Blow me down, Popeye. And mind you, she said this with glee!

What came next was a bit tricky for me to follow, but Jennifer went on to explain that off and on over the years, she'd hired a private detective to check up on her husband. Two days ago, she was presented with incontrovertible proof he was cheating. Photos. Really good photos.

"I sat him down and told him about Stevie."

The expression on her face spoke volumes. She meant she'd told him about Stevie being gay.

"After my hubby finished stomping around the room, I brought out the photographs of him and his latest sweetie. He tried to explain the pictures away. Like I'm stupid or something," she rolled her eyes. (This time I felt eye rolling was totally warranted. I was rolling mine, too.) "When he finished ranting and raving, I gave him the terms. He had two choices. Either come to family counseling and accept Stevie as he is, or find a new job. After all, I'm his boss."

That's when I knocked over my cola. The two of us took turns mopping up until a

Bread Co. employee noticed our dilemma and swooped in with a cloth rag.

Jennifer and I changed booths, which gave me the chance to settle down. For the second time in one day, I learned how other women handled straying husbands with binding negotiations. I could foresee a whole new career for Jimmy Carter if he ever got the Middle East to grab the olive branch.

I was forced to reconsider my opinion of Jennifer. First of all, the woman was a CEO. Secondly, she was not, as Nana would say, a flibbertigibbet. Instead, she was one tough cookie. She knew exactly how to get what she wanted. What strings to pull on the puppet, er husband. The threat of a possible reversal of fortune brought her spouse to heel. Actually, it caused him to genuflect.

"Quick as a flash, he was on his knees begging forgiveness and promising to go to counseling. He didn't even propose to me on his knees. He'd blown out his patella playing high school football. That's why he likes hanging around athletes so much. Relives his glory days. He's not a bad man, but he sure can be stupid. I knew he loved my daddy's company more than he loved me, but I owned the company, so it didn't matter."

She was so matter of fact, I nearly toppled my cola again. Jennifer was much more calm than I could have ever been. In my secret heart-of-hearts, I admit: I'm a believer in true love, love at first sight — or even at first sigh — and all that hogwash. But the woman sitting across from me was a clear-eyed, cold-blooded realist. She explained that to her mind, a long-lasting marriage is based on more than immediate attraction. Her philosophy was that to keep it together, you had to have a strong commitment. (Which I agree with.)

"Besides, our kids need two parents. Despite Stevie's sexual orientation, he still needs a dad." She summed it up nicely. "Love comes and goes. The marriages that last are those where there's more benefit to staying together than to going it alone."

How did Detweiler feel about his relationship to Brenda? That there was more benefit in staying married than divorcing her? If he did, I'd better make other plans.

I shook my head and told myself to focus on the present. Stay in the moment, I chided myself.

I'd obviously been wrong in my assessment of Jennifer Moore. I vowed not to undervalue another woman again. I especially promised myself I'd be more careful in assessing those who seemed on the surface to be very different from me. Looks certainly could be deceiving! Hadn't Nana always said that?

Besides, hadn't people done the same to me? Underestimated me? Judged me by my looks? And their face value perception of my worth? Indeed, they had.

I also made a mental reminder to put a higher value on my daughter's taste in friends. I could learn something from my kid. Anya obviously has good taste. My boss and my mother-in-law had been right: I needed to make a concerted effort to get to know the CALA parents.

"Jennifer, you sure are practical about this whole thing."

She grinned. "Cheating is not about sex. Men just want to feel powerful. Needed. Important. Younger women, especially younger women who act all dependent, make them feel that way."

"How's Stevie handling this and the situation at school?" I sincerely wanted to know. While I was pregnant, George and I discussed how we'd parent a child who was gay. We agreed that the hardest part would be helping and guiding our child through life. Being gay would add yet another layer of worries and concerns.

Motherly love brought a glow to Jennifer's face. She misread the conflicting emotions on mine.

"Stevie will be fine. I've known about him for ages. Practically since he was a baby. How could I help but know? He's the spitting image of my brother Phil."

The spitting image of Phil? The same Phil who dated Ella? How did that work?

This time the cola came out my nose. I rasped out an apology as I choked, and she slapped my back.

"What about him and Ella? I heard from Mahreeya that they used to date."

Jennifer waved her hand — with its nearly healed fingertips — in the air. "Phil broke up with Ella because he couldn't stand living a lie. My dad pushed him to be a macho, alpha-male type of guy. Dad thought Ella was the perfect mate for Phil. She was Phil's best friend. She knew all about him. That's why she went places with him. They covered for each other while she was involved with that guy from Vashon High. She even agreed to pretend she had broken up with him when Phil decided to come out of the closet. He needed to buy time before he told Daddy."

Her face grew somber. "Of course, Daddy refused to accept the truth. He made Phil's life at home so miserable that Phil signed up for the service to escape. I begged him not to, but Daddy refused to pay for his college, and he didn't have any money. What else could my brother do?

"That's how I came to own fifty-one percent of Hallback Entertainment, Inc. Phil wrote Mother and instructed her to leave his portion to me, in case anything happened. See, Daddy never thought I'd go into the business. He convinced himself I'd be a happy little homemaker. Daddy never thought Mother would make a move without his permission. She also left her shares to me. It was her money, after all."

Jennifer dabbed at her eyes. "Daddy forced my brother to be someone he wasn't. He forced Phil to run away. Gave him no option but to join the service. What happened to my brother is never going to happen to my son. Never. Over my dead body."

FORTY-THREE

After my meeting with Jennifer, I raced home to let Gracie out and headed over to Triple A. My dog wanted a ride, but with Anya's golf clubs and backpack, the car would be too crowded. Besides, I figured I owed Anya a sit-down dinner at a restaurant. We needed some bonding time. We needed to talk.

A drab shade of gray infused the sky. The heavy rain the weatherman had promised was on its way. The leaves on the trees — so richly colored in burgundy, bright orange, and gold — would be knocked to the ground. We'd go from our heart-stoppingly gorgeous fall scenery to the stark emptiness of winter. I hoped it held off a few more hours because I hate driving in storms. I always worry a limb will crash through my ragtop. It could happen. If it did, with my luck, I'd be in the Beemer to see it.

I slipped free of the seat belt and yanked

my hoodie over my arms as I idled at a stoplight. As usual, I was running late. But at least I was sober and drug free. I drove along 40 through the heart of St. Louis to Triple A. The golf course boasted a fascinating history. In order to accommodate the 1904 World's Fair, it had been relocated from the center of Forest Park to the edges of the green space. The park itself had been created in 1876 from 1,293 acres of land, which means our crown jewel is larger than Central Park in New York City. Mounted police patrol the grounds around the zoo, a tennis court, the Jewel Box (a glass conservatory), the St. Louis Art Museum, the Lindell Pavilion (a former streetcar pavilion), the history museum, the World's Fair Pavilion, the Norman Probstein (Forest Park) Golf Course (not to be confused with the Triple A Golf Club), trails, and various playing fields.

While the police presence is reassuring, I wouldn't come here at night anymore than I'd go walking in Central Park after dark. The park is too dense with trees and sits too close to transitional areas of the city.

Anya saw me pull up. If she noticed me limping — I was off the Bextra, after all — she gave no indication. Good moms are invincible, always on call, and easy to ignore. She threw her clubs into the back-seat. I knew she was tired. Jennifer had sheepishly admitted to me that she'd let the girls talk late into the night. Anya was a kid who needed her eight hours of sleep to stay up-beat. My darling hopped into the car with nary a "Hi, Mom, how was your day?" Instead, she chugged her Gatorade, demolished a bag of SunChips, and started snoring lightly. We crested Highway 40 when a strange cell phone ring broke the silence. Anya opened one sleepy eye and looked at me.

"Mom? Is that your cell?"

"No. Did you download a different ringtone?"

"No."

The phone was insistent.

"Ah, shoot," said Anya and she dug around in the backpack at her feet. "Hello? No, Elizabeth, this isn't Natalie. Sheesh. It's Anya. Anya Lowenstein! Huh? I don't know. Hey, wait —" she rummaged around through papers and books in the pile, finally yanking a stapled sheet of paper. "What the heck? I must have picked up Natalie's backpack. Talk to you later — yeah, yeah, I'll tell her you called. I can't tell you the homework 'cause I've got it in my stuff. How you feeling? But wait — aren't you sick, Elizabeth? Your mom said you were when she picked me up. Really? That's weird. Okay, well, bye."

Anya folded the phone closed and tried to get comfortable. "Better call Mrs. Walden, Mom. If this is Natalie's backpack, she's gotta have mine." Before I could argue about this being her responsibility, my daughter turned to the window to doze off again. A wave of exasperation swept over me.

"Anya, you need to be more careful."

"It wasn't my fault, Mom! Mrs. Bigler was being really weird. She kept telling me how she wanted to carry my backpack. I didn't even want to ride with her 'cause she's so weird, and Elizabeth wasn't even at golf today."

"What do you mean her daughter wasn't at golf? Mrs. Bigler called me and offered to take both of you." My daughter had already rolled over, as far as was humanly possible to do with the seat belt on, and snuggled against the car door.

Her sleepy voice drifted back over her shoulder, "How the heck should I know how grownups think? After school, she was standing there and she made a big deal out of how I had to ride with her." With that, Anya cranked the button to drop the passenger seat into the horizontal position.

Number three on my speed dial was Ella's phone. The number rang and rang. Ella's voice mail picked up. I hung up. Desperate, concerned that I'd pass her on the road, I tried once more. This time Ella broke through, "Hello? Oh, Kiki, it's you."

"Natalie's backpack —"

"I know. I'm already pulling into Forest Park. Patricia's meeting me there with it. Can you believe Natalie walked off without it?" she said. Her voice sounded weak and tired. "Tonight of all nights. With the weather like it is. And the visitation's tomorrow."

I had missed that. I hadn't heard. "But Patricia doesn't have Natalie's backpack. We have it. It's here in my car."

"But she says she has it. Patricia called to ask if Natalie made it home yet. Of course she was. Frederick had picked her up. Patricia has Natalie's backpack. She offered to wait for me at Triple A in the parking lot."

I thought a second. "Then she must have Anya's backpack and I have Natalie's. They all look alike."

"Tell you what . . . I'm almost at Forest Park. How about I wait for you at Triple A?" Ella sounded so weary.

Thanking her profusely, I ended the

conversation. I veered off at the exit ramp and headed back the way I'd just come. Nice as it was for Ella to pick up the backpack, this whole escapade didn't make much sense. Patricia lived a few blocks from Ella's house. And tonight of all nights when Ella was so totally in a mental fog.

A light sprinkling of rain covered my windshield, splashing concentric circles in the dust. I turned on the wipers, wishing I had a switch that would clear my brain as easily. I joined the bottleneck toward 40 east. Anya snuffled in her sleep. I tapped the steering wheel impatiently, trying to puzzle out why Patricia had been so eager to get my daughter into her car, so eager to be in charge of her backpack, especially when Elizabeth was home sick.

Or not.

Then it hit me. Ella would be there alone. In the dark. She wasn't thinking straight. It wasn't a good place to be alone at night.

Something Detweiler had said . . . what was it . . . Danny Gartner's attorney's name was Krupp. And that comment Patricia had made to Bonnie at the crop about people sticking with their own kind. Donald Krupp defended bigots. His sister Patricia Krupp Bigler had sounded mighty prejudiced as well.

"Oh, no," I whimpered.

I flipped my phone open and dialed Detweiler. "I've got a bad feeling. Get to Triple A in Forest Park now!"

Thank goodness he didn't waste time questioning me. "I'm on it," he said and hung up.

I hit the speed dial for Ella. The call went through right to voice mail. Either she was on her phone or the phone was turned off. I panicked. I could think of one reason and one reason only that Patricia had gone through so much trouble to drive my daughter to Triple A. She planned to swap Anya's backpack for Natalie's.

I glanced at my sleeping child. I had to make a choice. If I continued to Triple A, Ella wouldn't be alone. I hadn't asked where Detweiler was. Could he get there in time? If not, surely, he would call the mounted police. Or phone a nearby station and send the cops.

Maybe he expected me to do that.

I tried his number again and it went directly to voice mail.

I flipped open my phone and punched in 9-1-1. I lost my focus. My car hydroplaned — and I dropped my phone. I swerved in my lane, fought for control. Traffic swarmed around me. Horns blared. The rain started pelting the roadway. Oil from 170,000 cars making their commute rose to the surface. In front of me a car swerved, as I had done, fishtailing on the slick pavement. Brake lights blinked on and off. I calculated the speed of the cars on either side of me. I reached down fast and snagged my phone.

Now I was in the thick of rush-hour traffic. Rain impaired my visibility. Fog crept around the edges of my windshield. I flipped on the defroster. It worked very slowly in my old convertible. More brake lights flashed. We all slowed down. A car pulled into the lane in front of me and nearly clipped my bumper. I flipped open the phone with one hand and dialed. Nine-one-one. The cars in front of me sped up. I slipped into the far left lane, in preparation for my turn. The screen on my phone went black. The traffic ahead glowed with red brake lights. I slowed down.

And my phone beeped. I ignored it and tried to dial in 9-1-1. The screen went black. I glanced down to see the low battery symbol.

Setting the phone on my lap, I concentrated on pulling past the clog of cars. Would Detweiler call for backup? Should I leave this to him? What if I was wrong? I'd been wrong about Ella. And I'd been wrong about Connie McMahan. And Jennifer. Twice.

I needed to calm down. I was overwrought. I'd been drinking and taking painkillers. Surely I wasn't thinking straight.

I was probably just being silly. I really had no proof Ella was in any danger. None.

I just needed to pick up Anya's backpack.

Poor Patricia was so timid. So withdrawn. Surely this was just a mix-up. Besides, who knew her better than her friend Ella?

My mind was playing tricks on me. Patricia as a murderer? How far-fetched! I laughed out loud. I was really losing it.

Traffic was gridlocked on Highway 40. I couldn't exit because I couldn't cross three lanes of cars. Detweiler would get to the golf course before me.

Then again, the traffic was awful. If he was driving from Chesterfield or South County he might not. A low wail behind me forced me to check the rearview mirror. An ambulance threaded its way through traffic. Water flew from its spinning wheels. Cars refused to move onto the shoulder. The EMT driver beeped his horn impatiently as he attempted to work his way through the cars. The flashing red filled my rearview mirror. I pulled over as far I could to the side of my lane and waited. The sound of the siren caused Anya to raise her head and look around blearily, but only for a moment. She snuggled back down. With her seat back so far, you couldn't tell I had a passenger.

The backside of the ambulance passed. Were they headed for Forest Park? Was I already too late?

Me and my drama queen imagination.

Of course Ella was fine.

Or was she? She certainly wasn't thinking straight. Not with all she'd just been through. What to do? What to do?

At any rate, she shouldn't be there alone in the dark. She was waiting for me. If I didn't show up, she'd stay there how long? I couldn't stand her up. I had to meet her. Or call her.

I tried to dial, but my phone screen went black.

My foot eased off the accelerator involuntarily. Then I pushed the pedal to the floor again.

I passed all other traffic moving more cautiously, coming up on the Forest Park exit. Cars swarmed around me. I switched lanes, back and forth. I pulled out in front of another driver. He slammed on his brakes. I kept going. I felt sweat drip from under my arms. I slid through a yellow light into Forest Park.

Yellow, the color of caution.

FORTY-FOUR

Only one car sat in the lot. Ella's.

Whew. It was going to be all right.

Ella's car was angled so I couldn't see inside. I would tap my horn, but that would wake Anya. Instead, I pulled up next to the car.

Looked like it was empty.

Where was Ella? The rain let up a little. I parked my Beemer and turned off the motor. Anya was snoring loudly. Good.

I turned as far as I could in my seat. I scanned the area, trying to make out shapes through the swish-swish of my wipers.

I'd only been here once before. I couldn't remember how far the parking lot extended around the back of the clubhouse. That building was totally dark, as was the smaller shed ahead of me. As I recalled, the shed had a big overhang. Ella was probably waiting there. All I needed was to quickly grab my child's backpack and make sure my friend was okay.

The rain was pattering steadily now. Hitting my windshield with force. Splattering.

I pulled my hoodie up over my head and psyched myself to get out of the car. I was probably wrong about Patricia. So she was prejudiced. Big deal. My father had been also. That didn't make him a killer, just an idiot.

The place looked empty.

I stepped out of the car, shivered in the wet, turned my key in the lock, and locked my daughter inside the Beemer. At least no one from the outside world could hurt Anya.

I trotted to the shed. "Ella?" I called. "Ella?"

No one answered.

I huddled under the eaves and glanced around. No one was there.

I wanted to leave. I was tired, and it was cold. But I had to make sure Ella was okay. Her car was here, and she planned to meet me. She had to be here somewhere!

I stepped out into the open and made a visor with my hand to try to keep the water out of my eyes. I moved away from the cars and under the glare of the security lamp. I blinked. I couldn't see a thing. I tried to adjust my vision, but I still couldn't see. I needed to get out past the cars. My foot came down on a patch of grass. I moved soundlessly to another patch. These were islands in the gravel. Soon I'd run out of turf.

"Ella!" I shouted.

I blinked repeatedly, adjusting to the lack of light, and trying to get my bearings. My teeth chattered with the cold and the wet. I turned around, making a tight circle. Straining to see. Ella had to be here. But where?

"Ella! It's me, Kiki!"

No one answered.

I couldn't make out the clubhouse. I inched forward. I thought I heard a crunch in the emptiness ahead. Did I? I took another step and pulled the hoodie tight around my face.

BANG!

A shot rang out. Then a shriek of pain.

I turned toward my car, but then I tripped over someone. I fell onto my hands. I squinted.

It was Ella.

"Ella? Ella? Speak to me! What happened!"

She coughed.

"Help!" I yelled. But that was silly. No one was around.

But Detweiler was coming. He'd get this sorted.

I leaned closer to Ella. I slid my hands along the ground, crawling beside her, trying to see. I could feel a warm wetness. "What have you done?" I asked. Had her despair led her to shoot herself? Had she accidentally misfired a gun? I smelled traces of car exhaust and overtones of iron. My stomach roiled.

You don't die of a gunshot wound unless it hits your spine or brainstem. You die from loss of blood. She made a weird noise. Did that sound mean she was bleeding in her lungs?

Ella grabbed my arm, startling me. Her grip was surprisingly strong. "Run! Get away!" The smell of iron embraced her. Saliva flooded my mouth. I swallowed hard. This was the wrong time to puke. I ran my hands over her and touched a warm wellspring of wetness by her shoulder. "Run," she whispered. "She got me. In the chest."

"She? She who?"

"Run . . ." Ella wheezed.

But I didn't need to run. Detweiler was coming. So I pulled off my hoodie and wadded it up, pressing it hard against the warm, wet spot I'd touched. "Hold on. Don't panic. Help's coming."

"Go . . . please." The words came in a hiss. She tried to raise her head but couldn't. I stuffed the bundled-up fabric under her bra strap trying to get some pressure on the wound. It was tough going because I shivered so hard in the cold and wet.

Crunch.

I looked up, expecting to see Detweiler. "Thank good—"

I stopped. Patricia stepped out from behind the shed. She moved away from the security lamp's glow. She came over to where I was trying to stop the flow of Ella's blood.

"Patricia! Ella's shot! She needs help!"

"Of course she is! I shot her!"

My jaw dropped.

A maniacal laugh came from the figure standing before me. She threw back her head and crowed with delight. I could barely make out the rainwater streaming over her face.

"Call an ambulance!

"Or what? Huh? You'll do what?" Then I saw a glint of light on metal. Patricia waved a gun at me.

I tried to sound calm. "Look, I know this was an accident."

"Ha!" She brayed like a lunatic. "You stupid dope! I planned this! I tried to warn you! I tried to scare you after the book club. I put that message in Anya's backpack. I caused you to wreck your bicycle. But you wouldn't quit poking around, would you?"

"I guess not. You're right. I sure can be stubborn."

Ella moaned. I huddled over her body trying to shield her from the rain. I reached down and took her hand. It wasn't much, but perhaps it would encourage her to hold on.

Detweiler was coming, I told myself.

"They were going to take the baby away from me. Christopher! He needs me! Sissy and that . . . that black . . . they were going to take him! She didn't deserve that little boy! He loves me!" Patricia emphasized her words with a jab of her thumb toward her chest.

"I know he does," I said reasonably, which was hard to do with the mounting panic I felt. "So let's just calm down. Think about Christopher. He needs you. You don't want to go to jail."

"Calm down?" she shrieked.

Oops.

"I hate you!" she screamed, stepping closer to me. "You and your filthy half-breed kind! You have babies with Jews and blacks! You're scum! Scum! We need to cleanse the world of vermin. Filth like you!"

"Okay, I'm scum. But you're important.

Especially to Christopher. The police are on the way," I said. "Hand the gun over, Patricia. Give it here." And I extended my palm toward her. She was now near enough that I could smell the gunpowder. "Come on. You don't want to get hurt, do you? Christopher needs you."

"Oh, and I'm really scared." With that she backhanded me, using the gun flat in her palm as a club.

I staggered backward, falling over on my knees and landing alongside Ella's prone figure. The rain was pelting down now. It was like standing in a shower.

"Ow!" I pressed myself up. I rolled on my butt. I hurt. Every cell of me was in pain. I shook with the cold. I wanted to give up.

Then Ella moaned and I got mad. I was her one chance. Anya was asleep — and Patricia probably wouldn't hurt a child. At least, I hoped not. But Ella was dying. I snuck my hand up to her chest. The warm wetness gushed against my fingers.

With my free hand, I rubbed my jawline. Patricia laughed. "I got you good!"

I felt a surge of adrenaline. I could do this. I knew I could. I needed to outwit this crazy woman. I had to end this now, or Anya was in danger.

"What did you do?" I whimpered like a

child to Patricia. "It hurts so bad." I made more mewling noises. "Did you really hit me?" I sounded pathetic, even to my own ears.

Patricia stood between me and the light. It was getting darker by the minute, and the rain was coming down hard. I needed an advantage.

Behind me, Ella groaned and went silent.

Then I realized, Patricia couldn't see her victim. And she wanted to. She was bent on revenge. She needed to gloat.

"Ella's dead," I lied.

Except, maybe it wasn't a lie.

FORTY-FIVE

Patricia stepped forward, closer to Ella and me, and stared down.

"I'm bleeding," I whined, shifting my weight to free my legs.

Patricia moved even closer.

I sobbed, "I think you broke a tooth."

Patricia took one more step, angled against the light to check me out. To investigate and preen over the damage she'd done. I turned my face up toward her and pointed to my mouth.

I had to keep her busy.

Behind Patricia, in the glow of the security light, a figure crept toward us. A gleam of silver twinkled. I knew who and what it was, and I turned sick with fear. A wave of protective instinct gave me extra courage. Despite the pain, I had to hold on.

I had to keep Patricia occupied. I couldn't let her turn around.

"See? See what you've done? How could

you do this to me?" I sobbed. "How? I'm your friend, Patricia! I can't move. It hurts. It hurts so much."

But she didn't come closer.

I had to get her nearer. I needed to distract her. To keep her focus toward me and the body on the gravel next to me.

I glanced over at the quiet form next to me. I sobbed, "I think she's dead! I can't tell if Ella's breathing or not."

The darkness, which had before seemed impenetrable, now yielded shapes. The tail of Patricia's blouse must be a light color. A flash of it alerted me to where she was. I stifled another urge to cry out loud. The noise would have broken the spell. I had to be quiet. Had to let her think I was down for the count. I did a sidewise push up, every muscle shrieking with pain. A small rock dug into the heel of my hand. I had to bring her down. Otherwise Anya was in danger. And Ella?

Was she dead?

I didn't know.

Of course, Patricia wanted to check out her handiwork. She bent over to peer down at Ella. I waited as she moved more and more parallel to the ground. Then with an explosive burst of energy, I kicked my legs forward. I kicked at her knees — hard. My feet connected. Hers flew out from under her. She did a half-somersault. Her hands rose as she pawed the air. In a full layout position, she started coming down, her arms flailing in the air.

But she didn't turn loose of the gun. A spark of light glinted off of it. I traced the arc with my eyes. Rather than turn loose, she'd held on, just as I had done when my bike and I careened down the hill.

Anya jumped out from behind Ella's parked SUV. The silver shine of the golf club traced a half-circle through the air. Swish, the shaft cut through the night. A metallic clunk told me she'd connected with Patricia's gun. The weapon flew high overhead, crashed to the ground, and skittered along the gravel a good ways behind me.

Anya pounced forward, carrying the golf club over her shoulder like a bat. She smelled of fear, salty and pungent.

"You leave my mom alone!" she screamed at Patricia. "I'm warning you!"

The club swayed over my daughter's head. I had no doubt she'd bash Patricia's brain with it. A tone in Anya's voice sounded feral, animalistic. Frightening. Even to me.

I didn't doubt my daughter would whack Patricia — and beat her repeatedly. Neither did Patricia. Patricia raised her hands in surrender. "Please, please don't hurt me." She tried to roll away.

I made it to my child in two steps and yanked the driver from her hands.

Patricia scooted back from us, her hands over her head.

Now it was my turn to raise the club and threaten our assailant. "Anya, go grab her gun. Patricia, you move again, and I'll knock your head into the center lane of Highway 40. You see if I don't. I've had it with you. Hear me? Had it!"

In the distance, I heard a car.

A bright light blinded me.

"Police! Freeze!"

I froze. Every muscle ached to grab my daughter. Anya. My wonderful Anya. She was just out of my reach. How I wanted to hold her! But I did as I was told. I froze.

Men in uniforms ran past me to get to Patricia. I watched them jerk her to her feet. Finally, I couldn't help myself. I dropped the club and reached for my baby. From far away a voice said, "It's okay. I'm here. It's okay." I blinked into the light and watched as Detweiler trotted toward us. He pulled us both into his arms and hugged us tight. Beyond him, tires dug into the gravel as an ambulance pulled up, red lights flashing, the rain causing them to flicker like old-time movies.

"Ella —" I said, pointing weakly.

"They're on it," he finished.

I watched two EMTs race toward the supine figure.

A cop walked past me and picked up Anya's golf club from the ground. In the half-light, I could see how young he was and the grin on his face. He extended his palm to my daughter for a high-five. The slapping flesh made a wet splashing sound. "Hey, young lady. That's some golf swing you've got. Woowee. How far do you hit the ball?"

She said, "Two hundred-thirty yards. But I have a mean slice."

"I'll bet you do," said the cop. "But this time you made a hole in one."

The paramedics lifted me into a second ambulance. We followed the first emergency vehicle carrying Ella up Kingshighway, Anya moved away from me only when the EMTs suggested, firmly, that they'd be able to care for me better if they had a clear path to my messed-up face.

My daughter called her grandmother to explain that I'd been hurt and we were on our way to the hospital. I didn't hear all the conversation because the paramedics were

asking me what I was allergic to.
"Guns," I said. And I meant it.

FORTY-SIX

Shock started to set in once I was in the emergency room. My memory is a little patchy about all that. At one point, a doctor turned to Anya and said, "Young lady, you need to go sit down outside," and a nurse took my daughter away. I heard hollering and yelling and realized dimly that Sheila was on the premises.

Boy, was she mad.

With me.

One of my caregivers wore a green smock with animals on it. I tried to focus on those cavorting cartoon dogs and cats. Briefly I wondered if I'd been taken to a veterinary clinic. That's how loopy I was. The nurse started an IV, shined a penlight in my eyes, asked me questions, and took my vitals. "You're off to get pictures taken, Mrs. Lowenstein. We need a better look at that skull. Seems to me you've got a bit of that Humpty-Dumpty action happening."

I tried to nod, but the motion brought a body-curdling pain. I whimpered instead. I was alone. My fingers crawled across the starched sheets for . . . what? I realized I'd been holding my daughter's hand throughout the ambulance ride and most of the intake procedure. A pair of eyes in a mask introduced himself as Dr. Pedro. He peeled back my gown to give me a thorough going over. "Good Lord, woman, you have bruises all over your body." Dr. Pedro decided I was the victim of domestic abuse. He stepped outside and grabbed the nearest police officer. I heard Detweiler's voice and caught words like "bike accident . . . run off the road . . . happened yesterday."

Dr. Pedro's bushy eyebrows were nearly up in his surgical hat-thingie when he came back to me. "Have you considered a more sedentary lifestyle? Usually I'm suggesting more exercise, but this isn't agreeing with you. Off you go to get those pictures taken." Over my head, to the orderly, he said, "Make sure you strap her down tightly. She's having a bad couple of days."

Gunshot wounds generally move right to the top of the triage tree. Seconds after my arrival, the emergency team discovered what I already knew. Ella had taken a hit. The bullet collapsed her left lung. She'd been really lucky because a few more minutes and she would not have survived.

Me? I had a concussion. See, you only hope you'll pass out from the pain. But you don't. And the nice people in the ER want you conscious as long as possible so they can ask foolish questions like, "Heck of a night, eh? What on earth were you doing facing down a woman with a gun?"

Fortunately the pictures only showed a terrible bruise where Patricia had whacked me with the revolver. She'd split my lower lip, which required two stitches, and she'd loosened my teeth. My upper right front tooth now had a tiny chip in the bottom. I'd also bitten through the inside of my lower lip, so that took four stitches. And my skin had ruptured at my left temple, so they slapped on a couple bandages. All in all my face was a crazy quilt of cat gut or whatever they use these days and plastic do-hickeys that functioned basically as photo splits.

But Dr. Pedro seemed pleased with the results. "You've got one heck of a hard head. Lucky girl. Only a minor concussion. Pretty good, considering."

A young man in blue scrubs walked my bed down a long hallway. I was definitely there for an overnight. Detweiler caught up with us and took my one free hand. The other had tubes attached. The medic and he exchanged glances. The detective dropped my hand and walked alongside.

The vein in his forehead pulsed. "A near miss in Ladue, a wild bike ride, barbecue with white supremacists, and a shooting in the park?"

I lisped, "Yeth, it-th been kind of a biz-thee week."

"Got anything I can use on Patricia?"

I'd been thinking about this. The pain had actually sharpened my reasoning. I hoped for some nice drugs when I was settled in my room, so I had to talk fast. "Check out the commemorative paving brick in the display case on Coach Bosch's mantel. That's the murder weapon. Patricia took it back from Coach, killed Sissy, rinsed it clean, and had it framed."

"Will do. What was her motive?"

"Love," I said sadly.

The medic maneuvered me into the elevator and gave him a long look. "I'll be taking Mrs. Lowenstein past the nurses' station." Detweiler nodded to him.

"I've got to go," he said. "I'll check on Anya and follow up on all this." With the precision of an about-face, he peeled away from us.

It seemed a bit abrupt, but he did have a murder investigation to close.

EPILOGUE

I spent the next morning pretty well out of it. I burst into tears twice while getting up to use the restroom. I dozed off frequently, but woke up to a bad dream, about something I couldn't pin down. My mood was dark, and of course, my whole body hurt from the banging around I'd had. Dr. Pedro reminded me I'd conked my head twice within days, counting my bike crash. He checked me and decided I should stick around another twenty-four hours.

Chief Holmes, I believe, was pleased the hospital decided to keep me off the streets. Patricia Bigler's arrest was taking longer than expected. Her family hired a good criminal attorney, who kept her out of custody and tried to negotiate for some sort of diminished mental capacity charges.

The chief stopped in to see how I was doing. "Patricia Bigler had been treated for severe post-partum depression after each of her miscarriages. Later she had what we used to call a nervous breakdown. Frankly, I think her problems were much more extensive and long lasting than anyone realized. But her family is very well-connected. Her doctors were part of her social circle, so her mental state was kept under wraps. She managed well in certain environments, like helping out at school with supervision and limited stress. There, the relationship between Ms. Gilchrist and Coach Johnson exacerbated her racial prejudices and tipped her over the edge."

"The idea that Corey and Sissy would move to another state and take Christopher away from her must have been the final straw," I said.

"No. I think the final straw for Mrs. Bigler was her teenage daughter Elizabeth pulling away from her."

I must have shown my surprise. The police chief smiled at me. "It's hard for everyone, Kiki. Watching your child pull away. Elizabeth was tired of her overbearing mother. I remember when my boys were teens. They gave my late wife fits. She used to say that we parents are the bones on which pups sharpen their teeth. My boys sure let us know they were ready to be independent," he chuckled.

"If a woman sees her whole purpose in life as being a mother, she can fall apart when her children no longer need her. Not that it excuses murder. You know, Kiki, over the years I've come to believe it's almost a waste of time to ever try to second-guess people. They do what they do for reasons I'll never understand."

"I hear you, Chief."

Ben showed up with flowers. I didn't know what to say. He suggested we'd have a talk later, but meantime, he added, "I was wrong to try to boss you around. I'm sorry." He kissed my cheek very tenderly and asked if he could give me a ride home when I was released. He told me about the progress made in shutting down the Crusaders for Racial Purity's CD launch. "We covered it, sent it out on the wire, and got it halted immediately. You've given our paper the biggest scoop of the year. More importantly, we've struck a blow against hate-crimes and bigotry. The backlash is sure to make the white supremacy movement think twice before trying this again."

Mert brought brownies from Johnny, and news that she was taking good care of Gracie. My friend clucked her tongue at me. "Girlfriend, we need to talk. Dodie and Horace are worried sick about you. Even

446

Bama called. Leastways, you need a new hobby. How about you and me going to the shooting range once you get shed of here? Now that's a skill you can put to good use."

Clancy sent a huge yellow and orange sunburst mum, a cluster of Mylar balloons, and a teddy bear wearing a helmet. To his chest was pinned this message: "You need protection like this!"

Anya and Sheila dropped by briefly with a bag of iced cookies from Kaldi's. Anya was a little weepy, but Chief Holmes had talked with her. He told her she should be proud of herself. After all, she probably saved my life and Ella's too.

My daughter also brought me a new book I'd been wanting and a huge "get well" card. I could tell Sheila was biting her tongue to keep from scolding me. I knew she couldn't wait to chew me out for putting Anya in danger. She was probably well within her rights.

Maggie came by that evening with an armful of tabloid magazines. "Mindless reading."

"Appropriate for a broad with a scrambled brain, eh?"

We sat quietly for a few minutes. Finally she said, "I owe you an apology and an explanation. I overreacted to what you told me about Sissy Gilchrist's parents' decision not to press charges when she was molested. When I was a sophomore in high school, I was attacked when I'd stayed late after school to work on a library project. It was November. I missed the second bus. My parents both worked and couldn't come get me. I stepped outside into the cold and drizzle. It was nearly dark. My scarf and hat covered most of my face, so I couldn't see clearly. A man jumped out from a clump of bushes."

She struggled with her emotions. "He hit me over the head with a baseball bat. I needed twenty stitches. See?" She parted her hair to expose a pink line. "That's why I always wear my hair parted like this. To cover up. I was violated.

"The news traveled fast. The stories, well, they were pretty lurid. I went back to class, a week later, but everyone whispered behind their hands. I couldn't take it. I crawled into bed and I didn't come out for a long time. Missed all kinds of school. I had to be tutored to catch up. That summer my dad took a transfer, and we moved to another state."

"I am so sorry," I managed to whisper. This put a new face on Maggie, sturdy Maggie.

After she left, I reflected on how falsely secure our lives are. We don't want to believe evil exists right alongside us. We picture the devil as wearing horns, smelling of brimstone, and generally announcing his presence with sound and fury. But a smart demon cloaks his face in a bland smile and flies beneath the radar.

We believe trauma survivors will look scarred and different. That they will wear their pain openly. But we're wrong. Their struggle is not to get by, but to return to normal. Camouflage is not only a survival tactic for the animal world. It's an important asset to the human species as well. It allows us — good and evil, whole and hurt, sane and unstable both — to blend in.

Because when we don't blend in, when we stand apart, we're at risk of being culled from the herd. It is when we stand alone that predators can pick us off.

I snuggled beneath the too-crisp sheets of my hospital bed. I took note of the brownies, the magazines, the new book, the big "get well" card, the shiny balloons, the silly teddy, and of course, no one could miss all those flowers. Woo-wee. My room was awash in the sweet floral fragrance. All around me were signs that I was not alone.

That I had friends and family, and I was loved.

Everyone had been by to see me.

Everyone, that is, except Detective Chad Detweiler.

I closed my eyes and drifted off. My room was dark. But my cracked door let in a little light. A movement at the foot of my bed aroused me. A nurse was readying the blood pressure cuff and the finger monitor of my blood gases. Her back was to me as she worked. Something about her seemed familiar. Then she turned and smiled down at me.

It was Brenda Detweiler.

AUTHOR'S NOTES

Don't go looking for a book showing a photo of Ella Latreau Walden protesting and holding hands with her African-American boyfriend. This is a work of fiction.

However, the Veiled Prophet is real. You can read more about this colorful and spectacular St. Louis organization at my website (www.JoannaSlan.com) in the resource section. Just follow the links. You'll find information about the V.P.'s history as well as photos and videos. There's also a list of the resources I used to research this book. My intent was to do justice to an organization that has changed with the times. Who knows? Maybe this year I'll get one of their coveted invitations in the mail.

Congratulations to Claudia Skwiot, who won character-naming privileges for her granddaughter, Addison Kobe, by making a donation to the Guardian Angel Settlement Association in St. Louis. The organization provides many social services to families, senior citizens, those with disabilities, and young people in the inner city. Olivia Kormeier facilitated my opportunity to help this worthy group raise money. Thank you, Olivia, for always looking on the bright side and for being such a dear, dear pal to me.

Congratulations to Joyce Casaldi, who won character-naming privileges for herself and her daughter Ashlynn through a contest at www.SpottedCanary.com, a website sponsored by EK Success.

I want to thank Mike Spahn, Gus Castellanos, and Jane Campbell for their help with medical questions. Karen DiGasbarro helped with proofreading an early version and a later galley; I can't thank her enough.

I extend my appreciation to the St. Louis County Library and their reference librarians, especially Paul Steensland. The United States Holocaust Museum helped me nail down the fact that George Lincoln Rockwell was, indeed, the nephew of Norman Rockwell.

Kiki has a lot of friends. Special thanks to Jessica Martin, Andrea Silva, and Joy Macdonell at EK Success; Angela Daniels at Fiskars; Katie Franceschini of ANW Crestwood; Tina Hui of Snapfish; the kind folks at Bazzill Basics; the dynamic sisters Angela

Rhyne and Diana McMahon; the Mid-Atlantic Great Dane Rescue League and Joan Schramm; the entire ScrapFest 2009 team from Archiver's, who make me feel so welcome every year! Extra big hugs to all my Barnes & Noble Bookseller friends, including Jolene Carter, Christina Pohl, and the wonderful Lynn Oris. My deep appreciation goes to Lori Jane Perdew at Borders, Nikki Furrer from Pudd'nhead Books, and Danielle Borsch at Left Bank Books. Many thanks to Kathy Jones and all the wonderful people at Jellystone Park Resort at Eureka. Send a round of applause to Cassidy Renick, and everyone at the St. Louis County Police Department.

My gratitude goes to Connie Hill, senior editor at Llewellyn. Her thoughtful discussions have helped me shape my characters. Thanks to my publisher Bill Krause for his faith in me and the coffee he buys me whenever I'm in town. (Bill, if you think this was your favorite Kiki book, wait until you read the next one!)

Last, but certainly not least, I want to thank my readers. I have been blessed with the best fans in the world. Thank you for telling your friends about Kiki Lowenstein. I am truly gratified by the multitude of ways you've spread the word. Whether it's buying a book, giving a copy to a friend, making a blog post, sharing on an online forum, or writing a review, you honor me with your enthusiasm. I hope that someday I'll get the chance to thank each of you in person —

Joanna

PS. Visit my website, www.JoannaSlan.com, for book club questions, newsletter subscription form, recipes, resources, and trivia questions based on the Kiki Lowenstein Mysteries. There's even the script for a Kiki Lowenstein Mystery Dinner Theatre play. You are welcome to use it at your next crop or event. (Thanks to Debbie Chabot at ScrapbooksPlus! in Chantilly, VA, for hosting the premiere.)

ABOUT THE AUTHOR

Internationally recognized scrapbooking expert **Joanna Campbell Slan** is the award-winning author of fourteen books, including the mystery series featuring Kiki Lowenstein. The first book in the series — *Paper, Scissors, Death* — was an Agatha Award nominee for Best First Novel. Joanna and her husband David live outside of Washington, D.C. with their two dogs.

You'll find book club questions, newsletter subscription form, recipes, resources, trivia questions based on the books, and a script for a dinner theatre play at her website, www.JoannaSlan.com

We hope you have enjoyed this Large Print book. Other Thorndike, Wheeler, Kennebec, and Chivers Press Large Print books are available at your library or directly from the publishers.

For information about current and upcoming titles, please call or write, without obligation, to:

Publisher
Thorndike Press
295 Kennedy Memorial Drive
Waterville, ME 04901
Tel. (800) 223-1244

or visit our Web site at:

http://gale.cengage.com/thorndike

OR

Chivers Large Print
published by AudioGO Ltd
St James House, The Square
Lower Bristol Road
Bath BA2 3BH
England
Tel. +44(0) 800 136919
email: info@audiogo.co.uk
www.audiogo.co.uk

All our Large Print titles are designed for easy reading, and all our books are made to last.